CONFESSIONS

OF A

CRIME SCENE

INVESTIGATOR

Bill Moloney

Confessions of a Crime Scene Investigator

Cover photo by Vincent Boyd. Special Thanks to Betty & Verl Ringgenberg and Cindy Herbert for helping create an amazing cover photo.

Book layout and design by Andy Grachuk - www.JingotheCat.com

For the Loves of my life.

You know who you are…..from here and there!

CONTENTS

1.	No Glamour Here, Slick	7
2.	The Roads Not Taken	13
3.	Wearing the Gray Bag	29
4.	Blood and More Blood	55
5.	Frozen	81
6.	To Be or Not To Be	95
7.	Oops!	109
8.	All in the Family	129
9.	Just Gross	139
10.	WTF!	149
11.	The Tough Ones	161
12.	On the Table	187
13.	Bits and Pieces	205
14.	Murder in the Catskills	223
15.	The Whodunit	235
16.	The Big Picture	253

Chapter One

No Glamour Here, Slick.

wo of my fellow crime scene pals were there before me. The small house was on a hill about a hundred and fifty feet from the road where I parked my big black van. Marked and unmarked State Police cars littered the driveway and roadway shoulders, but they always left a couple of parking spots up close for our arrival. A mild August breeze fluttered the bright yellow crime scene tape that kept small groups of uniform troopers and plain clothes investigators away from the scene. I grabbed a box of disposable latex gloves and started to put on the white Tyvek suit before slipping under the yellow tape. Scott and Joe were heading towards me from the house. They were already suited up. Smirks on their faces seemed to grow as they got closer. About ten feet away from me, I knew exactly what they were about to say. I beat them to it, "Aww that is awful!"

"Oh no, big guy. It gets better," came Scott's response.

That familiar odor was now upon me, having already stuck to these two guys from being inside for only a short time. And boy, was it strong.

Scott continued, "Hasn't been seen for two weeks. Every window is closed and it's gotta be at least 90 degrees in there."

Joe chimed in, "He's been baking for a while."

After a collective combination groan/chuckle, I asked, "Anything to it?"

"Don't know yet. We photoed everything as it is. Wanted to wait for you before moving anything," Scott said.

I sneered back, "Gee thanks."

We squatted under the crime scene tape and made our way up the hill. I couldn't help but notice something strange. "What's with the blacked out windows?"

"Youuu'll see."

I wasn't crazy about the way Scott said that.

That smell was heavy duty even standing outside the closed front door. As expected, the opening of the door produced an overpowering wave of death's awful stench. I was surprised at how dimly lit the house was on such a sunny day. There were no curtains on the windows so why were they so--- And then I heard it. A second later, I saw them. Flies. Every single window was covered with buzzing, black flies. My amused co-workers were getting a kick out of my "You gotta be fuckin kidding me" expression.

Now let me clarify something here. Yes, this is pretty gross. I can't imagine anyone wanting to be in my shoes at that particular moment, but then on the other hand, it certainly isn't something you experience every day. Standing inside the front door of this darkened house with the reek of decomposition almost knocking you out and listening to this unearthly mass buzzing as you witness thousands of winged insects all flapping together, tapping on and masking every pane of glass in the place, really was something straight out of a Stephen King novel. And we hadn't even seen the body yet.

After fifteen seconds of this, it was time. "OK. This is bullshit. We gotta air this place out. Open every friggin window in here." We went to it. When the windows were opened, the cops outside said that it looked like one of the seven plaques happening in reverse. Every lawman beat feet backwards away from the approaching stink.

Back inside we stood over the source of it all. There on the kitchen floor were the bloated and badly decomposing remains of the homeowner. It was tough to get close to him because decay had caused bodily fluids to leak and cover the entire kitchen floor. We'll often refer to this as "melting". Melting onto the floor is a helluva lot better than melting into a fabric sofa. At least we had that going for us. We got called because there appeared to be an electric cord from a box fan wrapped around the guy's neck. With the body's current condition, it was difficult to tell if there was any other obvious trauma present. I stress the word "obvious" because there might always be that small caliber bullet hole you can't see in a guy's hair or bruises that decomposition starts to hide. We had an elderly man in very poor health who lived alone. A check of the residence showed no signs of forced entry, but we had to see what this cord around his neck was about. To get a better look, we had to make our way a bit closer to him. The goo covered the kitchen floor and made it slick as hell. Even in our Tyvek suits and booties, nobody wanted to slip into this mess. We also didn't want to track this stuff all over the house. We grabbed a wooden board from outside and laid it down across the kitchen floor sludge so that we could get closer to the body. The flies had had their way with this guy. The maggots left by the flies were working it under all of his clothing. They don't like being out in the light so they'll work their way under the clothing out of the light. You'll actually see a slight wavy movement. Oh yeah. It was there. He was infested with them. This would definitely be one of those scenes that you wouldn't release until after the autopsy was done. The post mortem examination may give you more to look for if it turned out to be some kind of foul play. Right now, it was looking like the box fan had been plugged into the wall and the cord was probably suspended in the air when the fan was placed on a table as far away as the cord would let it go. We figured that it was possible that our guy collapsed or fell for some reason and his body went down onto the suspended cord. His weight would've pulled the cord from the outlet and sent the fan off the table and across his body thereby wrapping the cord around his neck. Of course, we weren't sure of this yet. Interviews told us that he was a loner. There was lots of money sitting undisturbed on top of his bureau, so robbery wasn't a motive. His advanced age and poor health started to lead us toward a natural death, but we'd still like to have a forensic pathologist give him the once over and confirm a cause of death for us.

After searching and documenting the rest of the house, the county coroner was called. He would subsequently notify a funeral home to transport the body to the morgue. Since we really didn't want to have anyone else inside a potential crime scene, we decided that we'd bag the body and bring it out to the funeral home. How do ya get this melted muddle into the body bag? Believe me, a disintegrating, mushy mess of a body is not an easy thing to just pick up and put somewhere else. And it didn't help that he was a rather large man who was made even larger by decomposition's bloating process. Imagine three of us, each taking a hand or foot and side stepping through goo and putting him down inside a body bag that barely fit him. Try doing this when everything you hold onto is slipping away in your hand. Now comes the worst of it. As you do this, you are exerting yourself and sucking in lung fulls of that newly disturbed decomposition aroma. Well, it got me. It got me good. It was the only time in my entire career when I thought I was gonna hurl. And I know better. I know not to breathe deeply when the muck gets disturbed, but my feet started to slip as I lifted and then I sucked it in. I held it together until the body was on the body bag and let go of him immediately and backed away. I remember thinking, "Do I toss my cookies right here or run to the kitchen sink and throw up?" Joe took one look at me and said, "Go outside. Quick."

I stood motionless for a time and the feeling passed. I was fine. The color returned to my face and I helped carry the zipped up bag out to the waiting funeral home.

The autopsy showed a massive heart attack. We released the house to family members.

And that, my friends, was only a natural death.

Death is a morbid curiosity. Mayhem and destruction intrigue us. Like a train wreck, we can't look away. Rubber-neckers cause enormous traffic jams. We'll curse and scream out the window at them. That is, until we roll up on the wreckage and do the exact same damn thing. Slow right down to a crawl hoping to catch a glimpse of a stray body part. We want to see something ghastly, something dreadful, something shocking. We pray for a gust of wind to blow away the sheet that covers what must be a dead body. Was that blood? Was that a hand? Oh, to have just a peek.

We are truly fascinated by death and all of its horror. Why? Is it the unknown? We've been taught what science says, what the Bible says and now we live to hear what mediums say. We love true crime novels, movies, TV shows and websites with graphic images of death scenes. Even the most grounded person on the planet will steal a glance at a grotesque snapshot of one's final destination.

Why?

People often ask, "Doesn't it bother you, seeing all of that gore?" or "How do you go to a horrific murder scene or pull mangled remains from a demolished tractor trailer or photograph every part of a brutalized victim's body?" or "How do you watch the autopsy of a child? Don't you have children? How do you do that? Do you get nightmares?" My answers to most questions like these are pretty much the same. "No, it doesn't bother me and it's my job." But a different question stood out from the rest.

"Does being around all this death make you look at life a little differently?" And the answer to that is a resounding, "Yes! Yes, it does!"

The opening scene of this book wasn't chosen to turn anyone's stomach right from the get go. The fact is that these are the kinds of things we deal with day in and day out. Television doesn't even begin to describe or portray this very basic element of our job. Anyone who thinks that they are going to join some badass CSI Unit with a police department or medical examiner's office and not have to deal with the things I have just described is living in la-la land.

This is what you see, touch, hear and smell. There's also a lot of interesting, sad, funny, frustrating and really cool stuff you'll experience. Indeed, death teaches us so many valuable lessons about life. But let's get one thing straight. There ain't no glamour here, slick! It's a downright, dirty job. So let's roll up our sleeves and get busy. That is, after coffee. Always gotta have my coffee first.

Chapter Two
The Roads Not Taken

For the record, I didn't bite the wings off flies or burn frogs when I was a kid. Gothic or satanic wasn't my style. I was actually quite straight laced. To me, dead bodies weren't cool, although the original black and white Frankenstein is still one of my favorite movies. In my youth, I didn't dream of growing up and being surrounded by death. During my elementary school and altar boy days, the priesthood was a goal. Then my love of animals brought veterinary medicine into my sights. Our house had a dog, three cats and a rabbit. Later, my father had horses. I even went so far as to memorize and test myself on the contents of veterinary manuals. One morning, during senior year of high school, woke me up with the very vivid realization that I was never going to put in all of the years of college and medical schooling needed to become a vet. I knew I wouldn't do it. My father used to tell me that school was the best years of your life and that I'd miss them. Don't get me wrong. That age was fun, but I do not miss going to school at all. I wasn't a troublemaker or had a hard time learning. I just wasn't crazy about sitting in class all day, studying stuff and doing homework. No, four years of college and more years of medical school were out of the question, so I finally came up with a reasonable career choice. I was going to be an actor!

During senior year of high school, I was in three shows. I had done some stuff before that but senior year cinched it for me. Yes, I would become an actor. Finish high school, hit the "Big Apple", a year of college taking film and theatre classes, pictures and resumes, and then pound the pavement knocking on doors so that I could inspire agents and casting directors to put me to work. At night, I'd work part-time to pay the bills and go to auditions during the day.

Well, I think you can tell how that idea turned out. In truth, the theatre (and writing) have become a huge part of my life. But the one full time job that I just knew I had to have was being a Dad. I wanted a family. I needed to be a hubby and a Dad. If honestly asked whether I wanted to become as famous as Elvis or have a couple of miniature human beings call me Dad, well, I knew that signing autographs wouldn't be in my future.

My sights were now set on a steady income career job that would provide health benefits for my future family and a pension for a relaxing retirement. Ah yes. Civil service! I was already familiar with union jobs having done a couple stints in residential and commercial buildings in the city where I worked as a porter or concierge (yes, very fancy). Health coverage from these jobs would be a must. I learned the importance of this when every dime had been paid after I was involved in a motorcycle accident. It took one of my toes and hospitalized me for a little while. I now have nine toes and my grandchildren think that it's so cool.

Yes, a steady job would put show biz on hold, but directing school and community plays would eventually become a part-time passion.

The security of these union jobs was very attractive, but the pay wasn't great and many weren't the type of job I'd want to make a career. So the quest to take as many civil service tests as possible began. The Post Office was first, but they were only hiring part-time. I heard good things about the Port Authority Police so I took that exam. I heard nothing but horror stories from older New York City cops so I refused to take that exam. Then finally the career above all careers posted its exam dates. I signed up to take the New York City Firefighter exam.

Growing up in New York City constantly brought me into contact with firemen. Besides walking by a firehouse, you'd see their fire trucks parked outside a supermarket while they grocery shopped. They'd be out in the street washing down the trucks and laying out equipment. And the one thing you couldn't help but notice was that they always seemed happy. It was evident in every fireman, no matter what age or rank. They seemed to love their job. And everyone loved this group of good looking, jolly guys in great shape. Especially the ladies. Remember that this was a time when gals weren't yet on the FDNY. It was still an all-boys club. Here was a life of living together in the firehouse, sliding down the pole, riding in the fire trucks, battling out of control fires and saving babies! Wow! That was the job for me!

I signed up, took the civil service test and did well. I aced the physical test and was number two thousand something on a list of 22,000 names.

"Don't worry, kid. You're in," a local fireman told me.

But then hiring got put on hold when a group of women (who were now allowed to take the test for the first time) filed a lawsuit that called the physical portion of the testing unfair to female applicants. They felt that it was geared towards men who have more upper body strength, so women subsequently scored lower. The list was frozen. While arguments were made in court, the FDNY would have to petition the court every time they needed to hire. This meant that the hiring process would slow waaaay down. I started to worry that I'd never get called at all. Would the whole list eventually get tossed by the court? Would I have to take the test again? Would I score as high the next time around? There was no choice but to wait it out. I still wanted to be a fireman in the worst way.

I did realize that firemen had their share of death to deal with. Their job included lots of calls to fatal and life threatening emergencies, and of course, burned bodies. It isn't difficult to walk through a charred building and literally step over a badly burned body and not know it. Again, the smell might help you identify it. A different smell. A burning meat smell. I'm sorry, but that's what it's like. When a fire chars every surface black inside a house and the lights go out, well, everything sorta blends together in a dark blackness throughout. With a person, it doesn't help that the first things burned away are hair, clothing, then the fingers and toes. As the skin blackens, the muscles contract and tighten so much that the body starts to take on unusual shapes; most times, the pugilistic stance (like a boxer). In many cases, it takes a much closer inspection to see that two bodies are entwined together. Often, a parent hovered over a child.

Fire scenes are very difficult to process in the crime scene world. In an attempt to locate any kind of evidence whatsoever, you could be sifting through ashes and debris for days. And I mean manually sifting using wire sifting boxes and visually examining every little thing you come across.

Years later, I would work a fire scene and see this first hand.

Local firefighters responded to a house fire at a beautiful estate in upstate New York. It appeared to be contained to the expansive master bedroom. Once the fire was out and firefighters began their investigation, two bodies were found on the floor inside the bedroom. A sharp eyed fire official noticed what looked like lacerations to the two bodies. The cuts weren't like the normal tearing of the skin and muscles that occur in many burn victims exposed to extreme heat.

The lacerations and the fact that the family car was gone bothered him. He held the scene and called the cops. As is the case in so many of these situations, the local emergency personnel like fire departments and ambulance folks are a tremendous help; not only doing the job they were called out to do, but helping us out afterwards. In rural areas, the vast majority of this special breed of human being is volunteers. They will always offer any kind of help or support and will man emergency equipment for use, shut down roads, and conduct searches. They are an amazing species.

Fire personnel inspected and insured that the remaining structure was safe enough for us to work within. It was a gorgeous home. The master bedroom was almost completely destroyed. Most of the bedroom ceiling and roof was gone which actually helped with lighting conditions, but it was cold outside. Real cold. We were told that the fire had not burned through to the basement because the entire bedroom floor was laid with marble. This was a huge advantage for us. Although we had piles of ash and rubble that ranged from five or six inches deep to three feet deep, at least we had a bottom to it. So often the upper floors burn down to the lower floors or basement and that creates a mess. The marble floor would prove very beneficial.

The bodies of the husband and wife were both located on the floor of the bedroom only a short distance from each other. They were badly burned and difficult to identify. Once the bodies were photographed, documented and given a preliminary examination at the scene, they were transported to the morgue under police escort. Now began the painstaking task of going through every bit of debris in this huge bedroom. The rest of the extensive home would be done a day or two later.

Eventually, a serrated kitchen knife was found on the marble floor between the locations of the husband and wife. This was where the marble floor had done us right. The knife had what appeared to be reddish brown stains on it. We hoped it was blood. It would be later discovered that the knife belonged to a set of knives from a knife block on the kitchen counter.

Conversations with our State Police investigators on the case told us that the couple's adult son had been home prior to the fire. He was now in New York City with his parents' vehicle and seemed stunned at the news of his parents' death. He stated that everything was fine when he left that morning with their car. Interviews with relatives led our guys to suspect the son because of some disputes he was having with his parents over his drug addition. The early twenties son had just been told he was going back into rehab. Tracking the son's cell phone put him on the road sometime after the fire, but it wasn't enough to lock him into the exact timeframe. He denied having any arguments with his parents and added that they had allowed him to take their vehicle to New York City to see some friends. He swore that they were alive when he left.

The case immediately drew media attention and the pressure was on to solve it. The son stopped all communication with us and hired a lawyer. Back at the office, we began to go through the mountain of evidence collected from the scene. But of course, we zeroed in on the knife. Autopsies of both victims confirmed their identities and concluded that the cause of death was the fatal lacerations consistent with the serrated knife we found. (Pathologists have a much fancier name for it than that.)

A closer inspection of the reddish brown staining on the knife verified that it was blood, but it also brought something else to light. There was a faint impression on the blade as well. Holy shit. There was a partial fingerprint on the blade and it was a partial fingerprint in the blood. Numerous photographs were taken of the knife, the staining and the fingerprint. An examination of the fingerprint photograph determined that the print had enough visible detail to be considered an identifiable partial fingerprint. An inked fingerprint card related to a minor, prior arrest of the son was requested and compared to our blood print. The comparison matched the print on the knife to the son. When the district attorney advised the son's lawyer of our findings, his immediate response was, "So what? You found my client's fingerprint on the blade of a knife from the kitchen of the house he lives in."

The DA responded, "Did I forget to mention that the fingerprint on the blade of the murder weapon is in his mother's blood?"

The case never went to trial and the son is still serving a double murder sentence in prison.

A quick thinking Fire Chief who thought the circumstances were a little suspicious got us on board right away before valuable evidence could be trampled, destroyed or lost.

Getting hired by the New York City Fire Department would be put on hold. The women's lawsuit was just beginning and I had a pretty good idea that the court system wouldn't be moving along too quickly. With the FDNY only allowed to hire fifty candidates at a time, I'd have quite a wait where I sat on the list at number 2015.

I kept checking "The Chief", a civil service newspaper, for upcoming tests. There were all kinds and they usually listed a brief job description, the education needed and the salary range. A friend of mine said that his sister's fiancé had taken the state trooper test. State troopers? Did you have to know how to ride a horse to be a state trooper? I'm not kidding. This was the 80's and I was a city kid. The only photographs I'd ever seen of troopers were on horseback. I equated them to Canadian Mounties. I did remember them marching in the New York City Saint Patrick's Day Parade. Not a one of them ever seemed to smile, but they did look sharp. Those cowboy hats looked pretty cool. What the heck! I'll take the test. I heard it was pretty hard, so I probably won't score high anyway. That was 1982. I was right. After completing the written test, I was number four thousand something. Never heard from them. There were a couple of other lists I was sitting on, but still no job offers.

If I wasn't getting any calls for a steady job, I figured I'd try my hand at show biz. Why not? I could always look back and say I tried. I left the union job I had, bartended a few nights a week to pay the bills and went knocking on doors or "making the rounds" as they used to call it. I did a few showcase plays (no pay), a few paying magazine gigs for advertisements or story photos, but it's a tough business. I put a lot of miles on my shoes, handed out a ton of pictures and resumes and read a lot of copy (a short script) for commercials. It was fun working on the shows, meeting new people, learning the craft and, of course, performing. But it wasn't paying at all. My parents were very, very supportive and helped out here and there. Dad always believed that most jobs were the same old day in, day out 8 hour dirge that you'd work for 30 or 40 years. "When you're young, you should be trying to do something different. Do it now. Do something you like."

My parents have always been my biggest supporters. They'd come to every performance whether it was on a stage or in a basement. Even to this day, they will show up at anything I'm doing whether it be directing a school play or acting in some community show. And I am still most nervous on stage when I know that they are in the audience. It would bother them to know that. As a parent, they still want only the best for their kids. On the opposite end of that, it's obvious that their approval and opinion of what I do in my life is still important to me. In my lifetime, I will never, ever be able to say "Thank You" enough for how much they have loved me by supporting what I do.

A couple of years later, the State Troopers would give another written exam. The closest test location to me was Saint John's University in Queens. I overslept and actually thought about blowing it off. Once I was awake, I figured "What the heck." and hustled out there. This time my number on the list was 137. I have no idea why I went from four thousand something to 137, but I got called for the first academy class in September of 1985. No other jobs were calling and part time bartending was barely paying the bills. The Troopers' pay wasn't great, but the benefits were. I knew that if the FDNY called I could always leave the Troopers. The decision was made. I'd be a state trooper for a while.

To be honest, I never really wanted to be a cop. I had friends growing up who dreamed about becoming cops, but not me. Don't get me wrong. I didn't dislike them. I just never saw myself as one. The concrete jungle of the NYPD really didn't appeal to me, but there was a little something cool to the whole trooper thing.

During my adolescence, my parents had saved and saved until they could put a down payment on a house in upstate New York; a place to bring my brother and I on weekends and summers. A home away from the city. They moved us up there permanently after my junior year of high school. It was during those two and a half hour trips upstate that I'd see troopers fly by on the highway pulling people over. Then living up there exposed me to them a lot more. Their crisp gray uniforms and stiff brimmed Stetsons always looked sharp. Silver .357 magnum revolvers hung from their hips. I swear they looked like modern day cowboys. They were in great shape and were all business. I didn't know if I would fit that mold. I was a pretty easy going guy. I liked having a good time, a laugh whenever I could. They seemed a bit serious for me. I'd never been in the service, so this para-military organization stuff might take a little getting used to.

My first three years after elementary school were spent in the all boys Jesuit Catholic Saint Francis Xavier high school in Manhattan. My father worked a second job to send me there. Xavier had an ROTC program that wasn't mandatory, but the first four weeks of it was. After the four weeks, you would make your decision as to whether you wanted to continue it. I opted out. But I had a number of classmates who continued it and went on to careers in the service. Some of them went overseas and I have thought of them often. Thank you guys so much for the sacrifices you have made to serve our country.

It wasn't for me, but now here I was years later about to start the

Academy. I wasn't sure how I'd handle the constant leather polishing, never-ending push-ups, sit-ups and drill sergeant types screaming at me. Now add to that six months of intense studies while you lived Monday to Fridays in their dorms. Believe me, I know this is nothing to you service guys who did real boot camp, but I wasn't used to this shit. And then the final straw. A high and tight haircut! Come on! Really? I had longish red hair and I liked it that way. It was the 80's, man!

Three mile runs every other morning? What? Are you serious? Hey, I'll run a block to catch the 7 train, but 60 blocks? For no good reason? I was a lanky, thin frame city kid. Today's fitness crazy mindset was no where to be found. Watch old baseball games from the 80's. Nobody was juiced up. They were all thin and wiry. I started working my way up to a mile and a half a couple months before the Academy and that was killing me. Three miles? That's insane. That's when I realized that marathon runners really were superheroes. I finally got to about two miles and Thank God I did. I figured that would get me to consistently be somewhere in the middle of the pack. I was still dying, but at least I wasn't dead last and abused. I've heard that once your body gets used to it, the running gets easier and your body looks forward to it and you can go longer distances and run longer times....that's a whole lotta bullshit. If I didn't have to run another three feet, my body would be very happy. Ecstatic in fact. I still loved running to first base or doing a post pattern in touch football, but that long distance nonsense? Not this kid.

But I said yes anyway. Here I was in Albany, New York doing a six month stint in a police academy. What was I thinking? And I got exactly what I expected. The first few weeks was filled with screaming, push-ups and stress. There were lots of "Recruit Trooper, that's a sorry excuse of a salute to our nation's flag. Get down and gimme 20 push-ups right now!" (Again, you service guys were probably given 50 or 100!) Or "I didn't like the way you looked at me! Gimme another lap around the track. At double time!" You were barraged with instructions and you'd better remember them. "Attention to detail!" was the mantra. And if you failed to follow the instructions in any way at all, there were consequences.

A favorite routine was to give the whole group a task that could never be completed. You'd be told what to do and given so much time to do it. It could be to run so many laps around a track and everyone had better be done within a certain time. Another one was to assemble the entire Academy class into the main lecture hall. An announcement was made that every single recruit was to return to their room where they would find a new room designation written on a piece of paper. Each of us had fifteen minutes to return to their room (without running), gather all of our belongings and carry them to the new room which was usually in the other dormitory. Every belonging had to be back in its proper place (every piece of clothing, footwear etc had a specific spot in the room) within the fifteen minutes or there'd be hell to pay. Throughout this clusterjerk exercise you were still supposed to square your corners (ask a service person) and salute any officer who just happened to be walking the halls during this fiasco. If you didn't, everything in your arms and on your back wound up on the floor as you did push-ups. Then you picked it up again and went on your way. It was pretty comical at times to see these halls of hell full of panicked, young recruits tripping over other recruits who were doing push-ups all the while being screamed at.

The runs were similar. "All of you had better complete the run during the allotted time or you'll all do it again and again and again." This was stupid. We're just getting more and more beat up. There's no way we can all finish together....Or is there? It took us a while, but we finally got it. The point was to get all of us across the finish line together, even if you were late. It took a little convincing to get the track stars to slow down and join the rest of us, but eventually we all limped across together; the stronger carrying the weaker along. We formed a tight knit pack, a group with no stragglers, and we crossed the finish line as a group. No, we didn't make the time limit, but we stuck together. We did it together as brothers and sisters. As we all stood past the finish line, doubled over and panting, you could see a few trooper counselors nodding their heads as if to say, "By Jove, I think they've got it!"

Think as a team, not individuals. That was a lesson I always remembered.

After a few short minutes of rest came the next blast.

"Double time. Back to your rooms for inspection!"

I've always considered myself somewhat neat and organized. Organized was an understatement when it came to your room. The rules in your room had better be in place when inspection came along. Any straying from the rules got you a plethora of push-ups and a trashing of your room so that you could do it all over again. The right way. This was another "Attention to detail" drill. I can look back and agree that this motto was huge in police work, especially crime scene work. We were each given four pairs of pants and four shirts. They had to hang in your closet alternating shirt, pants, shirt, pants and the hangers had to be spaced exactly four fingers apart. Your one pair of sneakers and your one pair of highly polished, lace up shoes had specific spots on the floor inside your closet. Certain clothing went into certain drawers inside the closet. You had one side of the closet and your roommate the other. The sliding closet door had to be left open four fingers wide. Your desk was allowed one personal photo frame. Mine was of my girlfriend, soon to be fiancé, soon to be wife, Siobhan. And of course, it goes without saying that your bed had to be made exactly the way you were shown. Not a wrinkle better show in the wool outer blanket or the whole bed would be tossed. I knew some guys who actually slept on the floor so as not to ruin a perfectly made bed. The hell with that. I wanted some kind of comfort after a long day of abuse.

Along with room inspection, you were always subject to a personal inspection. Your clothing was to fit you properly. A plain black belt held up your pants with the belt buckle off to the left side, not centered, so it wouldn't interfere with the future gun belt's buckle. Your shirt's excess and gig line had to be proper much like the armed service does. Your shirt pockets were always buttoned and in your left breast pocket was your Miranda warning card which was to be read out loud upon request at any time. Your shoes. Oh yes, your shoes. Did I say that they better shine?

I'm not going to lie. This was starting to be a bit much for me. Yeah, it wasn't as bad as what service guys went through, but it still sucked as far as I was concerned. I was getting into the best shape of my life and the food was pretty good, but the yelling and standing at attention in long lines waiting to eat at every meal, seven hours of schooling, two hours of studying in your room at night was all getting very, very old. Luckily, the guys I met there were aces and that helped pass the time.

I cherished Friday nights and going home for the weekend. I dreaded Sunday nights when I had to return to that place and start another week of hell.

Finally, a ray of sunshine. A dash of hope. The FDNY called me for the next phase of candidate processing. The interview. I lucked out that I was scheduled for a weekday just before Christmas when we had a week off from the Academy. It usually took an Act of Congress to get a day off from the Academy and it wouldn't go well to tell them you were considering another job.

The interview went very well and the FDNY officer assured me that I'd be getting called soon. "Any idea when? The State Police Academy is killing me," I inquired.

"Nope," came the response, "The list is still frozen by the court. The case could be settled tomorrow or go on for another year."

I guessed that I'd be making my Academy bed for a while yet.

The camaraderie among the recruit troopers was fantastic. We definitely shared that "Misery loves company" mentality and we looked out for each other. There was one particular stretch of time when I was done with this routine. My immature state of mind decided that I was sick and tired of being harassed. Who needs this bullshit? So I made a phone call to the bar restaurant where I used to work and asked if there was a full time job behind the bar available. The manager was glad to hear from me and said a spot was opening up in a couple weeks and that he'd love to have me back. I was ecstatic. I confided to one of my Academy buddies that I was now a short timer. I was gonna be outta here. He tried to talk me out of it. Tried pumping me up with "You can do it. Don't quit now. We're so close." I told him that my mind was made up.

That was just the beginning. My buddy then went on to spread the news of my plans to all of the guys in our tight knit circle of friends. Now I had every single guy grabbing me and telling me that we were going to get through this together. Guys pleaded with me to stay. One pal admitted that I was the reason he stayed because I had helped him through some tough times. I know to this day that it was the upbeat and complimentary bombardment of "You can do it" and "We're not going to let you quit" and "You have the right stuff to do this job." comments that made me stay and finish. These true friends bonded together to keep me from quitting. I owe my career to them.

I finally graduated with the 158th session of the New York State Troopers. It felt good. I was sent to scenic Sullivan County, the county where my family had moved. I didn't have to ride a horse, but there were plenty of rural farms and back country roads. It was the area of the original thriving Catskill resorts of the 60's and 70's. But they were dying out. Atlantic City was drawing in the crowds now. Highway Route 17 ran through the center of the county and connected the New York State Thruway out of the Big Apple to upstate cities like Binghamton,

Syracuse and Buffalo. It was a very busy highway and I learned car stops pretty quickly.

I had to ride 12 weeks with senior troopers. It was a lot to take in. I remember asking one of them how long it would be before I'd feel comfortable walking into any of the countless calls we get and know what to do.

"About four years." he answered.

Four years! You gotta be kidding me. I had no idea what I was doing and this was going to go on for four years? Well, it did get easier. But there'd be one more tough career decision to make.

After about eight months on the road, I got the call. A letter in the mail advised me that I was being hired by the New York City Fire Department. I was being offered the job of my dreams. Seems like a no brainer, right? It's the job I wanted. I'd get to go back to the city. But I had worked so hard to get here. I made it through that Academy. Here I was a city kid driving fast police cars, wearing a cowboy hat and carrying a shiny six shooter on my hip. Yes damnit, I did feel like John Wayne. And yes, the girls did seem to stare a little longer at a guy in a sharp uniform. And there was one more thing. I found out very quickly the high regard held for troopers. Growing up in the city, I wasn't exposed to that. City cops were always taking all kinds of crap. This was something new to me and it made me very proud to be a part of such an organization. Most people were always very respectful.

One day, my father and I were walking along a rural town street. I was in uniform and a teenager passed by us saying, "Hello Mr. Moloney." After he passed, my father turned to me and said that he had no idea who that young man was.

I said, "Dad, he wasn't talking to you."

Chapter Three
Wearing the Gray Bag

have never regretted the decision to turn down the FDNY. It was a tough choice at the time, but I took the right path. Living and raising my family in the rural upstate countryside was a dream and the State Police helped me achieve that dream.

Wearing the gray uniform as a brand new road trooper quickly brought you up close and personal with your share of death and destruction at car accidents. Seeing someone deceased that you know was alive and driving down the road a few minutes earlier at first seemed a bit surreal. Looking into lifeless open eyes intrigued me at times. "Did they see it coming?", "What was the last thing they saw?", "What did they see that could help us figure out what happened?" Evidence at a crash scene would sometimes answer those questions.

Pedestrians and bicyclists struck by cars or trucks caused very damaging results as did head-on collisions with motorcycles. It amazed me that the simplest car rollover could end in a death, while a 100 mile an hour police chase could have the bad guy's car flip end over end and he'd walk out of it with a bump on the head. Some people believe that those scenarios support the old "When your time's up, it's up." The jury is still out on that one with me.

Later in my career, as a crime scene investigator, I'd show up at traffic scenes after everything had settled down. But as a road trooper, you're arriving seconds after it happened. You're there in the thick of it. It's uncertain who's dead or unconscious or who's about to die. You'll usually find out quickly whose hurt real bad because they'll be screaming or moaning in pain. It's a mini-disaster and it's all on you until help shows up. Cars are stopping all around. Some are continuing to drive right through the scene and past people lying in the roadway. You have to keep your head and prioritize, sometimes walk away from the injured, and momentarily leave those who need you the most to call for assistance. People will stop to help and you have to delegate. Victims cry out questioning whether their kids are breathing or not, and others look like they are about to check out if you don't do something right now. We're not paramedics, but we are trained as first responders and that training has been invaluable to me ever since. Stop the bleeding. Open an airway. Get the blood circulating. Continue this until a professional shows up.

There have been adults or kids pinned inside a crushed vehicle, begging you to get them out, and all you can do is be there for them. Talk to them. Find out their symptoms to advise the responding medical folks.

One of the hardest things I've ever done in my life is to look into a child's eyes with a reassuring smile, telling them that they are going to be all right. Promising them that they will be okay when you're not really sure at all if they're going to make it. But you need to keep them calm. You need them to believe you.

I knew a trooper who arrived on the scene of a car accident where the twenty year old drunk driver had been driving over 100 miles an hour and hit a guard rail. One of the young adult passengers had been thrown from the vehicle. Both of his legs were completely severed. The trooper attended to this conscious young man, trying to stop the massive bleeding below his waist. The young man was awake and once he could see what had happened to him, he began to plead with the trooper.

"Please shoot me! Please sir. Please shoot me! Kill me please! Please!"

The trooper was only a few years older than this young man on the ground. An experience like that matures a person. This trooper remained cool. He reassured the victim as much as he could. The young man survived.

This poor young man was obviously in shock and disoriented, but there are many accidents where victims are trapped inside a vehicle and very aware of what's going on. Some are caught under vehicles and the slightest shift could crush them. Others get stuck in the passenger compartment as the gas tank leaks out all over the road, praying that a passing motorist doesn't toss a lit cigarette out a window. In so many of these instances, all you can do is be there for them. Talk to them. Keep them calm as emergency folks try to get them out. We've crawled under flipped tractor-trailers to get close to the trapped person, talk to them and let them know what's going on. It's kinda funny how some of these conversations go. You want to keep them calm, so you talk about anything. Sometimes it'll be awhile so you get them on topics like where they're from, their family, their jobs and even throw in there "How about them Mets?" The point is to let them sense that you're not worried about anything, so they shouldn't worry. Many victims have gone out of their way to track down the cops who spent all that time with them easing their minds and thank them personally. In one emergency room, a victim, being wheeled by me, grabbed my arm stopping the gurney.

"Hey, thank you. I would've been an absolute mess out there without you. Thank you."

When a fifty-something year old man says this to you, a twenty something year old kid, it grows you up a bit and makes you realize that so many little things can mean so very much to someone in need. So many little things that can make a person's tough time that much easier to deal with.

I retrieved a little girl's doll from a car wreck and brought it with me to the ER. The mother and daughter were a little banged up, but they'd be ok. In the emergency room, I gave the little girl her doll. She cried out the doll's name and hugged it. Before I knew it, the mother was hugging me.

"Thank you. Thank you so much for thinking of my little girl."

I didn't think it was much of a big deal, but it meant the world to that little girl.

Working the road lends itself to a number of dangers. The everyday, routine act of pulling a car over for speeding or a busted headlight puts every cop at very serious risk. People speed, read, send texts, talk on the phone, drive tired, drive drunk and just don't pay attention. Now you step out onto the macadam of a busy roadway after pulling someone over where drivers are doing any number of the above mentioned tasks while driving and you are putting your life in their hands.

New York State did the right thing a few years ago when they wrote into law the "Move Over" statute. It has definitely saved numerous road cops from very serious injuries and death. Too many police officers are killed every year in some kind of motor vehicle accident. Unfortunately, I've been to a few of them. It's an awful sight that haunts every lawman. The horror of it is only equaled by the sadness of the family's loss. And usually, we know the family.

That's just the traffic danger to pulling cars over. Now walk up to the driver's window of that car you just pulled over for a busted headlight. That's all that you know about this driver at that moment. He has a broken headlight and he pulled over when you activated your lights. The cop will not know that there's ten kilos of coke in the trunk, or that there's a kidnapped kid in the back seat, or that this guy just left his house after killing his wife.

Officers walk up to a driver's window having no idea who this person really is. I can't tell you how many times I've had to defend a cop's actions because he walked up to the driver's window with his hand on his gun. "What's he gonna do? Shoot me for speeding?"

When I ask for a few particulars, I find out that the motorist was either reaching into their glove box or, my favorite, reaching under their seat. When I've come across this, I'd have my hand on the butt of my gun, lean into the window as their reaching under the seat and say, "I hope for your sake that's a radar detector you're hiding under the seat and not reaching for something that might hurt me."

They usually look back at me, see my hand and then realize what it does look like and jerk their hand out quickly. (Again, not a smart move.) "No, no, no. You're right. You're right. It's my radar detector. I didn't want to get caught with it."

Actions like these can create a lot of suspicion for any cop. Most people don't realize that when they get pulled over, they know exactly who I am. The red lights, marked police car, my uniform (especially the big cowboy hat) identifies me pretty quickly, usually accompanied by a fond phrase like, "Shit. A cop."

However, I'll say it again. The trooper or police officer or constable has no idea what state of mind you're in or where you just came from. He has to make a threat level evaluation immediately and then continue to make it the whole time he's dealing with this person he's just getting to know. We've all seen patrol vehicle dash cam videos that show car stops that started out somewhat cordial or even casual that turned violent and, many times, fatal. Those images run through my mind every time I see a car pulled over by a cop. It's also why many cops pull their personal car over and get asked by a spouse, "Why are you stopping here?"

"Just wanna see if this cop need's a hand. He's got three guys in that car." he'll answer.

This isn't to say that interacting with the public during car stops is all doom, gloom and scary moments. Car stops provided some of the funniest moments I've had during my ten years wearing the gray bag. Some days, we'd conduct a random road check on a safe section of a two lane roadway. Troopers would stand on the center line, slow cars down and check for expired registrations, inspection stickers and properly fastened seatbelts and child seats. Some road checks were during hunting season to make sure that the game was properly tagged, weapons unloaded and safely stored.

One approaching car had four elderly ladies in it. I could've immediately waved it through but figured I'd take this opportunity to have a pleasant social exchange with members of the community (How does that sound?). I leaned into the car, looking at all four of these ladies.

"Any loaded guns or illegally obtained wildlife in the car?"

"Oh no," came back one reply, "None at all."

"You ladies been out hunting?" I asked of the group all dressed in their Sunday best.

Another occupant piped back with, "Yes. We're hunting men and we've got you in our sights right now, young man."

Well, my head rolled back and I let out the biggest laugh that made everyone else at the road check stop what they were doing and look.

After I stopped laughing, I thanked them for making my day and asked that they let me go this time.

"Ok, but next time we come across you, you're ours!"

I know cops who have met their future wives at road checks or on a car stop. Some of these interactions have led to friendships. Every cop will tell you how many times he's heard at a party or function, "You stopped me once." It's interesting that most people don't get pulled over by a cop, so when they do, they remember every detail of the incident. We, on the other hand, pull over hundreds of cars in a year. We do it almost every day, so we're probably not going to remember your car stop as vividly as you do, or probably not at all if it went without trouble.

Every car stop doesn't result in a cop giving someone a ticket. We can use our discretion as to who we write and who we let go with a little talk. We all know that handful of cops who will write every single person they stop. The ole "They'd write their own mother" guys. It's good to let people know they broke the law and that we are out there enforcing it. Like I said, people remember being pulled over so it isn't a bad idea to once in a while let people know that we aren't all that bad. An occasional "Hey, this one's on me. Slow it down." or "Use the money you would've had to pay on a ticket to get that fixed." I was instructed as a young trooper that it is our job to alter people's behavior, not their attitude. I get that. But giving people a break here and there is also a good thing.

Sometimes you have to step back and take in the Big Picture. I'm a big believer of this philosophy and you'll hear about it later. I've tried to instill it in every young trooper I've ever been assigned to train. A car speeds by me. It isn't going extremely fast, but it is over the speed limit. The car pulls over and as I approach the driver's side, I see the driver's window start to roll down. As the window opens all the way, I hear the unearthly wailing of a young toddler. Once I get to the open driver's window, I see a Dad and a two year old in the car seat next to him. The days when you could do that. The tears are literally flying off her face like a cartoon; screaming and red faced. The Dad looks beaten and drained. He hands me his license and registration without a word. I tell him why I stopped him and he offers up no excuses. He just sat there, shoulders slumped and defeated.

"How long's this been going on?" I ask him.

With a big exhaled breath, he moans, "The whole ride."

Yes, he's speeding. Not a crazy speed, but he was speeding and he has a child sitting in the car with him. His child. Visions and screams from my own colicky daughter filled my head and all I could think was "This poor bastard." I hand him back his documents.

"Hey, slow it down, ok? I have one of those and she sounds like that quite often. Get her home safe."

This grown man looks at me like a kid who just got his favorite gift for Christmas. He let out a tired, but most appreciative, "Oh, thank you. Thank you so much. I will."

This is an incredibly simple example of "Looking at the Big Picture". Some guys I've worked with just don't see it. They see a blue Ford Taurus doing 70 miles an hour and he's going to get a ticket. They don't see a father who's had a rough two hours with a screaming child and just made a mistake. I know he broke the law, but so have you and me when we're running a little late for work. How many times have you driven a bit fast or had an expired inspection sticker and you didn't get caught. This guy did and by looking at the Big Picture, I realized that giving this guy a ticket would have been like kicking him when he was already down. I chose not to make this average guy's awful day that much worse. And he truly appreciated it.

Truth be told, I wasn't much of a ticket writer. I'd stop my share of cars for obvious traffic violations and write those tickets. College kids driving crazy or driving too fast with other people's college kids in the car always got a ticket. No breaks for kids driving like that. We'd seen too many tragedies and kids always need to learn the hard way. Kids never see a break as a learning experience. They see it as "I got away with that one." A number of these irresponsible young adults would tell me that their Dad was going to kill them when he sees his insurance rates go up. My standard reply was, "Better he kills you than you kill these three other kids whose parents are waiting at home for them."

Even though I wasn't crazy about writing tickets, I asked to be assigned to the Highway Task Force (HTF). The big advantage for me was that I wouldn't have to work the midnight shift anymore. I hated that shift. We had two week rotations of 11PM to 7AM, 7AM to 3PM, and 3PM to 11PM. They were referred to as the A, B and C lines. I never ate or slept right when working the midnight A line. So when the chance came along to work rotating B's and C's, I jumped at it. Now I'd be patrolling the Sullivan County section of highway State Route 17. It also meant a break away from complaint work. I didn't really mind going to the bar fights, larcenies, domestic disputes, or any of the hundreds of calls a uniform trooper would get called to. Nope, I'd be handling accidents, helping motorists, and writing tickets on State Route 17. Speeding tickets. That's what they wanted. The money from speeding ticket fines went to New York State. Fine money from other violations went to the local town or village municipality.

The HTF was created to enhance highway safety and it certainly did. Having patrol cars constantly out there did slow people down and assisted countless stranded motorists (before cell phones came along.) But a huge purpose of the HTF's existence was to generate speeding ticket money. The deal in being assigned to the HTF was that you had to write at least a hundred tickets with the vast majority of them being speeding tickets. This is definitely a good example of a quota. Yes, the HTF guys had a quota, but the average trooper really didn't. Everyone always thought we did, but we didn't. Like any job, a road trooper has to show that he's performing some kind of police enforcement during his 8 hours (now they're 12 hour days), every day. We had weekly activity sheets to fill out and had to sign through a blotter at the end of every shift. The blotter contained your day's activity. If you had no investigations to follow up on or accidents to respond to or complaints to handle, then you'd better show that you did something for 8 hours and that would usually be writing tickets. Some guys did have a "number" in their head that they'd like to hit every month. But if you were busy with other investigations or details, you simply didn't get your number, and most State Police supervisors were all right with that.

The HTF was a different story. 100 was the number. That was the quota. No excuses. If you want a break from complaint work and not have to work midnights, you better give them 100 tickets a month. It was a nice change of pace, but for me, it got old. I missed going to calls with the other guys. At heart, I really wasn't a ticket writing guy. After a year and a half, I asked to come off the detail.

A good sergeant always knows his individual guy's strengths and weaknesses. Some guys or gals can write 200 a month. Some are great with paperwork. Others excelled at training new recruits. Certain troopers were great at school speaking assignments. Still others were your solid complaint guys; the ones who could be sent to any one of the many disputes, problems or hassles that people get themselves into and handle it.

With a few years under my belt, I felt pretty comfortable responding to any complaint. There would be the same old "problem people" that you'd have to deal with and that could get tiresome. But there were also lots of funny situations you found yourself in. One call sent me to a mobile home park. The trailers were lined up one next to the other along a circling driveway. I had to respond to one particular mobile home to question a guy about a case I had. I pulled into the one parking spot next to the trailer and got out of the car. I walked around the trailer and knocked on the back door. As I walked back around to the front, I noticed a few young ladies in the next mobile home peeking out their window at me. That's not unusual. Everyone wants to know why the cops are around, so I went about my business attempting to find out if my guy was home. I soon realized that he wasn't and headed back to my patrol car. Just as I got to it, the door of the next trailer opened up and a couple of nicely dressed rather attractive young ladies stepped out. Upon catching my eye, one of them asked quietly, "Are you here for us?"

"No, I was looking for John Smith who lives here," I answered.

"Are you sure you didn't mean to come here?" she insisted.

"No, it's definitely this one, but is there something you need?" I asked.

She stepped a little closer as if about to tell me a secret and asked, "Are you here for the bachelorette party?"

Still confused, all I could utter was, "Ahhh, I don't think so."

She then cleared up my confusion with, "We ordered a stripper dressed as a cop for my girlfriend's bachelorette party and we thought you were him."

I must've blushed because her apology was immediate and repeated. I just smiled, told her that I wasn't and headed back to my car. For the life of me I couldn't come back with a single witty thing to say. I was speechless. But I can tell you that I have often wondered what would've happened if I.....well, you know.

Taking on the task of training new people always cut into your daily routine, but I did enjoy helping out new guys and gals who wanted to join our "NYSP Family". I've met many of my dearest friends as their training officer. It's a bond you'll always have. I also enjoyed any kind of break from the road. Going to speaking assignments, the State Fair or being sent to problem areas whether it be Indian troubles on the Canadian border or hurricanes on Long Island taught me pretty quickly that troopers were appreciated, respected and held in high regard. It's a nice change of pace to interact with members of the public outside of the usual, "May I see your license and registration" routine or showing up at their door to solve a problem. In a job like ours, when the vast majority of our interactions with the public result in some kind of discipline, it's easy for cops to become guarded all the time. Cops will be suspicious. That's the fact. The "What's this guy's problem?" attitude is always going to be at the forefront of our initial contact with people. It's what we deal with every day. We drive to where people are having problems and try to solve them. Many times it's a pretty serious problem. As a result, it's very refreshing to meet people and talk to them in a non-problem environment. It's during these times that people graciously express their appreciation for what we do. Having a Grandma walk out in the rain to hand you a plate of cookies as you stand on an escaped prisoner road check for hours is something very special. In a job that often times seems thankless, nice people step up and make the world a better place.

All in all, I really enjoyed working the road. Wearing the uniform meant something, donning the big hat. My kids loved seeing their Dad in uniform. They loved wearing the hat. It was a nice life. It paid the bills, provided health care and put our family into our own house. It was the American Dream; the front yard to play catch, the deck for get-togethers, even the tire swing hanging from a tree branch. Working overtime paved the way for simple vacations with the kids and a few extra niceties.

Every so often, I'd wonder if I wanted to move up the ladder within the State Police. Inside the rank structure of the New York State Police there is a uniform force. From the day a new recruit graduates the Academy, he is the rank of Trooper. As a uniform Trooper, you "work the road". From Trooper, there are two options for promotion. You can study like hell and take the Sergeant's test and be promoted to the rank of Sergeant within the Uniform force. You will now supervise uniform Troopers. The other route for promotion is to express your interest in being promoted to the rank of Investigator. Most departments title this position as Detective. We call it Investigator. After a process of researching your work history, work ethic and conducting interviews, you can be promoted by appointment to the rank of Investigator and put into the Bureau of Criminal Investigation (BCI). This is the non-uniform side of the house. As an Investigator, you will be assigned to a squad of other investigators who are all supervised by a Senior Investigator, (an awful lot of syllables in our rank titles). Every State Police station will have two sides of the house; a uniform side that patrols and the BCI side whose squad of investigators handle the more serious crimes. Since every guy started the job as a uniform trooper, the main dispatch area and uniform squad room were always considered the main part of the building or the front. When uniform Troopers had a serious case to turn over to the BCI, they'd take that walk down the hall, or to the "back rooms", where the BCI offices were usually located. Hence, the phrase "back room guys" became the household tag associated with the Investigators assigned to a station's squad. You'll hear me refer to them as such throughout this book. There are other Investigators who wind up in special units like Drug Enforcement, Child Abuse, or the Forensic Identification Unit. They are not part of that nuts and bolts group referred to as the "back room".

Both sides of the house have Officer ranks that go above uniform Sergeant and BCI Senior Investigator. These ranks go from Lieutenant to Captain to Major. Ranks above Major are stationed in our Albany Headquarters.

Let me get something straight right now. The uniform Trooper on the road stopping cars, going to domestic disputes and being the first one on the scene of a serious crime is the very backbone of our job.

And that's true of any police department. A very close second are the back room guys who run out on capers with our uniform Troopers and investigate the plethora of cases that cross their desk. Their workload is monumental and includes every kind of crime that you could imagine. The countless miles they put on their tires, their shoes, the vast amount of ink they expend into notepads; and the never ending number of interviews they conduct make them worth their weight in gold to this organization. Without them, we become a highway patrol.

Soon a sergeant approached me with an overtime opportunity. He didn't sell it to me as such, but I thought of it that way. Our troop (a five county region) had a crime scene unit. The unit was starting a new program that would train uniform troopers in the various stations within Troop F. The training would include some basics of crime scene work. Troopers could then assist with minor investigations at the stations, thus lightening the load that full time crime scene investigators were handling.

I wasn't a hundred percent sure if this was something I wanted to do. Remember that there were no CSI shows on TV and the OJ Simpson trial was years away. Most people had really no idea whatsoever what the work involved. Then the sergeant said the magic words.

"You'll probably see a fair amount of overtime in this gig."

That did it. I told my supervisor to put my name in for it.

So began my introduction into the world of fingerprints, dusting, evidence collection and lots of paperwork. I was sent to the FBI fingerprint school and then assigned to one-week rotations working out of the Bureau of Identification in Headquarters (as it was called way back then). This would give me on the job training under the direction of the full-time crime scene investigators who were all certified fingerprint examiners. I learned the basic patterns and details of fingerprints and how to process evidence for prints. If a call-out came in while I was working in the office, I went with them. If I was working the road and the crime scene unit got called to something heavy in my patrol area, I was called to the scene to assist the guys. Being sent to these scenes and working with the "guys in ID" soon appealed to me. Of course, I wondered if I had what it takes to do this important and meticulous job right.

My own higher education was barely a year of college, let alone any sort of degree. These days you need at least 30 credits of college to even take the State Police exam. I wasn't much on biology, chemistry or any of the sciences and here I was embarking on a career that would feature the debut of deoxyribonucleic acid. But the science of fingerprints was the bread and butter of ID guys when I started.

Thus I was thrust into the academia of bifurcations, ending ridges, loops, arches and whorls. You gotta be kidding me? I have to look through this little magnifying glass and try to pick out these miniscule markings on a smeared partial fingerprint? And then compare that mess to ten impressions on a fingerprint card? Remember that this was 1989. There were no computers yet! Can your young minds imagine this? Computers were high-tech, monstrous-sized machines in NASA or technology companies. There were none in the average office, let alone in your home or pocket. There was a fingerprint computer system in law enforcement, but it was still in its infancy stage. The State Automated Fingerprint Identification System (SAFIS) wouldn't make a real impact until years later.

Once the basic fingerprint schools were completed, the uniform crime scene technician job entailed dusting the scenes of burglaries and larcenies for prints, and then sending my lifted prints down to the full-time ID guys who were certified examiners. They would determine whether the prints were good enough and make all subsequent comparisons. These full-time crime scene guys did it all. When an FBI evidence team showed up at anything, we soon discovered that their people had individual specialties. Each team had one or two people who were the evidence collectors. That's what they did. They would also dust for prints, but the actual examiners were other people back at the office. The team had a photographer. That person only took the photographs. In our NYSP crime scene units, every full-time investigator was required to complete the FBI Photography courses, know how to collect evidence, how to dust, how to reconstruct a scene, and they all had to be certified fingerprint examiners. They did it all.

The one-week rotations through the crime scene unit office opened my eyes to a field that was clearly understaffed and overworked. Pleas for more training meant more cost to the state and thus fell upon deaf ears. It became obvious that this highly technical unit wasn't understood or managed properly by the hierarchy in Albany.

A veteran road trooper had put in for a promotion to Investigator. Many promotions meant "taking a ride" to a far away opening and waiting your turn to get back home. This trooper had been told that he was going to be "... taken care of. We're going to keep you in Troop." He had put fifteen years into the road and was glad to hear the news. The list of promotions came out and he scanned the list to see what "back room" he was headed to. He was quite dumbfounded to find out that he was promoted to the rank of Investigator and sent to the Bureau of Identification. His immediate response was, "ID? I've never lifted a print in my life? What the fuck am I gonna do in ID?"

I was a uniform crime scene technician working my one-week rotation in the ID office when Tom started as an Investigator in ID. The other ID Investigators were pretty overworked and not always in the best of moods. Now add the revelation that the new guy had no training whatsoever in crime scene work and you've got some pretty miserable guys. Tom was a poor soul who had been thrown into a lion's den. I had been a CST for a while so the ID guys had let me know how unhappy they were with this new jack that didn't know shit.

One day-shift, while I was working on evidence in the lab away from the other guys, Tom approached me.

"Hey, can you show me what you're doing there? I have no fuckin idea what to do, and these guys bite my head off anytime I ask them something."

I certainly knew the feeling of being the new guy in the dark. We hit it off immediately and began a friendship that lasts to this day. Tom would go on to learn every aspect of the ID world and, in my opinion, become one of the most professional and thorough crime scene guys I have ever worked with. He was a hard working guy who got the job done and always made time for a few laughs along the way.

Although overworked and beaten up by a dictator like commissioned officer, the other veteran ID guys were always great to me. They truly appreciated any young troopers who wanted to be there, who wanted to learn, and who would buckle down and help tackle the tremendous backlog of cases to be processed. Once you showed a genuine interest, they would go out of their way to stop what they were doing and teach you. No one epitomized this sentiment more than Don.

Don was an accomplished crime scene guy who put in tremendous hours to make sure the job was done right. Add to that a tyrannical boss who constantly called him away from home to respond to scenes we had no business being at. It was a time when Investigators had a higher base salary than Troopers, but didn't get overtime pay. Troopers did. This higher salary was supposed to pay for getting called out at night. Unfortunately, some bosses felt that since it wasn't costing the State any more money, they could call in everyone and keep them out as long as they wanted. It became obvious that the higher Investigator salary didn't even come close to the amount of time they were working in overtime. It wasn't right, and it turned many great cops into bitter men who couldn't wait to get out. The biggest shame was that experienced veteran cops in back rooms and ID wanted out.

But Don hung in there. He worked as the lead crime scene investigator in countless big cases. His knowledge and expertise were priceless. This was the guy that always took the time, often putting down whatever report he was working on to shuffle away from his desk after an hour of sleep to show a new guy like me the ropes. No question was ever too stupid and, believe me, I asked a lot of stupid questions. The man's patience was saint-like. Even as a know-nothing new guy, Don always made a point of thanking me for helping out. I learned so much from him; about ID, being a cop, a boss and about life. It's guys and bosses like Don that make you want to do a good job. Their appreciative and "whatever you need" attitude pushes you to do more, to learn more, to do the job right. Taking the time to treat people right, especially subordinates, goes a long way. I learned that lesson from Don.

I already said that these guys could be moody. Most of the time, it had absolutely nothing to do with co-workers. With some people, it's just who they are. A gruff, temperamental big guy of a cop can be somewhat intimidating to approach with a question or problem. It wasn't that they wouldn't help out in a second. But that tough exterior made the initial approach a bit risky. That was Terry.

An old school cop who had no problem physically taking care of business when he was a road trooper. Now he was in the tamer world of ID work, but that didn't mask his "I'm gonna kick somebody's ass" persona. It wouldn't be easy to approach a guy whose nickname was "Mad Dog" with a potentially bullshit question. You'd be taking your life into your own hands. But you know, sometimes you gotta live life out there on the edge. Every now and again, I'd throw out a few bombs to see if I'd get a rise. Sometimes I didn't and sometimes I had to run for my life.

Terry wasn't your touchy-feely type of guy so showing me how to develop 35mm film in a darkroom could be a little awkward for him. Remember, this was the 90's. No digital cameras for you out there who are asking, "Dude, what's 35mm film?"

And as a police agency, we didn't send out police film to be developed commercially. We did it all in-house. So teaching a new guy how to do this meant standing side by side inside a darkroom (Yes, total blackness). You were told to open up the metal film canister, take the roll of film out and then carefully roll the film onto wire spools. Now to teach somebody this, you could have them practice it in the light to see what it is they have to do, but once you're in the dark, very often the instructor has to put your hands onto the wire spool, get it started etc. etc. You get the picture? Did I say that Terry wasn't a touchy-feely kind of guy?

Well imagine having to stand right next to this serious, man's man sort of guy (you know what I'm sayin here?) in the pitch black and try to listen to his terse instructions that he is not going to repeat. Then comes the time in the dark when he has to take your hands in his to show you what has to be done and believe me, the hand holding was kept to an absolute minimum. Then he says, "You do it."

It was getting a bit tedious and I wasn't getting it as quickly as Terry wanted. He'd get a bit crotchety with me, but would always take the time to let me try it again. But again, this was getting a bit tiresome and frustrating. I figured it was time to break the ice a little bit. After a long lull in the instructions as Terry reached to grab another roll of film, I said,

"Terry."

"What?" came the impatient reply.

"I got my dick out."

I'm not sure if he had anything in his hands, but if he did, it was dropped immediately and I could feel his large frame pull away from me in a panic. He crashed into the photo table and I could hear him hit the floor. It was silent. I debated running out the door for my life, but didn't want to expose any of the film.

After a moment, I asked, "You okay?"

"You're an asshole." This was followed by a slew of profanities and subsequent laughter. But the ice had been broken.

Don and Terry were old time troopers who worked together on the road. Both wound up in ID. They became the best of friends and, although they were very different personalities, they created a dynamic duo that produced a fantastic crime scene team during financially strapped police times. It was a period with no money for training or equipment. They often bought their own supplies. They searched for free training anywhere they could find it. If there was essential training that the job refused to pay for, they'd lay out for it themselves. They were consummate professionals who always did the right thing. They'd get beat up on unnecessary calls just to appease a relentless Captain and still come to work early to finish up what was needed. They had good reason to be a bit grumpy. I'd come down for my one-week rotations, see that the boys had a bit of a rough time, and take upon myself to lighten the mood.

During another film processing procedure, Terry was showing me how to soak the film in chemicals. The wire spools would sit in these chemicals for a certain amount of time and then you'd remove the film from the spools and hang these 30 inch long sections of wet film inside a large dryer. The dryer was a metal container the size of a refrigerator. It was hollow and had lots of open space for the film to hang and dry. Terry was giving instructions as he took the spools out of the chemicals. He continued to talk with his back to me as he pulled the wet film from the spools. With several long sections of wet film in his hands, he turned around and continued to instruct that it was now time to put the film into the dryer. When he turned around, I was gone. No where to be seen. The cursing started immediately.

"Where the hell did that red headed prick go? Son of a bitch is supposed to be learning this shit and he's---"

As Terry opened the door to the dryer, I leaped out at him screaming bloody murder (Similar to Cato in the old Peter Sellers' Pink Panther movies). He jumped backwards out of his skin, dropping the film and grabbing his chest as if he was having the big one. He howled and staggered until he hit the wall. However, unlike the dark room incident, there was a look in his eyes..... Murder. It was on. Oh, it was definitely on and I was about to get a serious ass-kicking. My survival instincts took over and I bolted. I was like a gazelle who just saw that lion in the tall grass. I ran through the lab room. I could hear Terry thrashing behind me. I don't remember the curses, but there were curses. A lot of them.

Don was sitting at his desk in the office, as was our secretary. They were both typing. I ran by both of them like a flash of lightning (I was younger then!). A millisecond later, Terry bounded out into the office looking like a snorting bull, "I'm gonna kill that little prick. Almost gave me a friggin heart attack!" and out the office door he went. Don smirked and went back to typing. The secretary watched out the door and then turned to Don.

"I think he's really gonna kill him."

Don didn't even look up, "He'll be all right. Just another day in ID when Billy visits."

If the guys in ID liked your work ethic, then you'd get called to help them out at the scenes of major crimes. It was a nice perk. I was still a CST uniform trooper who worked under sergeants in my station when the guys got called to a woman's body found on a logging trail in the woods. If ID guys were called, then the scene was to be taped off with crime scene tape and no one was allowed into the scene until the ID guys got there. No one! The ID guys arrived, went way down the trail to the body and did their thing. A trooper was posted at the top of the trail with a crime scene log and told that no one at all was allowed to go down the trail. A cranky old sergeant was sitting in his patrol car nearby. I had heard about the body and was working the adjoining post so I figured I'd stop by. I pulled up and got out of my car. The crabby response from the sergeant's car was immediate.

"Forget it, Moloney. Nobody's allowed in there. If I'm not getting in there, you're sure as shit's not."

I went back to my car and pulled out the radio handset. I spoke in a nice loud voice, so that the trooper and his miserable supervisor could hear me. I was hoping the ID guys down at the scene were close enough to their van radios so that they'd hear me calling them. Don answered.

"Hey Don. Moloney here. You guys need a hand down there?" I asked.

"Absolutely. Sign in on the crime scene log and get in here," was the quick response.

I gave the irritable supervisor a smug, "Catch ya later."

The sergeant grabbed the radio from me and asked, "Do you need me to drive Moloney down to the scene?"

Don made it clear, "No, he can drive his troop car down. He knows what to do."

We've all had supervisors like that at some point in our lives. The guy that needs to be acknowledged as "The Man". I'm glad to say that the vast majority of supervisors in the State Police have been very competent professionals, but every profession is going to have a few jerks.

Stepping under the tape was always a nice feeling, and still is to this day. The respect for an expertise that allows you to be one of the select few who will walk under that "Do Not Cross - Crime Scene" border. As a young CST trooper, it felt cool. It really did. In later years, it would be the esteem held by other law enforcement professionals, whether it be State Police, other police agencies or prosecutor's offices, that made you feel good about what you did for a living. These incredibly hard working, underpaid and "committed to getting the bad guy" cops roped off a very serious crime scene and let no one at all inside it. And then they called you. They'd call for your know-how. They'd call to ask, "Hey, can ya help us out with this one? It's bad."

When men and women who put very bad people behind bars call for your input and help, it is unbelievably humbling. I'm not making an overstatement when I say that dedicated cops are some of the people on this planet who directly make the world a better place to live in. They do. They really do. But many citizens take it for granted. I don't. Being called to assist people like this is a true honor. A cop calls in the middle of the night and says that a little girl has been murdered. Then he asks if you can come out with your guys to process the scene.

"Right now, we have no idea who did it. We hope you can help us out, he continues.

"We'll be right there."

When the CEO of your company specifically asks you to run a project or head this particular presentation, it's a compliment. He has faith in your abilities. That makes you feel good. It should. When we cross under that crime scene tape, we're not always going to find the smoking gun. We're not always going to come back with answers. But I can tell you one thing. We're going to go to hell and back if we have to in an attempt to do every single thing we can for this guy who called us in the middle of the night. We'll do it because he's doing the very same thing to bring justice to a little girl's tragic and senseless death.

And when someone has this faith in you, when someone pays you this compliment, it's in order to say "Thank You". A lot of rough, tough cops don't, but they should. I will go out of my way to thank the cops that called us and the ones who tirelessly work outside the crime scene tape.

I soon learned that this was what I wanted to do. I loved the work. I had been a uniform trooper for about ten years, six of which were as a CST. Finally, my chance came along to get promoted and assigned full time to the Forensic Identification Unit. A lot had happened during those six years. The famous O.J. Simpson trial would bring evidence handling to the forefront of criminal investigations. Supposed screw ups in crime scene work soon opened the door to lots of training. No police agency wanted this media mess to happen to them. Now crime scene work became a hot item. CSI shows were right around the corner. We even changed our name.

I remember telling my wife, Siobhan, that yes it's a raise and I'll get a company vehicle, but be ready for those middle of the night calls. Don't be surprised when I'm called away from family BBQs, birthdays and anniversary dinner dates on a moment's notice. She was okay with it. She had been raised in a civil service family. She understood.

It was a bittersweet day when I turned in my uniforms and Stetson. I knew I'd miss wearing the gray bag. Even my young kids thought I wouldn't be cool anymore. I'd miss the patrol car, the diner with the guys, the interaction with the public. But most of all, I'd miss that camaraderie. I'd miss the guys. You always promise that you'll be back for lunch, but it has a way of not happening. You move on.

But it was also a very exciting time. CSI wasn't on television yet, so the job wasn't as in the spotlight as it is now, but I knew it would be fascinating. And I was looking forward to it. As a uniform CST, I was always an assistant, a helper, and then I'd go home. Now I'd be one of the case investigators doing this great job full time and doing it start to finish. I was eager. I had worked with all of the guys in the unit and knew all of them very well. It would be a smooth transition, but I also knew that I still had a boatload to learn.

This was the beginning of a career that would tutor me beyond my wildest dreams. I would receive an education not only about the crime world, but the real world.

Routinely seeing death in all its glory would teach me so much about life.

Chapter Four
Blood and More Blood

It's pretty obvious that to do this kind of work you can't be getting woozy at the sight of blood and guts. But for even the toughest of us, it can still happen at the strangest of times.

A week had passed before I caught my first case as a full-time guy in the Troop F Forensic Identification Unit. It was a particularly bloody scene. The male victim appeared to have been sleeping in his bed when he was attacked repeatedly with the claw end of a hammer. The repetitive blows to the head and face sent cast off specks of blood and tissue onto the walls, ceiling and furniture. It was interesting to note that blood had speckled clothing that was inside open bureau drawers, thus indicating to us that the perpetrator had been going through the drawers before attacking the victim.

The bed was a mess, as was the victim's head. The hammer's claw end left very distinguishable marks that made it easy to identify as the weapon. Believe me when I tell you that the claw end of a hammer can do some pretty serious damage especially if used repeatedly and with the right amount of force. The first one or two hard blows would incapacitate you almost immediately. I've seen a fair amount of homicides committed with hammers. It seems to be a favored (or maybe convenient) instrument and it certainly gets the job done.

In this case, our victim didn't even get a chance to hop out of bed. He was still under the covers and his hands and arms lacked any kind of defense wounds whatsoever. It doesn't matter if it's a hammer, a knife or a chainsaw coming at you, your natural instinct to survive is going to send your hands and arms up to ward off the threat. In addition to that defensive motion, your body will try to bob and weave away from the danger. It's tougher to hit a moving target. There were no glancing blows to this guy, no tears in the pillows from the claw, no hitting the bed. This guy did not see it coming and did not move at all once the onslaught started. The victim had definitely been asleep.

Cast off blood are the specks that are sent flying through the air when a bloody implement is quickly raised up and back over your shoulder or head to strike again. It's most prevalent with repeated blunt force trauma weapons like a hammer, baseball bat, or metal pipe. Anything that requires an arching swing of the object. It's the fast motion of bringing the weapon back in order to strike again that sends the blood and, sometimes, tissue flying off of the bloodied tool. You won't see cast off blood in cases where there was only one or even two strikes. The weapon has to be coming into contact with an already bloody surface to create cast-off patterns. The blood's location can often show you exactly where the attacker was standing.

While photographing the scene, we noticed that the cast-off blood had traveled quite a distance. There were trails of blood specks along the ceiling and inside an open closet at the far end of the room. This told us that the attacker was taking some pretty serious overhead swings at the victim's head. You can actually tell if the bad guy was taking short fast swings or long overhead haymakers. There was no doubt this guy was doing it the farmer's way.

As you could imagine, this left quite a mess. The pillows and upper end of the bed was pooled and spattered with blood and brain matter. We went about our job documenting the scene and the body. We photographed every pattern of blood and took numerous blood swabs. Once the determination is made that the body can be removed to the morgue, we will assist in getting the body into a body bag. That includes collecting every bit of bone fragment, brain pieces and torn flesh. It all has to go with the body for later autopsy and burial. Once the body is gone, we then have to go through every inch of the bed's blood soaked pillows, linens and blankets. This will include wading through pools of congealed blood for any possible evidence that may have fallen from the attacker. These soaked items will be collected as evidence.

Now I don't describe this gruesome scene in such detail to be overly morbid. I described it the way I did for two reasons: Firstly, because this is what we do. These details are exactly what we deal with all the time. Secondly, I started this chapter stating that you will find yourself getting woozy at the strangest of times.

After finishing this particular scene, I got home about 3:00 AM. My wife, daughter and son were sound asleep. Once inside, I heard a strange sound that had me peeking into my seven year old daughter's room. She had just vomited in bed. The vomit was all over the bed and around her mouth and face, but she remained asleep. Let me tell you. This girl can sleep. I gently picked up her sleepy form and laid her on the carpeted floor. I cleaned her face and changed her pajamas. I then wrapped up her puke filled sheets, changed the bed and put her back. She remained sound asleep. Mission accomplished. I took the puke filled sheets down into our basement laundry room sink where I ran the hot water and rinsed this kid puke from the sheets and down the drain. As I stood there letting the hot water spray away every remnant of puke, the smell of hot vomit rose up into my nostrils. My eyes started to roll back and I started to gag. Stepping back from the smell, I took a deep breath and waited. It passed. I'm sure the color came back to my face and I went back to the sink lowering the heat of the water, ready to complete the task at hand. The bundled up sheets and pillowcase were dropped into the washing machine. It was turned on and as I watched the machine fill with water, I started to laugh. And laugh. The biggest smile came across my tired face. I had just left the scene of a horrific murder that was committed with the claw end of a hammer. Brain and blood was everywhere. And I could stop afterwards for an early morning/late night breakfast on the way home with the guys. But the slightest whiff of my daughter's puke sent me into dry heaves. I got quite a kick out of that.

The murder scene I just described lends itself to a popular misconception that has been promoted by television. The presence of all that blood and mess inaccurately leads people to believe that the perpetrator must be covered in blood. In numerous cases, there will be some traces present on his clothes, in his hair, on his hands, but it is usually small transfer stains or some specks. But the idea that the bad guy must have blood all over him (as surmised by many people, including some cops) simply isn't true. It looks great on TV. It does happen here and there, but it's not the norm. If blood gets on his hands, he'll wash it off. If specks of blood hit his clothing, it usually soaks in and if it's dark clothing, you'll never see it.

Most cast off or blood spatter that lands on our bad guy isn't that noticeable and that works to our advantage. In one sense, a blood covered individual knows he will be noticed and has to do something about it. The guy who doesn't realize that he's wearing damning evidence gives us a chance to catch him.

We had a case where an elementary school aged girl was repeatedly stabbed in the school's bathroom and her body left in one of the stalls. She had just been dropped off for school by her father. The young girl died in the bathroom as the perpetrator walked out past numerous parents and school personnel.

It was apparent from the scene in the bathroom that there was a fair amount of blood spatter produced during the attack in very tight quarters. It was also obvious that the weapon was a sharp knife. In this situation, we did feel that some of this blood had to have gotten on the attacker. We also felt that there was a good chance that the person may have cut themselves during the attack.

Although you can't count on this in every case where multiple stab wounds are present, it does occur quite often. When you stab someone several times, it's likely that at some point you're going to hit something hard like bone or something hard in a pocket. When this happens, the very force of the stabbing motion will often send the attacker's hand sliding down the knife and across the blade. Pulling the knife back again can further damage the hand and fingers. If holding the knife one way, the pinky and ring finger will most likely be sliced. In another hold, it can be the index finger or the webbing of the thumb. With longer blades, it can happen to all four fingers.

Of course, the awful task of notifying the parents would have to be made as soon as possible. The father lived the closest and since he had just dropped her off, the guys would want to know if he had noticed anything suspicious at all before or after dropping her off. Uniform troopers were the first ones to his house, but before knocking on the door they noticed something strange. A small pane of glass to the exterior door of his house was broken and there was blood on the door. The quick thinking troopers called the case investigators to let them know about their find. The troopers swung the exterior screen door open as far as possible and propped it back to keep it out of the way and untouched. They knocked on the door. The father answered the door seeming calm. Upon hearing the news, he immediately became distraught. The troopers didn't ask about the broken glass or blood, but did notice a bandaged hand. They asked him to come to the station to help them in the investigation. He said he would. At the station, he would say that he had mistakenly broke the glass on the door and cut his hand. It was now important for us to know if he had incised cuts on the inside of his hand. The bandage covered his whole hand. The father immediately became a suspect; one of many at the time.

Early interviews revealed that the father was wearing a black leather jacket when he dropped his daughter off that morning. No one noticed anything strange or out of place as the father walked out past numerous people. The father stated that he had entered the school through the usual doors and dropped her off at the usual place inside and left. He went home, broke the window by accident and then went to the emergency room to tend to his hand, and then went back home.

Search warrants were obtained for the father's house and the emergency room medical records. The medical records indicated deep slicing cuts to two of his fingers. Once the search warrant was obtained for the house, the black leather jacket, among many other items, were secured as evidence. Upon an initial examination, we felt disappointed. We couldn't see any blood, but knew there had to be some present. What we could see was a lot of dried blood inside one of the pockets. And it was the same side pocket as his bandaged hand. The father was caught in a couple of lies, but would not admit to hurting his daughter in any way. Soon he asked for a lawyer and all questioning stopped.

When the jacket was brought back to our lab we put it under some high intensity lighting and there it was. Tiny dark reddish spots all over the chest area and right arm. The blood was subsequently tested and came back to his daughter. The blood in the right pocket was from his bleeding hand. The defense went so far as to bring Dr. Henry Lee to our station to examine the jacket. He was very cordial, a gentleman and a true professional. There was nothing he could dispute about our findings. The case went to trial. The prosecuting attorney did a nice job of describing the scene; lots of blood spatter produced during the attack and numerous people present as the defendant walked out past them wearing this jacket. In the courtroom lighting, it looked like a well worn black leather jacket. And then the photograph of the jacket under high intensity lighting was displayed. Eyebrows raised among the jurors. It was one of those "Holy shit," moments among the jury. The father was convicted and sent to prison for a very long time.

I know that many of you reading this are waiting for the "Why?" Why did he do it? There were some theories about stressful events going on in his life at the time, but we don't know his motive for sure. You, like us in the police world, will just have to accept that we may never know why. That's the way it sometimes goes.

Conversely, some blood does get on the attacker and he knows it. Now he has to wash himself and the clothing or get rid of it completely. Burning seems to be a desired method, but it can still leave remnants of evidence as well as neighboring witnesses who can testify that a fire was burning at that house ten minutes after the murder.

A small rural hamlet had a mentally unstable regular who wandered around town. He took a liking to a certain woman and found out where she lived. One hot, summer night he walked right into her house through the unlocked front door. (Lock your doors people! And don't leave your keys in the car!) With a knife in his hand, he walked up the stairs to her bedroom.

The woman's room was the only one with air conditioning so this divorced mother let her young son sleep in her room that night.

It's still unclear as to whether he was there to sexually assault her or murder her, but this guy got more than he bargained for. This savage didn't expect to see the son there or expect the fight he was about to get. This fierce mom did everything physically possible to save her son. It was evident in this bloody scene that the boy's mother put up a helluva fight that broke furniture and sent these two all around the room. All the while receiving slashes and stab wounds, she screamed for the boy to run as she fought hand to hand with this monster. The son sustained very serious cuts to his arms and wrist, but managed to get out of the bedroom, down the stairs, and out a kitchen door to a neighbor's house. In the bedroom, the stronger intruder wore the victim out. Her butchered body was left lying in the middle of her bedroom floor. The attacker fled the residence using the same front door he entered.

This was one of those scenes where you drive up to a very nice looking house in a country setting. It had a pretty front porch and manicured yard. But as soon as you entered the front door, it was like something out of a Friday the 13th movie.

The short foyer hallway floor had only a few drops of blood that went out the front door. Left of this foyer was a quaintly decorated living room. To the right of the foyer was a kitchen that was littered with blood. A trail of heavy blood drops ran from the stairway to the kitchen door. At this kitchen door was a huge pool of blood. The door knob was covered in blood. The stairway to the bedrooms had more of the same. Blood smears ran down the wall of the staircase. Blood transfers and bloody hand prints were visible on the hand railing. Doing the preliminary walk through to this point left you with the question, "If this is the exit route, how bad is the actual scene?"

It was bad.

At least one main artery had been severed early in the fight. Arterial blood sprayed the bedroom in several places. Blood gets onto the hands of both combatants and transfers to numerous surfaces as the altercation makes its way around the room. Bleeding from more and more wounds dropped onto the floor and got stepped on and tracked all over. Smears, transfers and spatters were on the floor, walls, and furniture.

I get a kick out of these TV cop shows like "Dexter" (although I really enjoyed this series) that have blood experts who can look at a bloody scene and say "This pattern indicates a blow to the head that happened in the middle of the room about 5 feet 6 inches from the floor. Then the victim was stabbed here causing this arterial spurting across the back of the sofa etc., etc."

There are scenes that can be accurately re-created because they're probably simpler scenes. Or scenes where you can combine some eyewitness accounts with the scene evidence and come up with a pretty accurate chronology of events. But when there were only two people who were present, a deceased victim and a bad guy who ain't talkin', there's a good chance you won't be able to completely re-construct a complex scene. If I point a shotgun at someone's chest and pull the trigger, there will most likely be a big, bloody spatter pattern on whatever is behind this guy as the slug exits his body spraying blood and tissue onto the wall, refrigerator or 70 inch flat screen TV. "Yes, Watson, you can deduce that the victim was standing in front of the 70 inch plasma when he was shot." But a deep bleeding cut might not bleed right away. Clothing soaks some of it up. An instinctive hand to the wound may stifle it. Physical exertion can open it up more and then it starts spurting. In bloody scenes, it's very difficult to exactly re-create the sequence of events in which they occurred. In most cases, it isn't that big a deal to know anyway. Learning that the blood spatter on the lamp is from the third time this creep stabbed the victim when he stabbed her 18 times doesn't really help much. If you're trying to determine that maybe this is the perpetrator's blood, that's a different story and very important. I also feel that sometimes we spend a lot of time attempting to re-create a series of repeated acts when we should be focusing our attention on other aspects of the scene; most specifically, other traces of evidence. We get a little wrapped up in the blood and "what it tells us", that some basic 101 evidence collection gets pushed off to the side.

"Hey, you can't dust that object. We need to keep that blood pattern intact."

"That object looks like it's been moved. Could have the perp's fingerprints on it."

"But the blood pattern? It tells us something."

"It's the victim's blood caused by the 9th or 15th time this cretin stabbed her. Fuck the blood. I'm dusting it. I might get his prints or better, his DNA off it."

That would be the written dialog for a CSI episode that I wrote.

We in the crime scene world get bombarded with these new ideas and cool concepts from television, real life crime shows and highly publicized trials. Some have merit, especially scientific ones, but many of them are all hype with no solid backing in crime fighting.

I have found that in most instances, if you keep focused on the job at hand, documenting, searching, and evaluating the scene thoroughly, then you can take that big step backwards and try to piece together what happened. As you do this, a light bulb in your head will get brighter and brighter, and open the door to lots of other goodies that may need documentation and collection. When you concentrate too much on one aspect, it's easy to disregard so much more that is right there for the taking. There are plenty of crime scene guys who will tell you that it's quite commonplace to get stuck on the room where it happened and disregard other seemingly uninvolved rooms that potentially hold very valuable evidence. Sticking to the basics throughout your scene work, and constantly stepping back and re-evaluating will result in the most accurate findings.

Veteran crime scene guys will agree with me when I say that there have been numerous times when I "thought" I had a pretty good idea of what happened at a scene, only to have my idea completely contradicted by a confessing bad guy. Don't misunderstand me. There are many times when we can say for sure and with complete certainty based on our years of going to these scenes that "this" had to happen before "that" and then "this" happened. Experience helps us do that. But the perfect re-creation of what happened in a complex scene is very rare.

The bedroom of the mother's attack was one of those complex scenes. It was clear that the altercation between the mother and the attacker began and ended in the bedroom. It landed on the bed, breaking it. The son got involved in the attack, got seriously wounded and fled for help, no doubt at the screaming behest of his mother as she held off this vicious animal. It probably didn't last very long. A scene like this and indications of a terrible fight could lead people to think that it went on for a while when in fact most of these interactions last less than a minute, two is a long time. When the victim was finally overcome, she collapsed onto the bedroom floor. The attacker fled.

We documented the blood that traveled down the staircase. At the bottom, it went in two directions. One towards the kitchen door, that we now knew was the boy, and a few blood drops out the front door.

The blood through the kitchen was a lot heavier and a later statement by the boy would explain all the blood at the kitchen door. He attempted to turn the knob on the kitchen door to get out, but his badly cut hands wouldn't work, so he stood there trying and trying to turn the knob using the palms and heels of his hands as the cuts bled all over the door and floor. Finally, this astonishingly tough kid worked through the pain and terror and got it open and ran to the neighbor's house for help. He was lucky to have not passed out from blood loss or shock.

Blood drops going out the front door had to be from our bad guy. It could be a cut he sustained, or possibly, her blood dripping from a weapon or him. A dripping weapon wouldn't leave much and there were only a few drops. At this point, either was possible. But one thing we felt sure about was that there had to be some blood on him or his clothes. This arterial cutting, fall on the bed, bang around the room fight brought him into close contact with this severely bleeding victim. There was no doubt that this was one of those perpetrators who had vital evidence on him and the clothing he was wearing. Time was essential. We had to find him and the clothes. The attack had only happened hours earlier, so we had a chance. We followed the trail out the door onto the front porch. Some transfer blood patterns from the bottom of a shoe were visible on the ground. The pattern didn't have much detail but it led to the woods in front of the house.

A detail of uniform troopers and K9's were brought out to track. Traces of more blood were found in the woods. The dogs did a great job. Soon a trooper smelled something burning. The trail led to a small house in the woods where this misfit lived with his mother. Upon getting closer to the house, a trooper spotted a burn barrel and smoke. A look inside confirmed clothing. Subsequent searching of his house revealed traces of the victim's blood. Remnants of the clothing were saved from the burn barrel by uniform troopers. Blood on the clothing was the victim's. Ownership DNA on the clothing confirmed that it belonged to our suspect.

In the first case, the father didn't realize that he had tiny specks of blood all over his dark jacket. In the second case, the suspect knew he had damning blood evidence on his clothes and had to dispose of them. There are times where the perpetrator knows he has to dispose of his clothes, but doesn't quite do a thorough enough job.

A woman was found stabbed to death in her residence by a visiting relative. The relative had gone out for a short time, so the murder had just taken place within the last few hours. The victim had been stabbed numerous times, but the scene wasn't overly bloodstained. The strained relationship between the victim and her estranged husband soon brought him into our sights. (You know the deal, people. The spouse, whether married, separated or divorced is always the first suspect!) Interviews of neighbors and the husband revealed that he had no alibi for the time frame of the murder and that a vehicle matching his was seen parked off the roadway a short distance away from the house.

He came in voluntarily and withstood hours and hours of interrogation. He had no one to confirm that he was home alone the whole time and denied that his vehicle was on that road. He was rather smug about himself, but a few things just didn't add up to our guys.

The crime scene didn't give us much. It was obviously a very quick assault that took her by surprise. She was incapacitated quickly and dropped where she was. Not much was disturbed. Again, it appeared that the front door was the way in and out. (Did I say, "Lock your friggin doors?") No weapon was found, but it was definitely a knife. All developed fingerprints would later come back as the victim's. There were slight traces of blood smears on a counter top and a unique, faint pattern left in blood on a piece of notepaper that was on the table. Uniform troopers scoured the surrounding woods and roadway shoulders in an attempt to find the knife or any discarded evidence. Nothing was recovered.

Next, we processed the scene where the vehicle was seen parked off the roadway. There was a good tire impression left in the wet mud. After photographing it, we made a plaster impression of it. It was pretty good, had a lot of detail.

The husband's lack of an alibi, the observed vehicle that matched his vehicle and a couple other things that didn't add up gave us enough to obtain a search warrant for the husband's house. Among many items, we secured whatever clothing appeared to have been recently worn or just washed, some footwear, and an open pack of rubber dishwashing gloves. We also took any knives that came close to the size of the knife blade that caused the wounds on the victim.

The search warrant included his vehicle. It said that we could search the vehicle and secure any evidence, but it didn't say that we could take the tires. Our search included any clothing or other evidence tying the vehicle to the estranged wife's residence, but we were hoping for her blood in his vehicle. Unfortunately, there was none. With the plaster cast in hand, we could tell that the tire tread design was the same design as the husband's vehicle. Same tread design didn't mean it was that particular vehicle that made the tire print in the mud, so clear impressions of a full rotation of each tire's tread design were needed. The plaster cast from the scene was only a short section of the tire. We had a good idea which tire it was, but you want to be sure and should get all four tires' exemplars if given the chance. The best comparison can be made with the plaster impression and the actual tire, but since it looked like we couldn't take the tires, we did the next best thing. We took a long thin board about 18 inches wide and 7 feet long. On it we taped a long section of rolled clean white paper. On another 18 inch by 7 foot board we spread out a thin layer of fingerprint ink. The inked board was placed on the ground in front of a tire with the white board laid out ahead of it. Now the vehicle was driven slowly over the first board transferring a layer of black ink onto that particular tire. The tire then continued to roll onto the white board and transferred the inked impression of one full rotation onto it. The white paper was removed and labeled as such and such a tire. Another piece of white paper was taped to the board. The first board was inked again and we went through the same process for the other three tires. Just like rolling your fingerprints (the old-fashioned way, now they have electronic fingerprints), we had four clear, rolled impressions of the vehicle's tires. The four lengths of paper could be rolled up and sent to the lab to compare to the plaster cast from the scene.

Unlike television, the best a lab criminalist can do is say, "The impression contained in item # 1 (the plaster cast) is consistent with the impressions found in item # 35B (the inked impression of the right front tire)". They can't say it was that particular tire from that particular vehicle because there are thousands of those Goodyear M&S P225/65R16's made and being driven around. What they can do is closely examine the tire tread design in the plaster cast and try to find specific details in the exemplars that match. It could be that they both show more than normal wear on the inside of the tire or maybe it looks like a nail is in the tire and four inches away from that is what looks like a cut to the tire rubber. Finding distinct characteristics that make this Goodyear M&S tire unique, is what will make it stand out from the rest of all other tires.

The case wasn't going very well. No admissions of any kind. No weapon. No fingerprints. No blood in his car. The husband didn't have an alibi and we found what certainly looked like his tire track nearby. That was all we had right now. The autopsy showed numerous stab wounds and many of them were to her back once she was down on the floor. We had secured her clothing and sent it to the lab hoping to find someone else's blood or DNA on it.

It was time to examine and review all of the evidence, as well as the scene photographs. Although the scene wasn't as scattered as the last one, it was still very obvious that it was an up close and personal attack. She had to have been overpowered, held in place and stabbed repeatedly until she collapsed. There was no evidence of a knock down blow to the head or drugging. She was attacked with a knife and died as a result of its wounds. There had to be blood somewhere. The vehicle was clean, so there's a good chance that the assailant's clothes were gone. We had to work with what we had, which wasn't much.

In so many professions, there always comes a time when you need to go back to the basics. The entire concept of crime scene work is based on the very fundamental principle first articulated in the early

1900's by the French criminalist Dr. Edmond Locard who stated that "Every contact leaves a trace." Locard's "Theory of Exchange" dictates that when two objects come into contact with one another, each will take something from the object or leave something behind.

As far as finding "something of the perpetrator" at the scene goes, we were striking out. We did have that strange faint honeycomb type pattern in blood on the notepaper in her residence. It would wind up being her blood, but what was the pattern? We then went to the evidence at the husband's house. We went through every bit of clothing. We lit it up with all kinds of lights. We examined every inch of every bit of clothing and footwear we took from the house. Finally, something jumped out at us. A faint red stain on the inside elastic band of the husband's underwear. It was at the back of the briefs and not easily seen. Is it possible that he got rid of the clothing he was wearing but didn't dispose of the underwear? Why should he? He probably assumed that only his outer clothing needed to be dumped. Is it possible that he reached back with a bloodied hand to pull up his pants and deposited a trace of her blood on the inside of his underwear? That was our hope. The underwear (along with other evidence) and a sample of the victim's blood were sent to the lab. We'd have to wait on DNA results. It took a little longer almost two decades ago. In the meantime, we wanted to figure out that weird pattern on the notepaper. No where in any of the blood on her clothing or inside the house was a partial fingerprint left. Not even a smear. He had to be wearing gloves during the attack. Gloves? We had collected an open package of dishwashing gloves at the husband's residence. When we pulled out the remaining unused gloves in the packet, we saw it. On the palmar surfaces of the gloves was that honeycomb pattern. It matched the pattern left on the notepaper in the woman's house. We'd still have to send both to the lab for a microscopic comparison, but we could plainly see that they were the same.

The lab results came back and the red stain on the husband's underwear was blood and it was indeed his estranged wife's blood. The case went to trial. The jury saw photographs of the evidence and heard testimony from our investigators relating to unaccounted for time frames and inconsistencies in the husband's story. He was found guilty and sentenced to a long time in prison.

As with any case I mention, it isn't only the crime scene unit delivering the evidence that puts away a bad guy. It's a combination of lots of great police work that's done inside the crime scene tape and outside the tape hitting the street and banging on doors. Then add to that the lab personnel who work tirelessly on piece after piece of evidence. It's a team sport.

"The victim really doesn't know anyone. She's new to the area and isn't married or hooked up. Seems to be liked by everyone she worked with." Hearing this can initially make you wonder if it's one of those random acts of violence. A lot of our work is for other police agencies that don't have a crime scene unit. This was one such instance.

A city police department had been called to a rough neighborhood by a family who lived in the ground floor apartment of a five story walk-up tenement building. This very religious family called the police when they woke up in the morning and found two streams of blood running down their apartment wall from the ceiling. The blood streams ran down the wall alongside a framed picture of the Virgin Mary. When responding cops got no answer to the apartment door above this family, the landlord was called in with a set of keys. Upon opening the apartment door, the source of the streaming blood was apparent. The nude body of the female occupant lay in the middle of the living room floor. You could not step into the apartment without stepping into a layer of her blood. Furniture had been trashed. Scissors stuck out of her left breast. The mid thirties aged victim had been stabbed numerous times.

The cops had conducted a search of the apartment making sure the perpetrator wasn't still there and that there were no other victims. They sealed the door and called us. That layer of blood on the floor had numerous footprints in it from cops checking the apartment. That can't be helped. The cops have to make sure the scene is safe. Responding crime scene guys like us are certainly grateful. The officers told us that certain prints were theirs and showed us the boots they were wearing, so it made eliminating a number of the footprints easy. These sharp thinking cops also told us that they made sure to wipe clean the bottoms of their boots when leaving the apartment so as not to falsely track the blood anywhere else. That's heads up thinking and we appreciate that. Naturally, we suited up and double bootied. (Put on another set of Tyvek booties over the ones that came with the Tyvek suit.) Walking in wet or dried blood was inevitable. We also brought in lots of extra booties and a bio garbage bag so as not to track blood into other areas of the crime scene or outside. In one spot it had pooled and seeped through the wood slat flooring creating the eerie image in the apartment below.

The struggle between victim and attacker knocked furniture over and resulted in the victim ending up on her back on the floor where the perpetrator continued to stab her. Her face had been beaten and her body showed other bruising. A closer inspection of her body showed that once she was dead, he had inflicted other wounds to her body. Some marks were cuts to her breasts and legs. There were post mortem cuts to her face. We could also see that a piece of her earlobe was missing. And high on the inside of her thigh was a clear bite mark. This was a sexually motivated attack. Seeing the bite mark made us wonder if the earlobe was bitten off. At this early stage, it was just a thought.

We processed the apartment for a while and then took a break to catch up with the case detective. He told us that the victim had moved into this second floor apartment only a few months earlier. She apparently didn't know many people. The few who did know her, knew her from local volunteer charity work. They related that she was a very sweet woman and that everyone who met her liked her. She was single and quite pretty. She didn't earn much money and couldn't afford the nicer part of town. Wow. Not much to go on here. It was looking like a random act, and random acts are very tough to work out.

At one point, we realized that whoever did this must've gotten some blood on the soles of his footwear. Some bodies will take a while for the blood to spread, so the perpetrator wouldn't necessarily be standing in it when he leaves. But it was obvious that our barbarian had stayed a while as she bled. We did have some unexplained footwear impressions in the blood. The tenement building hallways and stairs had old carpeting. We blacked out the hallways as best we could and used Luminol on the carpeting. Slight traces were discovered on the carpeting outside the apartment. Not really a big deal. That could be the bad guy or the first responding cops. We continued processing the hallway and down the stairs. We expected to find traces here and on the way out as it seemed that would be the logical escape route. We found nothing. Now you have to remember that finding nothing doesn't mean he didn't go that way. It just means there wasn't enough blood transfer left for the Luminol to pick up. We were striking out. The next step would be to expand the area, so we treated the carpeted stairs up to the third floor. We found a couple of traces on a few steps. When I say traces, I mean small spots or shapes. Unlike television, a beautiful footprint doesn't start glowing. You don't even get a partial impression that looks anything like a heel or the tread design of a sneaker. It'll be spots or lines or any variety of shapes you can think of. It reacts with the blood, so whatever remnant of the blood gets deposited, that's what you hope to see. We continued upstairs and found one more spot on the third floor. When we checked the carpeting in front of all the third floor apartment doors, we found nothing.

The detective stopped back again as we were wrapping up and we asked him if everyone in the building had been interviewed. He told us that most tenants had been contacted and seemed to be okay. That meant that nothing stood out about them, but of course, all alibis and whereabouts would be confirmed later. However, there had been one man on the third floor who appeared to be home, but wasn't answering his door. You could tell because the tenant used a huge padlock on the outside of his door when he left and would bring the padlock inside his apartment when he came home. The padlock was not on the outside. The landlord explained this to the detectives and further added that the tenant was a bit of a strange character who lived alone and had no job. When cops tried the door, it was definitely locked from the inside.

I joked with the detective that maybe he and his guys had better find some way into that apartment and see what's inside. You just might find a dead guy with a suicide note that explains all of this and we could all go home. We chuckled as cops do at these awful scenes knowing very well that things never get figured out that easily.

Back inside the apartment, so much blood on so many surfaces made it difficult to say if our attacker had been cut, so we collected lots of blood samples from all around the residence. Plenty of household items were secured for later fingerprint processing. We had already developed a number of latent fingerprints from various surfaces inside the apartment. The body was removed and we finished up with the scene.

An autopsy would be needed as soon as possible. The one piece of evidence we really wanted to process for prints was sticking out of her chest. As usual, our fantastic pathologist made immediate time for us and met us at the morgue. Once the scissors were removed, we'd preserve it for print development. Then we'd document every injury to her body in order to discern whether another weapon had been used. It didn't look like it. She was beaten by blunt force and stabbed numerous times with the scissors. The bite mark on her inner thigh came next. We photographed it over and over. It would be standard procedure to return to the morgue once a day as the bruising changed coloring and photograph it again in the hopes of getting more detail. Of course, the pathologist would also collect any and all evidence in relation to a possible sexual assault. Our pathologist agreed that this was a violent sexual crime. He added that the earlobe looked like it had been bitten off. We finished photographing and collecting as much evidence as possible. It had gotten late and we decided to hit the evidence first thing in the morning.

Nice and early the next day, we started on the evidence. We'd pack up and get certain things ready for the lab and prepare other items, like the scissors, for fingerprint processing, photography etc. As with all cases, it's customary to reach out to the case detective and ask for a few more specifics and see if any new leads had developed. He answered the phone at his desk.

"Bill, I was just about to call you."

"Hey, great minds think alike."

"You called it," he went on.

"What are you talking about?" I queried.

"After banging on that guy's door on the third floor several times, we went in one of his windows," the detective explained.

"And?"

"And you wouldn't believe the shit we found. Can you guys come over?"

He gave me a brief description that prompted us to return to the tenement building.

When we showed up, the front door of the third floor padlocked apartment was open. Lying on the floor, somewhat propped up against the sparsely furnished room wall was the apartment occupant. Next to him was an empty bottle of Drano, (Yes, the clogged pipe cleaning stuff). Apparently Drano will do quite a number on your own internal plumbing and it will hurt like hell as it does its work. Blood and foam poured from his mouth. There was also some blood stained clothing in the apartment. The detective had pointed these things out to us and added, "But no suicide note explaining it all, Bill." We had a little bit of work yet to do.

Our obliging pathologist (who I'll talk about later) agreed to come right back and do this guy. Upon opening the guy up at autopsy, you could clearly see that the Drano had done its job. It tore through organs and made a mess, so checking through the stomach contents wasn't easy, but once we did, there it was. The swallowed earlobe. Lots of photographs were taken and the earlobe was secured to be compared to the victim who was still at the morgue. Later DNA testing would confirm the earlobe came from our victim as well as the blood on his clothes in the apartment. Fingerprints in the apartment also came back to this solitary, mentally unstable man as the sexual murderer.

We, in the crime scene unit, get involved in big, high profile cases all the time. It's our world. And there are a lot of cops who can have a career made on one big case; a trooper who conducted a case changing interview, or the investigator who got the confession after spending countless hours in a room with a bad guy. Doing your job well and being recognized for it is a good thing. It's unfortunate that some employers or supervisors will recognize outstanding work and then "dangle the carrot" to make that good worker do even more. I understand the concept, but all too often it is used to abuse a good worker. A great work ethic provides good and honest results. You don't have to dangle the carrot in front of these workers. These hard workers are the ones who usually understand the idea that if you put in your time and do the job well, you can look for that move or that promotion and you'll get it based on your merit. But when the carrot gets dangled, we sometimes sway off course. We all chase the carrot to some degree.

The carrot comes in many disguises; a raise, a promotion, that big house, the dream job. We run, run, run toward the carrot. Run faster, work longer hours, make more and more money, trade in our perfectly fine car or house for a bigger and better one.

In our heads, we think that when we get to the place where that big, fat, juicy carrot is, we'll find that the grass is so much greener. It will be a paradise. It's going to be so much nicer than that rat race we've been running for years. And guess what? It's not. It becomes more running. It's still work. It's still a job. You might like it better and make more money, but it's still a job. Many times with higher demands on your life. I'm certainly not suggesting that you don't try to advance yourself. Doing better in your career is a good thing, but make sure your decision to do it is based on the right reasons. You have to want it because it's right for you in your particular life.

In our job, you can take a test to obtain the rank of sergeant and then later a test to become a lieutenant. In both cases, there's a good chance that if you do well on the test, you're going to take a ride somewhere across the state. If that works out for you, great. Wanting to move up the ranks is a good thing for most people. But are you sure you want to take a ride across the state and be away from home four or five nights a week when your kids are three and five? You don't get those years back. Then you take the lieutenants test and take another ride when your kids are 11 and 13. Sometimes it can turn into a pattern. The next promotion could send you to New York City or headquarters in Albany and you figure that it worked out those last two times so this'll work out too. The one ride becomes many rides. And then at a family get-together, you'll hear your son talk about some important achievement he had growing up and you'll remember that you were halfway across the state when that happened.

While I was still in uniform, I was having coffee with a part time constable. This guy had retired from the State Police after about a million years on the job and took a position as a part time constable for his town. He told me that his college age daughters were home for the weekend and that they were going to be doing something for the day with his wife. There was a quiet lull in the conversation as he stared silently out the diner window.

"Bill, I don't even know my own girls."

"What was that?" I stammered. This guy never spoke about family matters. He was all job.

In a rare moment of personal honesty, he opened up.

"They sit in my house and I don't have any idea what to say to them." He looked right at me now and continued, "Don't let that happen to you. Do the job right. But the job isn't everything."

A moment later, he cleared his throat, downed the rest of his coffee, stood up and declared, "Hey, I've got unsuspecting motorists to ticket." He bid me good day and was off. I watched this lifelong dinosaur cop get into his patrol car and drive away. He was a good man. A man a little broken by some decisions he made during his career. I've never forgotten his words. He has since passed away. I will always owe him a debt of gratitude for picking that day and picking me to open up to in one of life's rare moments.

All too often we blow off pearls of wisdom that come from our older generation. We don't pay enough attention to the advice of people who have clearly been through this thing we call "Life". Why do we do that? These people have lived through depressions, fought in wars, raised huge families without a husband, worked one job for 40 years, raised a family on next to nothing pay and have stared death in the face under all kinds of conditions. And yet, all too often we treat their words as nonsense. We're too busy to listen. We think we know the answers and don't need their advice. If we listened to a few more of these dinosaurs, we'd learn pretty quickly that the carrot isn't a place over the rainbow. It's right now. It's making the most of the journey and not putting it all off until you reach some imagined destination. Enjoy life at your job. Even if it's an awful job. Pass the day with pleasantries. Joke, talk about life, and "How 'bout them Jets?". Ask how co-workers are doing. Have lunch together and shoot the shit. When you get home, read to your kids, get tackled by their friends, go to their school plays, sleep on the hard floor in their room when they're scared at night. If no kids are home, have a few too many wines with your wife, husband, boyfriend or girlfriend at the kitchen table (even if you don't drink wine!). Visit Mom or Dad or call them, go see Grandma or Grandpa in the nursing home, call a friend or anyone you know who may be going through a tough time and bullshit for an hour. Read a book you've always wanted to, call a friend over for a few beers on the deck or in your living room. Then go back to work and do your job well with co-workers that you truly try to get along with even if it's hard to. I have met some of my dearest and closest friends in life during my time with the State Police.

When you have done that, there will be no pasture on earth that will have greener grass than the patch you're standing on right then and there.

Chapter Five

Frozen

nd I'm not talking about the wonderful Disney movie (my granddaughter's favorite... at the moment). I'm referring to instances when a human body freezes like the hunk of roast beef you tuck away in your freezer. The majority of cases I've been involved in dealt with a body (or bodies) being frozen solid as a result of atmospheric conditions. I know of only one case where a spouse went to the trouble of buying a full-size freezer to store the remains of his murdered partner. When frozen solid, he cut her into sections with a sawzall and then buried the pieces in the back yard. The loose ends left by the spouse were getting rid of the freezer and explaining why he rented a small excavator for a modest sized back yard. Yeah, neighbors tend to notice that. I never quite understood the freezer part of that plan. If you were going to bury all the parts together anyway, why bother with freezing and cutting it up first? Not everyone plans a murder the way they do on television.

Most of the cold bodies I've encountered have been exposed to frigid temperatures for a while before being found. I know of two times where people made the conscious decision to freeze themselves to death. One guy was an escaped prisoner who realized that he was surrounded in the woods and decided that he wasn't going back to prison. It was very cold out and authorities chose to wait him out for a while. He wore a single layer of clothing without an overcoat. Eventually police closed in around him and found his body. We were called in. It took us a while to hike into where he was. The immediate first question upon seeing him was, "Did somebody move him?"

The answer was "No". He had been found just the way he was positioned. We could see now why we were called. He was lying on his back in the middle of a densely wooded area with his arms spread out to each side and palms upward. His legs were close together. All three of us from the crime scene unit felt the same weird feeling and had the same question. Was his body posed like the crucified Christ by someone else's doing or his own? Did he hold himself in this position until he died of hypothermia, or was he killed and posed like Jesus on the cross by someone else? We went to work photographing and doing a preliminary walk through of the surrounding areas. Then we took a look at him. There was no obvious trauma to the body that we could see yet. No stab wounds, bashes to the head, gunshots or marks around his neck. We then went to check the back of his head. But we couldn't. He wouldn't move. His whole body wouldn't move. He was frozen in that position and stuck to the ground.

Well, that presented us with an interesting obstacle. How do we get him out of there? We had maybe three hours of daylight left and quite a trek through the woods. It was recommended to us that we call in the local fire department and have them use their tools to hack at the ground all around him and... then what? Pick up a 6' by 6' piece of frozen earth with him on it and carry it out? No, that was silly. We decided to have fellow troopers and other police personnel scour the entire area for any pertinent evidence. We would usually do this, but time was a wasting, so the three of us used chisels, crowbars, and screwdrivers to gently tap away at freeing each part of the man from the frozen ground without doing any post mortem damage to his body. It was a slow process. Battery operated lights had to be brought in for us to finish the painstaking job.

Once his body was freed from the ground, a funeral home was called. But then we realized that we had another problem. He wasn't a small man. His outstretched arms spanned almost seven feet. There was no way that this "T" shaped 7' by 6' tall frozen popsicle was going to fit inside one of their vehicles. We couldn't even get him into a body bag. However, the quick thinking funeral director ran home and came back with his four wheel drive open bed pick-up truck. We cut holes in the sides of the body bag for his arms to stick out. Before zipping it up, we wrapped his protruding arms with clean white sheets (funeral homes usually have these on hand). Then we zipped him up.

But even then our troubles weren't quite over. The pick-up truck could only get so far. Can you imagine trying to carry this big, cross shaped 200 pound package through dense woods? Through short clearings in the woods, four to six people could each take an arm, a leg, the middle, but once you got to lots of trees and rocky areas and inclines, he'd have to be turned sideways and balanced. If we knew for certain that there had not been any foul play, then we could have forced the arms into more workable positions. But we didn't know yet. It was imperative to keep him in the position in which he was found. We'd have to wait until the autopsy to have a much more thorough examination under well lit conditions. So for now, we relied on the extra hands and strong backs of young troopers to help us out of the woods with him. We loaded him into the back of the pick-up truck on some soft cushioning that the funeral home provided and covered him up. A trooper followed the body to the morgue. Some extra hands were again needed to get him into the morgue where he was laid on a gurney, with his arms outstretched, and rolled into a walk in refrigerator. Lucky enough, this morgue had one. He would never have fit into one of those refrigerated morgue drawers.

The autopsy pretty quickly concluded that the prisoner had indeed died of hypothermia. It appeared that this guy resigned himself to this form of death, and was strong enough in his final moments to hold a position that meant something to him. Some of you may ask, "How do you know that someone else didn't come along after he died and position his body the way it was?" With police surrounding the entire area, is it possible that someone, even an officer, made their way in there, found him newly deceased and positioned him before he started to freeze solid and then left the scene? In this line of work, you find out quickly that you can never say "Never", but that's very, very unlikely.

In many instances of suicide, when someone has made up their mind to go through with it, they can overcome obstacles that they would never have overcome during their normal lives. How often have you heard the accounts of depressed people who seemed to have perked up just before taking their own life? It's that' "I've made my decision and I'm good with it" feeling. Relatives and friends of these people have often said that during the prior days it seemed as if a burden had been lifted from the victim's shoulders. The subsequent suicide makes it that much harder for relatives and friends to accept.

The second of these situations involved a woman who had become distraught with her life. Severe depression set in and she frequently abused pills. All of the local pharmacies had her name as someone who should not be given any kind of prescription medications unless contacted directly by a doctor. During a cold December, she was reported missing. All attempts at locating her turned up nothing. Some interviews led our guys to friends and relatives that lived far away, but no one had been in contact with her. The snowy winter then began and blanketed the region for months. January was recorded as one of the coldest in decades.

March came around and one Friday had Paul, Vinny and I in the office. These two are a couple of my closest friends on the job and are guys that I steered towards crime scene work. Paul is a mountain of a man who I trained as a brand new recruit trooper. He immediately became a tenacious cop who never stopped until the job was done. He is one of the most professional and meticulous lawmen I have ever worked with. Vinny came along later. A little younger than Paul and I,

Vinny was just as persistent a cop, but with a decisive, quick wit that would have you rolling with laughter or have you chasing him down because he just threw some stinging barb your way.

Paul and Vinny had become good friends while uniform troopers. They had chosen different promotional paths, but with the passage of a little time, were once again united in the Forensic Identification Unit. They had a great time working together, however at any given moment the levity could very easily turn to, "What the fuck did you say?" I often equated Vinny and Paul to the literary George and Lenny of Steinbeck's classic novel. Paul didn't always like that, but it wouldn't stop the shorter than average Vinny from calling him names that referred to a prehistoric species. And it wouldn't take much. Paul could seem out of sorts one morning only to have Vinny sincerely ask, "What's the matter big guy? Did breakfast get away this morning?" Vinny's caring tone would almost have Paul answering in earnest until "BAM" the jab struck and Paul would be reaching out for Vinny's throat. Now the interaction between the two resembled the cobra and the mongoose; the big and powerful cobra being antagonized by the extremely quick and agile little mongoose. Several times I've had to be the Dad and break up the boys, always being very careful not to catch a stray swat from Paul in the process.

During one of Vinny's flights for his life sprints down the hall, I informed this dynamic duo that we had a body. A hiker came upon what he believed to be a fully clothed corpse in the woods. He said that he couldn't see any skin because the body seemed to be face down and was totally covered in clothing. Our back room guys responded to this section of woods that was only a couple hundred feet off of a well traveled road. It was a road our missing gal would often walk. The body was impossible to positively identify in its current condition, but our guys felt pretty sure that it had to be her. The snow had slowly melted over the past few weeks, but it was still a bit brisk that day. The layout of items around the body looked like the planned out scenario of someone who had prepared themselves for this.

A piece of discarded old carpeting was laid out under the body next to a short tree stump. The stump served as a sort of end table. Between the body and the stump was a nearly empty bottle of cheap vodka. Scattered all around the area were numerous empty packets of night time sleep aid pills. They weren't prescription, but the kind you could buy over the counter. A woman's purse was next to the stump and contained identification in the name of our missing woman. Of course, we'd have to confirm that. A small battery operated flashlight was clipped to a low hanging branch over her head. A plastic bag from a local pharmacy contained several more of the small cheap flashlights. The body was face down and was dressed for winter. The head was covered by a knit hat and a scarf that wrapped around the face. After photos, we did the routine gentle flip of the body onto its side for more photos. You try the best you can to photograph anything in place that you find under the body without disturbing too much. In this case, the clothed remains stayed intact, but a pair of eyeglasses fell from the totally skeletonized face and remained on the open notebook that had been under the face. The arms were tucked in close to the body with the elbows bent and the hands up close to the face. A pen was in one of the gloved, skeletonized hands. Her whole posture suggested that she had been lying on her stomach and writing in this notebook. She had definitely been there for a while. The skull's face and hollow eye sockets wrapped in a hat and scarf looked somewhat bizarre. The eyeglasses in place would've made it even more so.

The medical examiner's office was called. Placing these remains in a body bag was a lot easier than the frozen prisoner. The layered clothing helped keep all the bones together. The blanket of snow had also prevented the body from being scavenged by animals which would've scattered her bones all around. Once the body was gone, we set to collecting all of the evidence. The open notebook would be important. There was some kind of writing in it, but the pages were tough to decipher. It had been out there for months getting wet, then freezing, then thawing and freezing again. A decomposing head on top of it didn't help either. We secured it the way it was, being sure to keep it open to the page it was found on. Everything else from the scene was collected including what looked like a vomited mess alongside the body that contained numerous pills.

This would be one of those autopsies where the clothing would be as important as the remains, especially when all that was left was bones. Meanwhile back at the office, Paul and Vinny worked on the evidence, but most specifically the notebook. As usual, they did a helluva job. They managed to gently clean up the pages. Everything past that open page was blank, but prior to the open page was a detailed account of a sadly depressed soul who chose to end it all. She had written out her final wishes and made requests of certain family members. She went on to explain how she was going to end it all; taking lots of sleep aid pills with a bottle of vodka. If that didn't do it, she'd let Mother Nature's cold winter finish the job. The remaining writing chronicled what was happening to her as the booze, pills and cold took effect. She described getting groggy, tired and slowing down. It looked as if she continued to keep writing as long as she could. She wrote how the cold started to take over her body, numbing her and slowly sending her off into unconsciousness. The writing ended in mid sentence.

The power of the human brain coupled with the determination of a strong will boggles my mind. This isn't putting a muzzle to your head and pulling the trigger. This is enduring hours and hours of extreme cold, frostbite and pain until the end comes.

Are they better off? I don't know. I'll leave that debate to greater minds than mine. But I have stood over countless bodies, staring at the final resting place of what was once a life and wondered, "How did it come to this?" I mean how does a life spiral so out of control that death is the best answer? Did it have to end like this? Often times it seems so unnecessary because there were loved ones around them or nearby. Later interviews with parents, spouses, children and friends will reveal information like, "Yeah, he seemed kind of distant lately." or "I didn't notice anything at all." These deaths will place a huge burden of guilt on loved ones who will feel that they should've known or should've done something or should've paid more attention.

"Maybe if I took some damn time out of my busy schedule, I could've talked more to her and noticed. Maybe I could've gotten her help." That was the reply of one family member. The guilt plagued her for a long time. Is it warranted? Or would it have happened no matter what you tried? There's no stock answer to that. Each person and their situation is different. I've seen both sides.

Some of our frozen remains are the result of dying first and then Mr. Freeze taking over. (When I had more red hair, my kids said I looked like the Heat Miser in that movie!) One cold, cold evening Scott called me out.

Scott and I went through the crime scene world together as uniform troopers. He became my supervisor and would eventually move up the ranks to officer status and oversee all of the field crime scene units from Albany. He was a tremendous boss who always looked out for his guys. He encouraged input and valued veteran experience. He was a huge advocate of the team mentality. Scott became one of my dearest friends.

This particular meeting with Scott had us standing alongside a creek that ran under a highway overpass. A homeless man who lived under the overpass found the body and called police. The body had definitely plunged from the high roadway above. The fall could certainly kill him, but was he pushed, did he fall or was he hit by a car? The first two are the toughest to figure out. Being shoved off might show some other injuries if the person struggled a bit or got beat up prior to the fall. Then of course, what if the guy got roughed up earlier and decided to walk off the overpass on his own? As you can see, it's not easy to tell the difference. If he was hit by a car, the autopsy should show some damage made by the motor vehicle that would not be consistent with the fall. Interviews and any witnesses at all are very important.

He had been there for about two days and was frozen solid, but at least we could move him. The body was face down with his arms out to the sides and open palms facing the ground. There were no obvious injuries to his back. We wanted to take a look at his front. Scott stood on one side and I stood on the other. I lifted his right arm which raised his entire frozen body up onto his left side and arm. Scott then took hold of the right arm to keep him in place so that I could photograph and take a look. He was like a 4' by 8' piece of plywood being balanced on its edge. I took a good look at his face, his clothing, his entire body and his hands. The right hand stood straight up into the air, palm open as if reaching heavenward for something. I then stood up and we bounced ideas off of each other. Scott let the balanced guy rest slightly against his hips as we talked and looked upward at the roadway above. We continued to talk through the possible scenarios when suddenly out of my peripheral vision I saw the outstretched right hand reach for me. I jumped out of my skin about ten feet backwards and shrieked in horror. Scott had no idea what the hell was happening, but instinctively went to grab our frozen guy who was starting to lean toward me as if falling over.

"What's the matter?" replied a panicked Scott's voice.

"The hand. I thought the fuckin hand was reaching for me."

Scott had to lay the guy's body back on the ground because he couldn't hold it together. He was laughing so hard he had to sit down. I never heard the end of that one.

We've all heard that a cop's sense of humor can be quite dark. And it can surface at the strangest of times. An unfortunate accident left a man and woman dead in their bedroom when the fumes from a gas leak killed them as they slept on a very cold February night. When the gas tank emptied, the heat stopped and the interior of the house was colder than outside. This time we had two frozen bodies; the woman in bed and the man on the floor next to the bed. He was in a pair of underwear briefs and it appeared that he had gotten up during the night; maybe because he sensed something wasn't right or maybe to go the bathroom. In any case, he became overcome by the fumes and collapsed next to the bed. We were called because it looked a little suspicious, but it became apparent that this was an accident. The funeral home was called, but instructed to wait outside the small and very cluttered house. Both bodies were in the upstairs bedroom. The stairway was very narrow. The funeral home gave us a couple of stretchers and with strong backed young troopers we went upstairs to bring the bodies out to the funeral home rigs. I assisted with the woman who was the easier of the two because she was lying flat and straight in bed. We strapped her into the stretcher and maneuvered her down the narrow stairway, over jumbled piles of stuff in the living room and around more piles on the porch, and into the rig. The troopers went back upstairs to bring down the frozen solid man. I stayed on the porch so that I could get some info from the case investigator and catch up on note taking. In a few moments, I could hear the troopers making their way down with the man. I learned that he wasn't as easy as the woman. He was a big guy and had fallen onto his side with his knees bent, one leg back further than the other. One arm was extended outward and in front of him and the other was folded back alongside his body. An ID guy helped strap the guy onto the stretcher the best he could and sent the troopers on their way down the stairs. I was still on the porch when I could hear the troopers banging into things and tripping over stuff as they made their way around obstacles on the porch. A few curses may have escaped their lips. With my head buried in my clipboard, I asked the case investigator, "What's this guy's name?"

"Who? The Heisman trophy winner here?" came back the question to my question.

Upon hearing that, I looked up from my clipboard to see two troopers struggling with a stretcher that had flipped over during the transport. The guy's body was barely being held to the stretcher by the three straps that secured him to it. There it was. A frozen solid man in his tighty whiteys hanging from the stretcher in the classic college football trophy stance; arm out to ward off tacklers, other arm tucked back with the imaginary pigskin and legs bent in that running motion. Standing on the porch in below zero weather with troopers cursing and tripping, I let out the biggest roar of laughter that I just couldn't stop. I watched as they did everything in their power not to drop this posed symbol of collegiate athletic excellence.

The cold is a grim reaper that will claim any soul it comes across. It discriminates against no one. It isn't inherent to certain genetic backgrounds as some diseases are. It will kill you within hours. Every winter the news will throw out the numbers of casualties caused by Mr. Freeze. It can be storms or power outages, but there are many more that don't get reported. The crime scene unit got called to the previous cases because there was something suspicious. But there are many deaths attributed to the cold that never warrant our response. As a uniform trooper, I responded to a handful of these. In urban areas, metropolitan police forces have their share of homeless victims of the cold. In rural areas, people don't expect to hear about folks freezing in their own homes. There are government programs to assist people with heating bills. That's great. It's a good thing to help our citizens in their time of need.

But why doesn't an 86 year old lady call for heating assistance when her social security check isn't enough? Why doesn't an aging man who worked his whole life paying into the system call for assistance to heat the modest house he built when his small pension check doesn't cut it anymore? Is it ignorance? Pride? Stupidity? Is it the manner in which he or she was raised?

As a trooper, I would ask myself that question as I stood over a little old lady's frozen 91 pound body that was tucked in her bed under layers of blankets. I looked around and saw that she lived in only one room of the house she once shared with her long passed away husband. Framed photographs of this couple's younger days were close by on the night stand. Drapes and old blankets covered the windows and doorways to keep the grim reaper away. Water in the cat bowl was frozen. There was dry food for her furry companion, but barely enough food for herself. She didn't have much and her age and condition had made housekeeping difficult, but clothes were clean. Old and worn, but clean. Interviews with neighbors would reveal that she was born in Sweden and came to this country 60 years ago. She met the love of her life and married this hard working blue collar immigrant, and they became citizens of this great new country called America. They bought this small house decades ago and it's been paid off for years. They retired very late in life. Inflation turned his pension into a pittance. Their years of paying into the system would grant them a social security benefit that would soon turn meager. Cancer would take her husband a decade and a half ago. To the day of her death, her property taxes as well as any utilities she used were paid. She had no outstanding debts.

How does the American Dream end like this?

Why didn't she ask for assistance? Why would someone feel embarrassed or ashamed to ask for something she paid into her whole life? Has asking for assistance turned into something we don't want associated with us? Is there a stigma to it? If there is, why? Did she hear her husband complain about people who milk the system? Is it possible that she froze to death because she wouldn't dare be thought of as a cheat or freeloader?

These assistance programs came into existence because of people just like this woman. They came into being for single Moms whose dead beat Dads refused to pay for the kids they fathered. The programs are there for any of us who find ourselves thrust upon hard times. It can happen to any of us. But then I'll respond to some trailer where one low life kills another low life over the price of cocaine and I'll see a 60 inch television on the wall and the latest I phone next to a carton (not pack) of cigarettes and an eighteen pack of beer on the table. And guess what? It's not their struggling drug trade paying the bills. It's public assistance and it's been paying the bills for years. Yes, we do report it, but in years past it fell upon deaf governmental ears. Recently, our district attorney has taken it upon himself to place the Welfare Fraud unit directly under his supervision. He then put one of the most determined retired cops I've ever known in charge of it. The results were immediate. People who had been defrauding the system were being arrested. Thousands of dollars were immediately being saved and paid back. Then a little heat started coming from a bleeding heart politician (it's interesting to note that this politician was the opposite political party of the DA). Stories of unjust arrests were circulating. How could you arrest a single mother of two? This was bad press for local politicians. Of course, they didn't want to hear that this mother of two was living with a boyfriend who owned his own house. She claimed that she was paying rent to this homeowner and so received some assistance on top of the child support she was already getting. The assistance was paying this guy's mortgage. Meanwhile, boyfriend/homeowner had a decent paying job. This scenario happens a lot. Some people may think this isn't such a big deal, but she has to fill out paperwork that states she lives alone with the kids. If she isn't, then she is lying. This truly hurts single Moms who really are trying to do their best. In my eyes, single parents are superheroes. I don't know how they do it. I feel for the women especially. They really should be getting all the help they can. Other single parents who get greedy make these Moms and Dads look bad. And we wonder why decent people don't want to be associated with public assistance.

My own daughter came upon some tough times when things didn't work out between her and her boyfriend. They had split up. My daughter had my one year old granddaughter with her. She didn't want to go to court yet, because she hoped that maybe there was a chance at reconciliation. In the meantime, attempting to work, taking care of an infant and trying to pay bills got a little tight. A close family friend told her (not suggested) to get public assistance. Her immediate response was one of uneasiness. She tried to tactfully tell this relative that she wasn't comfortable with that. The relative was insistent, "Everybody does it. That's what it's there for."

My daughter stopped by to see me and told me everything and then added, "I'm not going to lie, Dad. Yeah, things are tough right now, but that assistance is for people who really need it. I'll be okay. I've got people around me to help out. I wouldn't feel right taking it."

I kissed her and told her how proud of her I was. I also added that she was a hundred percent correct. It wasn't easy, but between odd jobs here and there and family members babysitting, it worked out for her. Unbeknownst to her, I kept a quiet, behind the scenes watch over how she was doing. But she wanted to do it on her own. I wound up taking care of a little bit of this and that, but she did the lion's share and made it work. She now appreciates every dollar she earns and shops smartly.

Would I have let my daughter and grandchild go on public assistance when I have the means to help them out? Absolutely not. You can call it pride or stupidity if you want. I have the kind of honest relationship with my children that prevent them from even thinking of taking advantage of me. It's the way they were raised. Family helps family out. That's what we're supposed to do.

It's that "Come on everybody, let's build the barn together" mentality that makes the community part of the American Dream real. We're supposed to help each other out, Damnit!

Chapter Six

To Be or Not To Be

personal shock to me was discovering just how many people take their own lives. The Center for Disease Control and Prevention reports that approximately 34,000 people commit suicide a year. That's two and a half times the number of homicides also reported by the CDC.

Every death leaves behind feelings of grief and sorrow for loved ones, but suicide tends to add tremendous feelings of guilt to these already soulful heartaches. Loved ones will often think that they could have done something, should have noticed. Other loved ones will live in a world of denial swearing that my child or spouse or relative did not kill themselves. They'll come up with all kinds of scenarios of foul play or accidents. Almost every investigator has one of these sad cases where loved ones will keep calling back with possible new information that will explain what they hope really happened. The public never sees the continual compassion these cops show loved ones when they repeatedly call or come in to see them, some of them years later.

Of course, the saddest of all are young people. I've seen young gals and guys end it all over bad grades, being dumped or feeling that nobody cares about them. One teenage girl wrote in the middle of a notebook that no one would notice she was gone. She put the notebook in her drawer under other books. It took a while to find it, but we did. She had gotten into her father's gun safe and used a revolver. We were called to this because a second shot was fired and it looked like it went through her foot. Her body was found lying on the floor next to the open gun safe. We determined that she had been sitting on the floor when she put the revolver to her head. As she delivered the fatal shot, she fell backwards. Her outstretched legs and feet rose off the floor as her body rocked backwards. The gun arm fell forward and the revolver discharged again. The bullet passed through her momentarily raised foot and then out the room's window pane.

The discovery of two and even three shots at apparent suicides will summon us to a scene. You can read all you want about suicides, but nothing beats experience when responding to questionable scenes like these. Most times, the second and third shots are chronologically the first and second shots. Quite often, the victim test fires the gun and then shoots themself. It might be someone else's unfamiliar gun and they want to make sure it's going to work when the final big decision is made. There could be bullet holes in ceilings, through a window or wall. Most times, it's fired right from the spot where they will eventually rest.

One woman was sitting in her bed with the covers up to her waist. The box to her husband's hand gun was open on the bed next to her. She loaded the gun, pointed it down into the mattress next to her and fired. Then she put it to her head and fired. She fell backwards onto the pillow of her bed. Her hand dropped the handgun and it fell right into the gun box that was next to her. Her arm lay alongside her body as if sleeping in bed. A local police agency responded and then our guys. Our first reaction to seeing the gun in the box was to ask, "Who put that in there?" It's quite possible that a new guy cop or civilian or paramedic may have moved it from a dangerous spot or checked it for some reason. (They shouldn't, but it happens) But all accounts stated that no one touched it. It was in the box when the first cop arrived. It looked very odd. That was why they called us in. We checked for any signs of a break in. There were no signs of struggle on the body. Once we looked everything over, we could see that from the sitting position, she could reach the spot where the test fire went through the mattress. For the fatal shot, her hand would be just about over the box when she pulled the trigger. An examination of her hand showed the tiny blood spatter associated with blowback from a self inflicted contact wound. The two expended casings were also in line with having been ejected from the gun's right side as she held it in those two positions.

It is interesting to note that generally women don't usually shoot themselves in the head. In these two instances, they did. That's why we use words like "usually" and that's why I'll say again, "Never say `Never'".

Out of embarrassment or feelings of shame, family members may sometimes mess around with suicide scenes. This can make our job a bit challenging at times. It could be a note that blames a relative or maybe the deceased is undressed or dressed inappropriately. A relative who finds a family member in one of these situations may instinctively move something. The very shock of seeing this could very well blur their memory as to what they did or didn't do upon finding the deceased. When your brain is trying to process a sight that is so unsettling, memory will have a way of filtering out what it sees as unimportant. This happens with cops involved in shootings where survival instincts prevent them from seeing anything else at all but the threat. A Mac truck could drive by them and they'll swear they didn't see it. The sight of something extremely traumatic can trigger a similar response.

A suicide committed when other people are present will usually warrant a call to us. Especially domestic situations. Boyfriends have done it in front of girlfriends and vice versa. One wife told our guys that during a number of their arguments, her husband would resort to threatening, "I should just kill myself." She admitted that she got tired of hearing it and this time came back with the response, "Go ahead and do it." She walked away from him and into the next room and heard the blast. She ran back into the living room to find him dead, sitting in his rocker with a shotgun between his knees.

This was one that we got called to because our guys weren't certain if she may have done it and staged it to look like a suicide. The first thing I noticed was that the firearm was a shotgun and the guy's head was intact. There was lots of blood on his chest, on his lap and on his pant legs. His head hung down, resting on his chest. Normally a shotgun blast leaves a huge exit wound. I've seen bodies where there was nothing but the tongue sitting on top of the throat. But this guy must've been shot in the chest. An inspection of the spent shotgun shell showed that it was bird shot; very small pellets.

But the first thing you have to ask at a suicide where a rifle or shotgun was used is, "Can the victim reach the trigger with the barrel pointed where they want it to shoot?" Past scenes have proven that victims can be quite resourceful. If they couldn't reach the trigger with a finger, then you might see one shoe and sock off so that they could use their big toe. If that was too tough, both shoes and socks would be off and a pencil or something similar would be held by the toes of both feet to depress the trigger. Still others have used a stick or broom handle to hit the trigger. In any case, we have to see something that indicates it can be done. In this case, he could definitely reach the trigger.

Next we examined the shotgun. There were some definite blood patterns on the barrel of the shotgun that suggested blowback. Blowback of blood and tissue occurs when the barrel of a firearm is placed right upon against any part of the body. You'll get a bigger blowback when the barrel is held up against a bony part. The gases resulting from the gun's blast enter the wound, hit the hard surface and bounce back towards the origin of the bullet. Trace fragments of blowback can actually occur in gunshots that aren't contact wounds as well. But they're more difficult to see. You can find specks of blowback on the gun, hand or sleeve of a shooter up to three feet away. In our current case, the blowback was obvious on the gun. We now looked at him and saw that the barrel had been in his mouth. His front teeth were gone, but we still couldn't believe his head was intact after that. (Never say "Never") A couple of back room guys had the wife in another room and had checked out her hands. They were clean as was her clothing. Could she have washed up and changed? Sure. Now we looked a little closer at the dark jeans our victim was wearing. With a strong light, we could see the small (and some large) spots of blowback spatter on the front of both thighs, his left hand, forearm and wrist. When we opened his tightly clenched left palm that had been found around the shotgun barrel, we found redness. It was all there. The victim had sat in his rocker with the butt of the shotgun resting on the floor between his feet. He held the, soon to be very hot, barrel with his left hand, bent over and put the muzzle in his mouth, and pushed the trigger with his right hand. His left hand, wrist, forearm and legs got spattered with blowback from the close contact wound. This was definitely a suicide.

Men will often use a gun if they have one. And even when they don't have one.

Sheriff's Department Deputies responded to an elderly man's death. He was found in a tool shed outside his house. He had an apparent gunshot wound to the right side of his head. His wife of a thousand years found him and called the cops. When they showed up, they were a bit taken aback by her indifference.

"He's out in that damn tool shed. He's always in there," she told them.

The husband was lying on his back against one of the interior walls of the small shed. He was facing a work counter on the other wall. There was a very polite note left in the tool shed on the work counter that thanked the police for coming and then said that the gun was in the car. The hand writing wasn't the most legible, but the last line was very clear. "Don't worry. I'm already dead." A bit of a sense of humor in his final moments. That is if he really was the one who wrote the note. The wife's uncaring attitude, and the fact that the car was about 20 feet from the shed, caused the cops some confusion. A look inside the car didn't uncover any weapon at all. They gave us a call.

We had the same question as the deputies. How could the gun be in the car if he shot himself dead in the tool shed? We gave the car another search and couldn't find any gun. The wife told the cops that they didn't own any guns. We looked the male victim over. It did look like a small caliber gun bullet hole to the right side of his head that did not exit. Maybe it wasn't a bullet hole. Maybe something else caused the hole. This was becoming a problem. A suicide note with no gun or obvious weapon. We asked for the note.

It was handwritten in script. The word "gun" was very clear, but the rest wasn't as legible. Did that say "car"? It really didn't look like "car". It looked like it read, "The gun is in the rice."…. Rice?…. Where? What rice?….. Maybe it's not rice. It looks like "nice". "The gun is in the nice." That makes no sense. What rhymes with nice? Mice, lice, dice, vice. Wait a minute. Vice? Vice! "The gun is in the vice." We ran into the shed and on the work counter was a small vice grip bolted to the counter. We looked at the vice grip. It appeared to be closed, but a closer inspection showed a thin piece of piping tightly held in the grip. The end of the pipe protruded slightly from the right side of the vice. And it had something in it. A bullet casing. Next to the vice was a ball peen hammer. This thin pipe protruded a little bit more on the left side of the vice. If you looked at the wall in line with the pipe, you could see two small holes that went through it. Test fires. This resourceful fellow had fashioned a gun out of a short section of pipe that was held tightly in the vice grip. He got the exact sized diameter pipe that would allow a .22 caliber bullet to slide in, but only up to the lip of the casing's rim. The rim held the bullet in place just as it does in a revolver's chamber. He used the very distinct end of a ball peen hammer to strike the rim fire type primer of certain .22 caliber rounds to fire the projectile. Once he knew it worked, he loaded the pipe with a new bullet, took the ball peen hammer in his right hand and lowered the right side of his head to the left side of the vice grip and in line with the pipe. He then struck the primer of the bullet with the hammer from this position.

I could've leaned over and kissed the guy right there and then for leaving us that thoughtful note. I'd like to think that we would've eventually figured it out, but finding that small piece of pipe in a closed vice grip on a tool shed counter, that was cluttered with all kinds of stuff, would not have been easy. With no weapon, this could easily have become an open homicide. And the wife would've had lots and lots of explaining to do.

I think you'd agree that finding a guy lying in the middle of a busy campground on a holiday weekend with a big knife sticking out of his chest would lead you to suspect murder as his manner of expiration. Especially when interviews would reveal that the victim had just been arguing with his two buddies back at their campsite. As good luck would have it, a diligent young campground worker happened to be making his morning rounds when he saw this man staggering toward him. It wasn't unusual for this young campground worker to see the effects of a hard night's partying on many of the campground's patrons. However, as the guy got closer the worker could see that the man was holding onto something at his chest. The blood wasn't yet noticeable because of the guy's dark clothing, but once the teenaged worker recognized a knife as the object sticking out of his chest, he then made the connection that his clothing was soaked with blood. The shocked teenager's involuntarily response was, "Hey, are you okay?"

"I think," our guy started, "that I should definitely have the heart by now."

The campground worker watched in horror as the guy was actually twisting and maneuvering the imbedded knife around in his chest as he groaned in pain. He finally collapsed as the teenager ran for help. An ambulance was called, but he died before their arrival.

Interviews with his buddies revealed the consumption of a ton of alcohol and a night full of depressed deliberations. They didn't know he was gone until cops woke them up.

Without this teenager's eyewitness account, this could've turned into a nightmare to figure out.

However, we still have our fair share of ones that need quite a bit of figuring out. A 14 year old boy came downstairs to find his mother in a huge pool of her own blood on the kitchen floor. The poor kid ran to a neighbor to call the police. We got called because one of our first responding guys described her condition as, "It looks like her head was almost cut off."

When we arrived, the body was gone. An ambulance had already taken her away, but all accounts related that she was definitely dead when they arrived. This sometimes happens. Emergency medical personnel are supposed to take anyone to a hospital that doesn't show obvious signs of death. It may have just occurred and maybe her body temperature was still warm.

One of our guys went to the hospital to get a preliminary look at her injuries and take some photographs. We went to the scene. There was a lot of blood. It was all on the linoleum floor of this small kitchen that was surrounded by three sides of white appliances and counter cabinets. The large pool of blood was right in the middle of the floor. Also on the floor was a large serrated kitchen knife. It matched the other knives of a set in one of the kitchen drawers. We photographed the kitchen, and all its surfaces, and the remainder of the house. In the adjacent, very tidy living room, a large textbook was on the coffee table. It was an anatomy textbook and it was left open to the section that illustrated the arteries in the neck. We called our partner at the hospital. He already had the answer. The ER doctor had said that the carotid artery on the right side of her neck had been completely sliced through. In fact, that was the only slice to her neck and it went very deep.

Something bothered us about the scene. There was a lot of blood, but in a way it was too clean. There wasn't a speck of spatter on any of the nearby white surfaces. There wasn't any smears at all or any blood transfers or signs of a struggle. Her clothing at the hospital wasn't torn or ripped and again no blood smears or transfers on her clothing. Only where the pooling blood soaked her clothing.

The subsequent autopsy showed the markings of the serrated knife and the angle of the deep cutting was consistent with her holding the knife herself. By this time, our back room guys had found out that this poor woman had been suffering from severe depression. A scene that, at first glance, appeared to be a horrific crime had actually become the resting place of a lost soul, and ever the homemaker, who picked the easiest place in the house to clean up.

Unlike the pristinely clean and well kept home of a little old man, who bent over the bathtub to shoot himself in the head, so that all of the blood would neatly run down the drain, most times cleaning up is not usually a consideration. Someone who places a shotgun to their head isn't worrying about the mess that it's going to make. That's where our Tyvek suits and lots of gloves come in handy. And when you've got hunks of blood and tissue barely clinging to the ceiling above you, you make sure you wear the silly drawstring hoodie that comes with the Tyvek suit.

We have a little more "collecting" to do in cases like this when it's time for the funeral home to pick up the body. We'll always help the funeral home gang in loading and carrying the body, but in addition to that every so often we have to find and gather the pieces that have been sent in various directions. I mean scraping it off of walls and ceilings and reaching behind furniture to retrieve fragmented pieces of scalp, bone and brain. I'm sure that being down on all fours in a bloody mess and reaching under a bed to grab an eyeball isn't one of the "cool" images you think of after watching an exciting episode of CSI on TV. But this is it. This is the job.

And we do have to take advantage of every chance we get at a bit of levity. Paul, Vinny and I were at one particularly messy suicide with our Tyvek suits all zipped and hoodied up. When we suited up outside, the more diminutive Vinny had told the more gargantuan Paul that he mistakenly had an XXL size Tyvek suit in his van and that Paul could wear it. So Paul put it on. We were working inside for at least an hour when Paul stated that he had to get something from the van. Vinny and I had been secretly giggling like little kids every time we looked at Paul since we got into the house. I looked outside and saw that there was a newspaper photographer parked at road side. I couldn't let Paul go out.

"Hey big guy," I started, "if there wasn't a photographer from the papers outside, I wouldn't care, but you probably don't want him to see you like that."

"I'm not that bloody. It's only on my feet," Paul replied.

Vinny was having a hard time holding it in.

"No, it's not the blood. It's ah.... ah...."

"What? What's the problem?" He was getting impatient.

"Let him go," Vinny snickered.

"What's going on? What's wrong?" Paul started to get suspicious.

"Take a look in that mirror.... and I had nothing to do with it," I defended myself.

A full length mirror was attached to the back of one of the doors. Paul went over to it and stared at himself. There in the mirror he could see a slight alteration made to the front of the Tyvek. It was a very clear drawing that started at the crotch area and ended midway down his left thigh. I'll let your imagination figure out the rest.

"I'm gonna kill you, Vinny."

"Where did that come from?" was Vinny's weak retort.

"What if I walked outside?" Paul growled.

"That was kinda the intention," he giggled and backed away.

I intervened, "But not with the press outside, so take it off just outside the front door and get a new one on."

Paul turned to go and looked again in the mirror. "I must admit, that's a very good likeness," and went outside.

A man in his thirties unscrews the flat base and blade guard from a circular saw and tapes the trigger in the on position. Then he kneels down in a closed room, plugs the saw into an outlet which automatically gets the blade running and pushes the reciprocating blade of the circular saw across his neck. When he falls backwards, it pulls the plug from the wall, stopping the saw. He dies and is found later when someone sees blood running out from under the closed door. This man had serious mental issues that one day sent him over the edge. No one in the world around him saw this coming.

Why? Is it anyone's fault? Are we too distracted by unimportant things in our own lives to notice?

Let's face it. We get bitchy when we have to stand in line too long at the store. We know very well that the college kid behind the counter just started this summer job and really is doing his best. Our kid gets an 89 instead of a 98 on a test after studying all night and we want to blow a gasket. We will get so worked up because someone else is getting something bigger or better than us.

And then there are other people out there who fight from the very moment they wake up in the morning. While we're struggling with whether it's a flats or heels day, they are having a massive tug of war with Shakespeare's famous question.

Our drama queen led lives will lead us to spout, "I don't know how I endure this crap!" And "this crap" usually entails everyday hold ups, misunderstandings, and problems that we all face. The kids broke our favorite mug. You missed happy hour because you had to work a little late.

"Oh my God. I can't believe she showed up here."

"What the hell did he mean by that comment?"

"Nobody picks up the slack around here more than me."

"I don't like to eat that."

"My job sucks."

"How do I put up with this bullshit?"

Okay, I do get it. I've had those feelings. I've had those days. But I've also had days where I've seen a beautiful young girl think no one loved her so she hung herself in her closet. Yep. Then the big picture comes into focus and I realize that I don't have it too bad at all. As a mater of fact, I've got it pretty damn good and I feel thankful.

Gratitude is something we should also feel for an unseen group of folks out there who deal with some tough situations. There are caring people out there who will routinely answer a phone call to hear a desperate voice say, "I want to kill myself."

They answer hotline calls, talk and really listen. It is impossible to estimate just how many lives these amazing people save. To be this exceptionally compassionate also means that you suffer great sadness when you do your best and it isn't enough. These people answer these calls because they truly care. They listen to others who are at the very end of their rope and ready to let go. And somehow, in some way, they manage to bring many of them back. It's never an easy fix and the road back is tough for most, but it happens because these people answered the phone. I know that there is a special place in heaven for every one of them.

Chapter Seven

Oops!

Imagine finding a bow hunter shot to death in his tree stand with his rifle lying on the ground below? I don't think that there's anything short of a crystal ball that would've figured this one out. Maybe one of those flashbacks that those CSI guys get on TV all the time. In all my many years of showing up at crime scenes, I've never had one of those flashbacks or visions. I must be doing something wrong. A vision is what you would've needed to close this case out if he had died.... but he didn't.

The bow hunter managed to climb down out of the tree stand and get himself to a hospital. The good folks at the ER called the cops as they're supposed to whenever someone shows up with what look like gunshot wounds. The victim got a little nervous upon seeing our guys. He didn't want to talk about it. He knew very well that you're not supposed to have a rifle in the woods during bow season. Bow hunters are dressed in camouflage from head to toe. Fellow bow hunters don't want a guy with a gun in the woods with them. Of course, our victim knew this was a big no-no and didn't want to admit that he had brought his rifle into the woods. The cops told him that a witness saw his rifle on the ground near his tree stand. So what happened? Was this an attempted murder? Was he covering up for the assailant? Was it a family member?

When the cops told him that family members would start getting pulled into the station and grilled, he finally gave it up. He admitted to bringing his rifle into the woods while bow hunting, but naturally it wasn't for illegal reasons. It would only be used for the humane purpose of putting a deer out of its misery. He had to climb pegs in the tree to get up to the seated deer stand. The bow and rifle were on slings and hanging from his shoulder. Within reach of the tree stand seat was a hook that was screwed into the tree. When he got close to the seat, he hung the rifle on the hook by its trigger guard. (You might see where this is going by now.) He then put his bow on the tree stand and climbed into the tree stand and sat. When he decided to reach for his rifle, he didn't grip it correctly and the movement pressed the trigger against the hook in the tree and BOOM. The bullet hit him in the shoulder. But that wasn't the end of it. The recoil from the rifle sent the trigger back onto the hook and BOOM it went off again striking our guy in the arm. The second recoil shot the rifle right off the hook and down onto the ground near the tree stand. Although feeling like a complete idiot, this guy was lucky to be alive and we were lucky we didn't have an open homicide that would still be unsolved to this day.

Accidental deaths happen a lot more than people realize. One of the most common of these is drug overdosing. Due to the very nature of the lifestyles these people lead, the scenes can be very confusing. People are often present when the overdose occurs and either try to clean up any signs of drug use and leave, or they pick up the deceased and deposit them somewhere else away from their house or hang out. I've seen supposed friends dump an overdosed buddy's body alongside a roadway or into a lake or stream miles away from where he died.

The big problem with this is that it's an accident, but doesn't look anything like an accident. Most of the time, an autopsy will clear things up, but unfortunately if the body isn't found in a reasonable amount of time, decomposition can start to destroy toxicological evidence that proves an overdose. Then the elements, animals or fish will destroy evidence and the body. It then becomes much more difficult to see needle marks or other signs of drug use.

What most of these supposed friends don't realize is that someone is usually going to remember that the dead guy was hanging out with them. Now they look like a murder suspect. Drugs make you do real stupid things like leave your friend's dead body in a cleaned up motel room and go charge up his credit card for all kinds of cool stuff. Then you can sell the cool stuff for next to nothing to pay for another motel room drug party. I'm not kidding. These jerks were his friends.

There are accidents that look like suicides. It's important for us to make this distinction, especially for family members. Some insurance policies will not pay out if the death is ruled a suicide. Although every death is hard for family members, accidents are a bit easier to deal with than suicides.

A disabled woman had shot herself in her bedroom and subsequently died before anyone in the house knew. It was a big house and a party had been going on. The small caliber gun didn't make that much noise. The first thought was homicide. Alibis cleared every family member in the house and the shot in her lower back didn't really go along with someone's attempt to kill her. Who shoots someone in the lower back to kill them? Interviews revealed that the woman was very depressed about her condition and the severe pain she was always experiencing. The pain in her back often disabled her completely. This particular night, she went to bed early after having a few wines. She had told everyone at this family get-together that she wasn't feeling well. Later toxicology showed that she had taken a good deal more than the prescribed amount of pain killers. She was in bed when we showed up. When we rolled her body, the revolver was under her back and her right arm was twisted behind her. She had been found lying on her right arm in bed. A bullet had entered her lower back, passed out the front of her body and entered her left thigh where it severed the femoral artery. She quickly bled to death.

After piecing together evidence at the scene and reviewing family statements we could see that stress, severe pain, alcohol and pain killers led her to place her legally owned revolver to the base of her spine and pull the trigger in an attempt to stop the pain. Can we know her exact thoughts during those final moments? Of course not. But she didn't try to commit suicide by shooting herself in the lower back. This suffering woman tried this desperate measure in an attempt to end the pain. Maybe she tried to paralyze herself. Who knows? But she didn't anticipate the bullet hitting a major artery. She died accidentally.

An early morning jogger found an SUV in a deep water puddle on a secluded access road used by town workers. A closer look warranted summoning the cops. The local police weren't sure what they had so we got a call. The SUV was in a huge, water-filled hole that was in the middle of this dirt access road. All four doors were about a quarter of the way submerged in the water and it had seeped into the passenger seat areas. The rear of the vehicle was a little more submerged than the front. Inside the vehicle a man was sitting in the driver's seat and a woman in the front passenger seat. Both were dead. They were leaning towards each other as if they fell asleep that way.

Local cops told us that the access road was sometimes used as a quiet night time place to park. It appeared that you could easily be driving along this road, see the large puddle, and think that you could drive right through it. Especially in an SUV. Then you'd find out that it's a deep hole and be stuck. Mud and water marks all over the vehicle demonstrated numerous attempts at getting out. The location of this hole was still a good distance from any houses on the main road. With no lighting on this access road and without a full moon, it would be pitch black out there. We took as many photos as possible and then called for a tow truck to pull the SUV from the water. It was difficult to get a good look without opening the vehicle doors. Once out of the water and with the doors open, we could take a closer look.

The man and woman had their legs folded underneath them so as not to have their feet in the water on the floor inside the passenger compartment. The seats were high enough to remain dry. Both front windows were open four or five inches. It had been a bit cold that night. They were wearing jackets inside the vehicle. A preliminary examination of the bodies showed no obvious signs of trauma. Keys were in the ignition and in the "On" position, but the car was not running. The gas gauge said empty. One of the first theories was carbon monoxide poisoning from the vehicle's exhaust, but both front windows were open. Would that be enough air to dissipate the fumes? Was it a double drug over dose? But we didn't find any evidence of drug use. Was it a lovers' double suicide? Maybe ingesting something poisonous? But why in a sink hole? The vehicle was held as evidence and the autopsies were scheduled for as soon as possible.

The autopsy resolved the puzzle pretty quickly. These two looked to find a quiet spot to themselves and got stuck in the water hole. After repeated attempts to get out, they settled in to wait for daylight. It was cold out, so they kept the car running with the heat on but figured they'd leave the windows open a few inches because of the fumes. But it wasn't enough. After all, almost the entire exhaust system was under water, but not the motor. As the motor ran, the exhaust fumes could only go so far and started to back up into the engine compartment. From the engine compartment, it seeped right into the front passenger area of the SUV. As they waited for daylight, they began to get sleepy, passed out and died from carbon monoxide poisoning even with the windows open.

We already know that falls from great heights always beg the question, "Did he fall or was he pushed or did he plunge intentionally?" Eyewitnesses and interviews are extremely important because the body may not tell us much. Loved ones and friends may insist that he wasn't depressed or suicidal. Could it have been an accident? Come on. Who walks right off a cliff by accident?....Umm, I've seen it happen twice.

One time two guys were vacationing in the country and had been drinking at a very rural establishment. After a few too many, they decided to walk back to where they were staying. At some point, they needed to make a pit stop and walked into the very dark woods to do so. After about fifteen feet, they both walked right off a cliff. One survived, albeit a bit busted up, and the other died.

The other instance was a woman who had met a guy at a campground. They started talking and realized that they were both nomads of a sort who bounced around here and there. Evening rolled in as they talked and drank. She had a little bag with her and asked him if she could stay the night with him. He agreed. She took her little bag and went off to take a shower. He tucked himself inside his tent, waiting for his guest to join him. More and more time went by, and the guy figured that he had been stood up. There was a group of guys at the next campsite having a good time. She must've stooped there on the way back from the showers. He resigned himself to a night alone and fell asleep. Morning woke him. He packed and checked out.

Cops got his information from the campground which included the car he was driving, and a couple hours later, pulled him over a distance away. He was brought to the station for questioning. He relayed his account of the evening's activities and repeatedly stated that the last time he saw her was when she went off to take a shower.

We had been called when they found her body floating face down in a wide, slow moving creek that bordered the campground. She was caught on a branch in the stream that prevented her from floating further down stream. Thank God. This creek was at the bottom of a long drop off that bordered the guy's campsite. It was night time of the next day by the time we got there and the campsite was lit by police cars. We asked everyone to turn off their car lights for a few minutes. We then took flashlights in hand and slowly walked the perimeter of the guy's campsite. The edge of this drop off was a very short distance through some bushes from the campsite. We turned off our flashlights and realized that you could barely see one foot in front of you. Three steps and you'd be off this cliff.

Down below, her face and head had been under water. Her hair was already gone and the water had done quite a number on her face. The normally small framed woman's body had already started to bloat, so it was a lot bigger than usual. A local fire department's row boat went out to get the body for us. I knew this wasn't going to be pleasant for these guys. They pulled the small boat up alongside the floating body. We were on the shore only 20 or so feet away from them, so we had a front row seat. The two young firemen started to reach into the water to pull her into the boat. They were disturbing the gases associated with decomposition as they labored to get her now big, slippery body into the boat. We yelled out the suggestion that they could just guide her body towards us and we would pull her to shore, but they wanted to do their duty. I get it. They were doing their job, but I don't think they were ready for the assault to their senses.

"You think he's gonna lose it?" my partner asked.

"Maybe he's done it before and knows the deal," I answered.

"Oh shit."

Then we saw it. The younger fireman inhaled a deep breath as he tried to pull the heavy body into the boat. He sucked in a lungful of decomp and his face started turning white. Now he tried holding his breath, but it was too late. He attempted to turn his face away and take a clean breath, but there was none to be had. He was trying his hardest to keep a hold on her and not vomit. We felt for this poor guy.

"Let her back down. It's okay. Take your time," I yelled.

"Let her down and give yourself a break. Take a few breaths from the other side of the boat," my partner added.

"I'm okay," came back the reply. We knew he wasn't. We had certainly been there and done that before. Now he and his partner gave it one more pull and that did it. It got her into the boat, but the exertion had him sucking in another lungful up close as she got dumped into the boat and he lost it. Luckily, he got his head over the side of the boat in time as he spewed. You hate to see anything funny in this because we had indeed been in his place before. But that wasn't the end of it. After vomiting, he turned his head back toward the body which was now basically in his lap and he spun back quickly and let loose again. We let out a stifled guffaw at that. You know, the type where you cover your mouth 'cause you don't want to let anyone see that you just laughed and said, "Oooh fuuuck!"

We met them at the shore with a body bag and thanked them profusely. They were both a bit woozy and the younger guy still had that pale pallor going. We made sure to take over for them. We photographed her body. Her face was unidentifiable. It was a mess, but she did have a lot of tattoos. That would be helpful. Tattoos stay visible for quite sometime after death. Her bright colored shirt said, "Help is on the way."

Along with the damage done by decomposition, there was some discoloration that was consistent with bruising, but her head had no obvious damage. We bagged her up and sent her off to the morgue.

She had been barefoot, but a pair of flip flops was found scattered nearby on the shore. Also on the shore, just under this cliff drop off, was a bottle of shampoo. Near that was a woman's toiletries bag. With our flashlight we looked up and saw something stuck on a branch. It was a towel. Next to the towel was a clearly broken branch that jutted out of the rock face. Looking up from the very short section of shore that bordered this creek, you could see the path of her fall. When she hit the sloped shore, her momentum bounced and rolled her into the water. The items she was carrying got scattered during the fall. We had already established that in total darkness it would be easy to wander a bit too far to the edge without even knowing it, especially after having a few too many drinks. Maybe she was going to hang her towel on a branch to dry. Maybe she could hear the stream and wanted to see how close it was. Who knows?

The poor guy had been grilled and agreed to take a polygraph. He passed it with flying colors. The autopsy showed fatal injuries consistent with the fall.

What we do in the privacy of our own home is our business. And that's the way it should be. That's why search warrants are required to enter a person's "castle". Everyone has a certain expectation of privacy. My job routinely sends me into the very private part of many people's lives. When someone is discovered dead in their home, it is the task of the police to find out why this person is dead and who or what is responsible. Sometimes it's possible to get an immediate feeling from the atmosphere surrounding the death. Rage can be observed in a violently bloody scene. Other scenes will give off a definite sexual vibe. It could be the clothing the body is wearing or its state of undress. Maybe it's the body's positioning or suggestive items found nearby. Furniture might be moved or, in some cases, a rather detailed set up put in place to facilitate a certain act. As with any death scene, we have to treat it as a homicide until we know otherwise.

A man in his fifties who is found dressed in women's panties and a bra and lying dead at the foot of his bed could have been suffocated by someone he met and brought home. He may also have had a heart attack or maybe he accidentally overdosed on pills and booze during an erotic scenario while he was alone or with a consensual partner.

I've witnessed several of the above and a few others. A drunken homosexual encounter that turned into murder when he sobered up and realized what he had done and couldn't face it. A guy videotaping the act of "having at himself" and suffering a heart attack right in the middle of his last episode, (Gave a whole new meaning to the phrase "Come and go"). And then there are the erotic scenarios that put your personal safety at risk at the expense of heightened sexual pleasure.

Auto erotic asphyxiation is the intentional restriction of oxygen to the brain for the purpose of sexual arousal. These deaths can look like straight up suicides, especially if a family member found them first and took away a few embarrassing items or clothes. If you find someone hanging from a door and there isn't any display of something sexual, it could easily be ruled a suicide. Some of these scenes are quite extravagant with toys, dressing up and magazines (now open laptops) nearby. Others will be as simple as a guy's pants down. I'm sure there have been auto erotic asphyxiation cases that have been ruled a suicide because a guy's open fly wasn't enough to convince anyone that it wasn't suicide. Participants will use any number of methods to "choke themselves" right at the point of orgasm. A lot of people will wrap something like a soft towel around their neck first and then a rope or ligature to prevent leaving any visible bruising or marks.

A pretty young girl didn't arrive for work one day. A relative was called who then went into her small house to find her hanging in the bedroom closet. The twenty-something year old victim lived alone and relatives were horrified because she was the happiest go lucky person who loved her job, her life and her family. She had not shown any signs whatsoever of being depressed and had been planning and looking forward to a big family get-together. Our back room investigators arrived and felt that it was a bit bizarre, so they called us.

Upon our arrival, we were told that there weren't any signs of forced entry anywhere in the house. Everything had been closed and locked. The small house was very tidy and clean. The main bedroom had a closet that had sliding doors on it. It was open at one side and upon entering the bedroom you could see a nude female's backside at the closet door opening. We photographed everything and every angle. At first, the most obvious question was: "What is she wrapped in?" Her body was completely nude and it was covered in a thin kind of plastic. However, her arms were free and not wrapped to the body. The arms had been individually swathed and hung down the sides of her body. A towel and a chain were around her neck. The chain was secured to the clothing bar inside the closet. This was at first difficult to see because her long hair covered the back of her neck as she was facing the rear wall inside the closet. Her knees were bent and her feet were touching the floor. She could easily stand up and take any pressure off her neck.

We like to get as much of a good look at everything as we can before we move a body. In this case, we couldn't see her face or the front of her body without moving her out. We used a mirror on an adjustable handle. It affords us a look behind objects that we don't want to move right away or things we can't move like looking inside walls. I took the mirror and reached to the back of the closet to get a look at her face, and then I shined the flashlight into the darkened closet right at the mirror. Her wide open eyes stared straight back at me in the mirror and, quite frankly, gave me a bit of a start. Once I began breathing again, I checked the rest of her and couldn't find anything out of the ordinary except for this thin plastic wrap that covered her. Inside the closet and up against the rear wall was a low bench style seat that had a lid you could open and store stuff inside of. You often see them at the foot of a person's bed. Her thighs, just above the knees, were resting against the front of the bench seat. On the bench seat inside the closet was a novel, one of those trashy romance ones. Next to the closet was a nightstand that had a pot pipe, a lighter and some loose marihuana. The pot pipe still had some burnt marihuana in it.

Everything was pointing to auto erotic asphyxiation, but what was up with the plastic? Was she strangled and all of this intentionally staged to look like an auto erotic asphyxiation? The other bothersome aspect of this scenario was that the vast majority of auto erotic asphyxiation cases involve men. Rarely do you see a woman, but hey, remember my mantra: "Never say never."

While one of the guys took notes, I looked around a bit. I called the guys into the bathroom. There on the bathroom counter were three empty boxes of Saran cling wrap and scissors. Stray pieces of plastic cling wrap were in the garbage. Above the bathroom counter was a very large mirror. Otherwise the bathroom was tidy and in order. There were no signs of struggle or altercation anywhere in the neat little house.

Now it was time to take her down. But before moving her, it's very important to document how the chain was secured around her neck and to the closet bar. In auto erotic cases, there has to be a way that the person can easily take the ligature off or be able to loosen it in case of a problem or once the desired results have been achieved. To get a better look at the chain, we took the sliding closet door off. We could now see that a metal carabiner had been used to secure the chain links around her neck. Heavy duty versions of these carabiners are used by mountain climbers and you'll see some people use the cheaper versions as key chains. They are shaped like a large chain link and have one side that opens and can snap closed. This one was located in an easily accessible spot where she could reach up and unfasten it if she wanted. Another carabiner secured the chain to the clothing bar inside the closet. The carabiner afforded her the opportunity to adjust the height of the chain.

After completely documenting the chain's positioning, we took her down and laid her on the bed face up and photographed her whole front. Things were beginning to come into focus now. From the front you could see that she had actually dressed herself in the cling wrap. It was wrapped around her hands and arms up to her biceps like long formal evening gloves. There was cling wrap around her head and under her chin fashioned like a fancy bonnet. Both of her legs were individually wrapped like stockings that stopped high up on her thighs. And then a dress. The dress started as a halter type top that wrapped around her neck and cradled her breasts. It then continued downward in a snug wrap until it stopped just above the knees.

Once we could see that her arms and legs were free, you could piece together the set-up. At some point before or during the dress-up, she'd smoke a little weed. Then she'd dress in the bathroom where she could do it right and enjoy the view of herself in the large mirror. She might have started reading a trashy section of her romance novel or might do it later during the act. A towel got wrapped around her neck to prevent any bruising. She knelt on the bench style seat in the closet and attached the chain that was hanging in the closet around her neck. In her marihuana buzz, she either read sections of her novel or pleasured herself in other ways while applying downward pressure on her throat. During the attempt of reaching that heightened climax, she unfortunately cut off the blood flow to her head and caused a loss of consciousness. She eventually passed out. Her knees would slip off the bench and she would hang herself accidentally.

A number of accidental deaths occur out of recklessness and pure stupidity. The most common ones are hunting accidents and the careless handling of guns. In my humble opinion, there are way too many people out there who have no business handling a firearm of any kind. As long as you're not a felon, you can buy a shotgun or rifle, and sit through a couple of short classes. Once a few pieces of paper are signed you can now shoot a weapon that sends deadly bullets across great distances.

Don't get me wrong. I have no problem with our Constitutional Right that allows law abiding citizens to bear arms. I have a serious problem with idiots bearing arms. There are people who just get it in their heads that they want to own a gun so they buy one and target shoot out back where houses are nearby. Others get the notion that they have what it takes to be a big game hunter. Sometimes it's just a bullshit macho thing. Carry a big gun and kill something. These guys do their 9 to 5 office jobs fifty weeks a year. Then those few weeks in November come around and they drive a couple hours away to find some woods where they will don their hunting gear and take their high powered weapon into the woods (usually after a night in a hunting cabin getting hammered). They take this brand new gun out of the box. They've sat through the minimal gun safety class that teaches them the safe way to hold and point a gun, the safe way to load and unload, and the safe way to conduct yourself in the woods. They get one class on this and are set free into the world. (What is it they say about needing to watch a TV commercial seven times before it sinks in to buy the product?)

They can now fire a rifle that produces a bullet that can travel a mile killing anything in its path. That's friggin scary. And don't think that these guys are always on huge parcels of state forests or privately owned hunting camps. Yes, some of them are and that's a frightening thought in itself; a bunch of these guys all on the same patch of woods. But remember that state lands border private property. Private property where homes and people and kids are.

Many of these guys know someone who has a piece of land

upstate. And often times these guys will get permission to hunt on a person's property, but that property usually borders other people's property. My house is on five acres in a very rural area of upstate New York. My property borders other five acre parcels with houses on each side. If you walk up the hill behind my house, and into the woods, there are properties with houses that border the back of my land as well. Numerous times over the years, I've had guys come trampling through my woods with gun in hand. I'd meet them as I walk in the woods behind the house and get that "Hey, what're you doing here? I'm hunting here." kinda look on their face. When I question them about what they're doing, I get the response, "I've got permission to hunt here from the owner." Depending on my mood at the moment, and this armed stranger's demeanor, I'll toy with him a bit instead of getting right to the point.

"Oh really? Who's the owner?" I'll ask or "Oh, are you related to the owner?"

I'll let him stammer through some lame answers before I let him know that I am the owner and that 300 feet right down this hill is my house and my family. I'll then also add that I happen to be a state trooper and that I'd like to see some identification and his hunting license. He is then told that he is trespassing. Whatever name he gives me as the person who gave him permission will get a phone call from me.

These are the same guys who dismiss the fact that a house is a thousand feet away, but their bullet can travel a mile. Simple arithmetic, I'd say. These morons figure that it's a thousand feet of woods in between, so that makes it safe to shoot in that direction. Believe me, there are guys out there with big guns who think this way.

Being a city kid who moved to the country, I have come to greatly respect people who grew up with guns; people who learned as kids how to treat them, and how to respect them. And I have a huge admiration for what I call the "Real Deal Hunters". The guys and gals who go out into the woods and play by the rules. These are true sportsmen. Personally, I don't have the patience for it, but I give a lot of credit to the real hunters who do. They do their research for a good spot. They make a plan, get out early (and not bleary eyed from the night before), and sit motionless for hours surveying every bit of movement. They will only shoot into areas that they already know are safe. These "Real Deal Hunters" will always wait until they can get a clear shot. They wait until they can actually identify their target and see it well enough to know that it is the right size and gender to take. And they will sit until it is in a position for a shot that will kill it, not maim or wound it. I knew a fellow trooper who passed on shooting a trophy buck because he never had a clean, clear shot. This beautiful buck was surrounded by doe as he passed through the woods. The only shot he could take would be through one of the doe. He wouldn't do it. He told me that there are lots of guys out there who would do it, but to him that would be breaking the rules. It wasn't part of the sport he loved. You shoot when you've got a clean shot. If you don't, oh well, that's part of the game. There'll be another day.

As a uniform trooper, I've stopped guys in their cars who drive around with loaded guns and shoot at deer they see in the roadside woods. There are guys who sit at their kitchen table with the patio door open and a cup of coffee in their hand. One clown actually followed the deer's path through the scope of his rifle as it walked behind his house. He forgot that he was looking through the glass of his patio door and fired. And these guys can carry guns around? Real sportsmen, huh?

I've witnessed guys unloading their rifles by ejecting the bullets and then pulling the trigger to double check that it's not loaded. (Yes, that's the wrong and very dangerous way to unload a gun.) Other guys will walk through the woods with their shotgun over their shoulder pointing at the face of the guy walking behind him. All too often, these weapons get momentarily pointed at people. It could be during its transport or putting it down or taking it out of a car. No matter how many times you tell these people to treat every firearm as if it is always loaded, they will repeatedly come back when challenged with, "What's the big deal? It's not loaded."

I know some of you are saying, "Yeah, he's a city kid who came to the country, but it's the city people like him that come to the country and hunt like assholes." And you'd be partially correct. There are a number of city folks who fall into the category that I have been bashing. Yes, they are the ones who make the exodus from their urban metropolis, venture into country woods and fields, and have shot cows. Their bullets have hit houses and wound up in cereal boxes inside kitchen cabinets, and they will get that dose of "Buck Fever" that has them shooting at movement without actually identifying what they're shooting at.

Yes, they are out there, but they are not the majority. Most hunters, whether they are local folks or travelers from the city, play by the rules for the most part. However, many locals will admit that they never see the city hunters who play by the rules and that's because they don't trespass. They follow the rules and go home. It's the problem child that gets all the attention. And very often the problem child is a local.

Most locals will be better at handling guns, but some of them will think nothing of driving around the back roads with loaded guns in their pick-up trucks or venturing onto other people's land. The mindset is that this was a great spot when they were kids. Well now this great spot is owned by someone else who put a house up on it.

I've had to talk to these guys and I get the "Well, my great granddaddy used to plow the----"

I interrupt with, "Hey, spare me the great granddaddy bullshit. You're trespassing. Stay off the land, or get arrested. Simple as that."

I know I've done a bit of bitching here about people who shouldn't carry guns, let alone shoot them, but I'm going to let you in on a little secret. If you're reading this and getting insulted and pissed off, or think "Who the hell is this guy?", then you're one of the problems. I've been involved in numerous tragic accidents that happened only because someone handled a gun recklessly. That doesn't take into account the countless times that haven't been reported. Bullets whizzing by someone, bullets hitting houses or passing cars, loaded guns pointed at people with a finger on the trigger, scopes used as telescopes with fingers on the triggers, accidental discharges that thankfully hit no one and the list goes on and on.

The reason I can say this is because I've had lengthy discussions with real hunters who are scared to death that these idiots will ruin the sport they love. A real hunter will have no problem with anything I've said. A lot of my comments come from the talks I've had with them. Real hunters have had to deal with these jerks trespassing through after they've sat for hours waiting for that buck they know is coming. In short, real hunters play by the rules, and they realize just how deadly a weapon it is that they're carrying and they treat it as such.

Some accidents, whether hunting or otherwise, are just that: accidents. But too many are tragic consequences of not thinking things through that get labeled as accidents. In most cases, we should know better.

So here is a list of careless behaviors that should make you think twice before doing it again.

FYI: I've seen every one of these end in death at least once. So be careful.

- Don't sleep with an infant. Even a small Mom can lean on, or unintentionally lay an arm across, its mouth that can smother it. It's very easy to suffocate an infant.

- Put life jackets on every kid in every boat (and the unsure adults as well).

- Do not carry infants or toddlers on your lap while operating machinery. Not even a riding lawn mower.

- As a pedestrian, walk on the shoulder of the roadway FACING oncoming traffic. Do not walk on the road at night.

- Learn how to operate deadly instruments like an axe or chainsaw or tractor before you actually use it.

- Treat and handle all guns of any kind as if they are always loaded.

- Hunt with people who know what they're doing, people you trust with your life and, possibly, the lives of your children.

- Don't walk through dark woods, but, if you must, then have a flashlight or even the light from your cell phone. Look before each step.

- If you're not an electrician, don't mess with electricity. It can burn your house down and, more importantly, can kill you and anybody near you.

- Don't mix medications without a doctor's approval and that includes booze.

- Do not text and drive.

Chapter Eight
All in the Family

I'm sorry guys. It's just the way it goes. If your wife or girlfriend or ex winds up dead, we're coming to have a long chat with you. So bring a snack.

The significant other of any victim will always be the initial suspect. And that's based on cold, hard, very convincing numbers. Sometimes it's a planned crime and other times an argument escalates to murder. The majority of murder/suicides are spouse/partner related. Again, it can be planned that way or the initial murder sends the perpetrator into the "What have I done?" dilemma and they complete the cycle of deadly acts.

Infidelity is the big one. It causes the hottest fireworks, but it can also be a rising number of fights and series of events that culminate in a volcanic confrontation. One guy who challenged his wife about her infidelities cut her throat when she got out of the shower. He wrote out a long suicide note describing what he did. Then he turned on every gas burner and pulled the knobs off the burners on the kitchen stove and started a fire in the house. He sat on the sofa waiting for the explosion that happens so often on TV. The gas just fed the fire and got the house burning hotter and hotter. He hung in there as long as he could and sustained third degree burns, but finally ran out of the house and collapsed. He told responding police a different story, but forgot that he had left the suicide note outside on the front porch.

Many arguments will finally result in a resolution. However, it might be a resolution that's unacceptable to one partner such as the other's decision to leave. Various stages of packing or packed bags at the door are often the scene we come upon. One party might make the final decision, but then that night while everyone is asleep, the double deed is done. In one horrific instance, the father decided to kill the children as well.

Sometimes the murder/suicide plans go awry. Finding a deceased elderly woman tucked under her covers in bed could appear like a natural death until a look around reveals that a laptop and television are missing. When the unemployed, down and out son who was living with her was interviewed, he said he came home and found her like that. It was good police work that finally cracked him into admitting that he used a slow choke hold on his mother in a mutually agreed upon murder/suicide pact. She allowed him to choke her to death and tuck her into bed. He was supposed to follow suit by drinking a poisonous mixture and then got second thoughts. He decided to sell the TV and laptop for money to buy drugs and went off to party with friends.

Feeling awful about doing the deed is also common. It happened and he or she is dead. Now what? Some try to cover it up and others really don't know what to do. A whacked out on drugs hubby strangled his wife during an argument. In his hazy head he figured he'd try putting her in a bath to see if that would revive her. After drying her off, he laid her in their bed as if she was going to sleep. He then slept next to her for the night. When an angry relative came banging on the door looking for the wife, he stood her nude body up in the closet and closed the door. Rigor mortis had made the body stiff as a board by morning so she stood up quite conveniently amongst the hanging clothes in the closet. The mad as hell relative called the cops and insisted that the wife was in the apartment and that the husband must've done something to her. The husband said "Sure you can search my apartment. She's not here." A few minutes later, a cop was surprised to open a closet door and see the naked slumping body of the wife. I'm sure it gave him a bit of a jump when he opened that door. By the time we got there, the rigor mortis had left her body and she was sitting on the floor in the closet. The husband confessed to strangling her after an argument. Some of the other details were cloudy because of the night's drug use.

When residents hadn't seen their elderly neighbor for a few weeks, they called the State Police. Responding troopers questioned the adult son who lived with his elderly mother. He told them that he hadn't seen her in a month. Knowing that the son was a bit of an unsavory character, they talked him into letting them search his house just to have a "look around" to see if they could find any kind of clue as to where she might have gone. One of the troopers made his way into the basement and found a large freezer chest. Oh yeah. You know what's coming next. Mom was in the freezer. This wasn't exactly a Norman Bates kind of thing and the autopsy did determine that she died of natural causes, so she wasn't murdered. Then why put her in the freezer and not notify authorities? Because that would've ended Mom's Social Security checks that were getting automatically deposited in their shared account. Besides collecting the Social Security money illegally, he was only guilty of not properly disposing of human remains and failure to notify authorities of the death. Neither of which would get him jail time, but he would have to pay his mother's Social Security money back.

Money problems, or the thought of getting lots of money, can lead family members to commit some pretty horrible acts. It's happened more than once that a strong personality boyfriend talked his weaker girlfriend into doing terrible things to get their hands on a relative's money. Like the granddaughter who choked her grandmother, took her cash and went driving around town in grandma's car with boyfriend having a good old time. But to make sure that no one would come to grandma's house and find her, they'd put her into the trunk of her own car. Now they were spending grandma's money and driving grandma's car around with grandma in the trunk!

But not all elderly folks allow themselves to be victims. Sometimes they have had enough. One elderly father lived with his adult son who constantly berated him. The son would take whatever money the father left out. When the father questioned him, and suggested getting a job, the son would verbally abuse him calling him every name in book. He'd tell the father that he was useless, stupid and had no idea what he was talking about. One time as the son began one of his vicious tirades, the father gently instructed him not to talk to him like that.

"What're you gonna do old man? Huh?" yelled the son. "What can you do? You can't do nothing cause you're useless."

The father pulled out a revolver, pointed it at his son and begged him to stop treating him like that.

"Oh you gonna shoot me, old man? No, you're not cause you're nothing but a ----"

BAM!!

One shot ended the tirade. The father called police and turned himself in. He admitted to everything, never trying any battered or psychiatric defense. We felt bad for this poor, abused old man who worked his whole life to end up in prison.

A number of these situations truly are acts of self preservation. Mental illness that goes untreated can lead to tragically sad stories. Many parents really try to do their best to raise their kids who have aggressive tendencies. But, without medical assistance these kids grow up into strong adults as parents age and get weaker. Some of these adult kids stay living at home because their condition makes it tough for them to keep a job and even harder to keep their own place. The frustrations from both sides build, and often the parents become the victims of physical abuse. In talking to these poor folks, it becomes obvious that the physical pains are nothing compared to the emotional hurts they endure.

An aging husband and wife's situation got so bad that one day the father had to pull out a handgun to defend his wife from being beaten. Constant cries to get him help fell upon the son's deaf ears. During an anger filled confrontation with his mother over unlaundered clothes, the quite large adult son went after his mother. Bruises on her face hadn't even healed from the last altercation. The father stepped in and pointed a gun at their son and demanded that he stop and leave. This only infuriated the son even more and it sent him barreling towards the father like a raging bull. It took three shots to stop him. This poor man had saved his wife from future beatings, and probably saved her life, but he now had to live with the fact that he had killed his own son. When the crime scene unit arrived on the scene, the mother and father were being taken to the station so that they wouldn't be present for the removal of their son's body. Words can't describe that sad, lost look in their eyes.

Whenever someone dies and family members are present, it stands to reason that everyone in the family will be questioned about what happened. But the tricky part is that we don't always know if we're talking to a victim of grief, or the potential perpetrator of an awful crime. It's our job to be suspicious of everything; no matter how clear cut it may appear.

A local police department had gotten a call about a man who was found dead on his sofa with a gunshot wound to the right side of his head. The man was lying on his left side on the sofa with his head on the armrest. The wound was adjacent to his right ear. A revolver was on the floor in front of the sofa. The man's wife and teenage son were home and said that they had heard the shot, came into the living room, and found him like that. The woman was his second wife and the teenager was her step son. The wife told the cops that her husband had been very upset about the family's financial burdens and that he feared he was going to lose his job. The son said that his dad seemed upset recently.

It appeared to be a suicide, but something didn't feel right about it so they called us and asked if we would attend the autopsy and look things over with the pathologist. The local cops had already handled the scene at the house and took lots of photographs. One of our guys attended the autopsy the next day. The pathologist was one of the best. She had worked many cases with us and was always an outstanding asset to any investigation. There was a lot of blood around the wound and on the right hand that held the gun. Upon cleaning up the blood on the right hand, the doctor immediately saw a problem. There was a small hole in the webbing of the right hand between the thumb and the index finger. A closer look revealed that the hole was an entrance wound that went in the webbing from the back of the hand and exited out the webbing on the palm side. The hole size on the palm side matched the bullet hole size in the right side of the man's head. It was now apparent that the right hand had to have been lying on the right side of his face or head when the bullet was fired. With his hand on the side of his head, the one shot went through the webbing and into his head. He couldn't have been holding the gun in his right hand.

As the autopsy was going on, a neighboring police department observed something that was a bit peculiar. This department had read about the suspicious death and knew the names, of the people involved. (It's great when information sharing works.) A sharp-eyed cop sitting on the desk remembered the names and noticed that the wife and step son were there in his police department's lobby reporting something trivial. They were sitting and waiting for some information. The cop then noticed something that made him notify his supervisor immediately. The wife and step son were having a pretty heavy make out session in the lobby. The supervisor immediately got on the phone with the detectives from the department investigating the apparent suicide. I'm sure it had to be one of those conversations that went something like, "Hey, you ain't gonna believe this."

Both the wife and step son were brought in and questioned separately under the guise of "a few last questions we have about your tragedy". At the proper time, our guys hit them separately with the autopsy findings and their rendezvous in the lobby. They both confessed to planning the murder so that they could have a life together. They waited until the father had taken a nap on the sofa, and then shot him to make it look like a suicide. The son had done the shooting and didn't realize he had hit his father's hand that was lying along the side of his face.

This was one of those cases that demonstrates how much can be accomplished with open communication between different agencies. The collaboration of a police department that wouldn't write it off as an obvious suicide, to the expertise of a forensic pathologist, to a heads-up desk officer at another police agency helped solve a premeditated murder.

Overall, murder/suicides and partner/family member homicides that happen at the spur of the moment are a bit easier to figure out. But when one family member takes the life of another, there's a little more homework to do. They usually live in the same house, or visit frequently, so finding their DNA or fingerprints doesn't help us. It's going to take meticulous interviewing and searching for a motive. Emotion is such a huge part of violent crimes that occur within relationships.

Many spouse murders are referred to as crimes of passion. You don't hear that phrase as much nowadays, but it's still quite fitting.

The word passion is appropriate, but I'd say that the word rage is more so. It's a fact of life that we are hurt the deepest by the ones who are dearest to us. When an acquaintance hurts or betrays us, it stings. But when a loved one does it, the pain sears like a red hot knife through the heart. The resulting plethora of emotions includes sadness, grief, frustration, and anger. And the expression of that anger offers us a release. Lashing out is a form of that ire. The lashing out created by anger's overwhelming power will be directed towards the provider of that hurt. A primal instinct takes over and we hit back. We hit back so that we feel better, even if only momentarily. We want to hurt that person back so we scream, curse and, sometimes, strike them in an attempt to rid ourselves of these terrible feelings. The reality is that it may feel good for a moment or two, or you may feel as though you "told him all right", but the miserable feelings are still there. They didn't go away at all, and it probably made the situation worse.

A little kid gets upset, throws a tantrum and gets put in the corner. When adults get deeply hurt, they throw a raging tantrum and get put in jail. There are many, many people in jail and prison because their anger got the better of them. And they all know it..... a little too late. Anger and frustration are emotions that people deal with quite often, but true rage is not. Extreme anger and rage can overcome you, and lead you to do things you would never even dream of doing when you're thinking normally. The other side of rage is extreme grief caused by some personal devastation. And in a number of cases, you have both hitting you at the same time.

I know very well that these emotions can be overwhelming, and all we want is to feel better and have the bad feelings go away. We want life back to the way it was before all of this happened. I do know. But I also know that lashing out in any way doesn't help that happen. Wanting answers now and not backing down are acceptable. You don't have to quiver and shake and cry and walk away. You're usually going to be a whirlwind of questions and frustrations and doubts, so you'll want some kind of explanation, some kind of answer.

Asking "Why did you do this to me?" is a lot better than "Why did you do this to me you lying, cheating bitch?" Spewing out the latter may momentarily make you feel better, but it does not make the situation any better. I have come to live by the motto: "Why make an awful situation worse?" If a certain action is going to make an already stressful problem harder to resolve, then don't do it.

Those feelings of wanting to attack will be there. But like the guy who wound up in jail, you too may do damage that makes the disaster tougher to resolve. There are lots of books out there, and self help advice online, that can assist you in dealing with, and releasing some of this unbelievably strong emotion that will seem to take over you.

Remember that there will be things that happen to you in this life that you will have absolutely no control over. But what you will be able to control is how you deal with it. You must acknowledge it and try your damnest to accept what's happened (which won't be easy), and then you must decide how you will let it affect you. You have to make the conscious decision to step back, take a deep breath, say a prayer if you want, count to ten and nip in the bud these unbearable feelings that want you to act out in a destructive manner. The hurt and grief and betrayal will still be there. That's something else you'll have to deal with, but summon up every ounce of strength and will power you have left to prevent yourself from doing something that will destroy you, and possibly destroy the lives of other loved ones around you.

It's not easy. But it's a mindset that once understood and put into practice can literally save your life and keep what remains of your existence whole and healing.

Chapter Nine

Just Gross

'm sure many of you want to know if as a kid I ever thought that I'd grow up to be searching through maggot infested dumpsters on a hot summer day. No, not quite, but life has a way of sending you down a particular path towards what you think will be your dream job or career. Then a fork in the path comes along and something down the less traveled way catches your eye. "Hmmm…I think I'll try that one."

I'm a big believer in experiencing as much as you can during this one lifetime we're given. I tell young folks all the time. Go. Travel. Try it out. You're young. It kills me to see kids stay in the same hometown and never see what's out there beyond the county line or city limits. I have no problem with settling in your hometown, but explore a little first. There are so many opportunities out there that may never have presented themselves as viable options if you hadn't put yourself out there.

Even when I first got involved in crime scene work, I had no idea of the sights I'd see and the places I'd go. I remember the first time that I saw a body in the woods. It had been a hot summer. The head and hands were skeletonized, but the rest of the body was fully clothed.

As I got closer, I thought I was seeing things. Was the body moving? Is it breathing? It was especially noticeable in both upper pant legs. A closer look revealed that the fabric of the pants was moving. The shirt fabric was moving too but not as much as the pants. The senior guy in the unit was with me and said, "Take a look. Pull up his shirt." I stooped down close to the body, being careful not to disturb anything nearby. With gloved hands I carefully lifted the bottom of the loose fitting shirt upwards toward the shoulders and beheld the ghastly sight of thousands of squirming maggots feasting on this guy's innards. Lifting the shirt exposed them to the sunlight, so they wriggled and began slinking around even more. They were like little vampires. I couldn't help but reply in disgust, "Now that's just fuckin gross."

"Welcome to our world," came back the seasoned reply.

It really was gross, but also quite fascinating. "Yeah.....yeah...I can do this job." I thought to myself. I'll be dealing with worse than this and again I thought, "That's okay. I'm good with it. I like the work." But I will tell you that I don't look at a fly the same way anymore. Stay the fuck away from my food. I know where you've been.

Plenty of you have watched shows like "Hoarders" that depict homes with mountains of stuff; items that people collect and just can't get rid of. Houses become jam packed with useless objects. Imagine a house where the mountains are made up of garbage. Bags of trash piled high, and loose garbage that towers over, and covers, the furniture so that only narrow little pathways are left that enable you to get from one room to another.

I know a trooper who got called to one such house because the little old lady who lived there hadn't been seen in days. When the trooper got inside, he couldn't believe his eyes. There was so much garbage, he couldn't see the walls or furniture or the floor except for the little paths. As he entered the main room, it looked like one large pile had toppled over and was now blocking the main path. When he climbed over the path as best he could to get through, he heard a little voice cry, "Help me!" He immediately pulled away a number of large garbage bags, and found the little old lady buried under the trash that had toppled over. An ambulance was called and she survived, but the house was condemned.

Think about what these conditions bring with them. The smell of garbage, and old food, and wrappers bring mice and all kinds of vermin into the house. Imagine breathing the air inside one of these places. And these aren't the worst. Many aging folks can't keep up with basic housework because of failing physical or mental health. For some of these people, their only companion is a pet or many pets. Cats are easier to keep than dogs, so we tend to see more cats with lonely old folks. But as with any animal, if you don't clean up after them, it can get quite offensive rather quickly.

My partner Paul, a bruiser who can pull a tree from its roots, will have a tough time with some of the smells that come with the job. Cats, and everything they leave behind, will send him into a heaving fit. There are other unpleasant smells that do it to him too, but this time it was cats.

We responded to the unattended death of a woman who was found in her upstairs bedroom. As soon as we entered the house, it hit us. It wasn't the smell of decomposition....yet. It was cats; cat hair, cat shit, cat piss. And it was everywhere. We made our way up the stairs toward the bedroom with me leading the way. When I reached the top step, I heard muffled gagging behind me.

"You gotta be kidding me? We're not even to the body yet," I stated.

A quick "I'm fine." pushed me onward....but I knew he wasn't.

There were two rooms at the top of the stairs. One to the left that didn't have much furniture in it, but the floor was covered in a thick layer of matted cat hair and cat feces. Once again, the gagging.

I offered, "You wanna go outside for a bit?"

"I'm fine."

Don't mistake me. It was nasty. I was having a hard time breathing myself. All the cat hair was already making my allergies act up.

So now we turned right and went into the master bedroom....and the other smell pounded us on top of the cat stink. Now there was a big gag. The gag that usually signaled to me something else was coming soon.

"Dude, go outside and get a breath of fresh air," I said.

Between heaves came back, "I'm fine."

"No. No, you're not. Don't fuckin throw up in here or on me. I mean it."

He took a beat or two, got it together, and calmly replied, "I won't. I'm fine. Let's do this."

The woman had been dead a couple of weeks and was pretty ripe. She was lying on her side. It was hard to tell if she had any obvious trauma because of the advanced decomp. We took a closer look at her face near the side of the bed and saw a thick black liquid that had poured from her mouth.

From behind me came, "What the fuck is that?"

"I'm not sure of the technical name for it, but I've seen it at natural deaths. Let's back out and start the photos," I started to retreat.

As we turned to exit the bedroom, something flew off of a high bureau towards us, almost knocking both of us onto the bed with our deceased. It scared the living shit out of the two of us. I mean race your heart scared.

"Fuckin cats!" Paul spewed and I knew right then that if he had gotten one of his mitts on that cat in mid air, he would've twisted its neck and hurled it out a window. The feline had been behind a TV that was on a high bureau and jumped out onto the bed as we turned to go. That's happened numerous times when opening a closet, or looking under a bed, and the damn beast leaps out at you. It can give you a friggin heart attack. But it's pretty funny to watch it happen to someone else.

The woman had died of natural causes, but that house would thence forward be referred to as "The Cathouse".

In this case the cats had plenty of food. In others, Kitty might get a little hungry and you walk into a scene that looks like something out of a zombie movie. Yes, you would be the only meat around, and Kitty has to do what she has to do.

And The Cathouse is again by no means the worst. You could have a scene where the condition of the house is worse than the bodies. From the outside, it was a brand new, two year old mobile home. Inside was a woman's body that had been discovered pretty quickly so she wasn't in too bad a shape. New mobile home, body not too decomposed. This wouldn't be bad..... Oh, was I wrong.

Envision keeping every food wrapper or packet you brought into the house for two years and piling them up on the kitchen counter or floor. And all pots, pans and plates in the house are in the sink caked with food and grease. The smell in this place wasn't cats or decomposition. It was something else. Scott had been around a while and seen quite a bit, so hearing uncertainty in his voice wasn't a good thing.

"Oh my God," is what I hear him say from down the hall. I walk towards him as he stands in the doorway of the bathroom looking in.

"Check this out," he tells me.

I peek in and see a brand new bathroom with a toilet that is full to the very top and overflowing with feces. Between the toilet and the far wall was toilet tissue. No, not rolls of it. It was a discarded pile of used and soiled toilet paper as high as the window. I mean a pile four feet high by four feet wide. That was the smell mixed with dirty dishes and rotted food. And guess what. That wasn't all.

I went to do a search of the living room and opened a closet door. I pulled open the door and the entire surface of the inside of the closet door was covered, and I mean every inch covered, with cockroaches. My knee-jerk reaction was to slam the door closed and, naturally, that caused hundreds of roaches to fly off the door into the closet and onto its floor, making that disgusting hitting-the-floor-and-scurrying away sound inside. I instinctively backed away, not quite gagging, but making the gagging face and shaking myself as if the possibility existed that a couple of them may have landed on me.

Scott saw me, "What happened?"

"You won't believe what's in there."

"I don't think I wanna know."

"Roaches. Thousands and thousands of roaches all over every inch inside that closet."

He just stared at me as if I was making it up. When he could tell that I wasn't, he just turned back to what he was doing and answered, "Screw that. I ain't going in there. Let's wrap this up."

The poor woman had severe dementia and had suffered a heart attack.

The smells that we encounter would turn any decent person's stomach. I have a brother-in-law who is as close to me as family can get, but he will throw me out of his house if I start talking about the stuff we see at work. Weak doesn't come close to describing Danny's stomach. Years ago, when we were younger lads and having a few drinks out at a bar, I started telling him about an autopsy I had recently attended. His face began to contort, so I asked him what was wrong.

"Can't listen to that shit, I'll throw up." he answered.

I didn't believe him. I thought he was messing around with me so I kept talking about how they stick a needle into the eyeball to extract the vitreous fluid. He asked me to stop or he would throw up. Having had a couple of drinks, I just kept on describing the cutting and sawing of the skull that happens at an autopsy. He then put his beer down and started heading toward the bar's back door. I followed him telling him that he was overreacting to some simple medical procedures.

"I'm telling you I'm gonna throw up," he insisted as he just about reached the door.

"You're being a bit dramatic."

At that he opened the back door, took one step outside and let loose a stream of projectile vomit that looked like Linda Blair in The Exorcist. I stood there a bit shocked and feeling like a jerk. He wiped his mouth, looked at me and said, "You happy?"

I stammered out a weak apology, and he told me not to worry about it.

"You owe me a beer," and back inside we went. I don't do it anymore in front of Danny.

The smell of death, of decomposition, is truly an awful stench. Other smells don't tend to stick to you like decomp does. I don't know what it is, but you could be in a room with a decomposing body for only a few minutes, and that stink will attach itself to you. We are inside crime scenes for hours, so it takes up residence in our clothes, our hair and in our noses. I got a kick out of one particular officer who pulled up in his car, rolled down the window and told me to get in with him to bring him up to speed about what was happening.

"You sure you want me to get into your car?" I made sure to ask.

"Yeah. Yeah. Get in here. I want to know what's going on," he instructed.

I got in, gave him a briefing of what we had thus far and then sat there. He stared at me debating something in his head, so I asked, "You want me to get out of your car?"

He blurted out, "Yes. Yes. Get outta my car. That shit smells awful!"

If we stop for a drink or something to eat on the way home from one of those scenes, we usually find ourselves with our own section of the bar pretty quickly. Arriving at home was no different. And all it took was the first time I walked into the house with that smell on me to be ordered by my wife to strip outside and get into the shower immediately. (Luckily, I lived in a rural area with no houses nearby!)

I can't tell you how many times I have come home in the middle of the night from places like that and stood in the doorway of my kids' rooms and watched them sleep. I'd find myself taking a deep breath and letting out a long slow exhale of everything I left that night. Places where I witnessed how some people lived, and how badly some people had it, and then I'd step through my door into the perfect world. And it was perfect! Healthy sleeping children and a wife who loves you in a house that you bought with the proceeds of a job you enjoy. Does it get any better? Can it be any better? No, not really.

Oh yeah, we'll complain about the bills, and the kids' school grades, and relatives who don't do their share. We'll hold grudges against friends and family members over the most ridiculous things. We will compare ourselves to others and wish we had more. We want to stay young forever and, in the process, miss out on the enchanted surprises and treasures that age and experience offer. Like the respect of being "The Dinosaur" at work or hearing the most beautiful phrase in the world, "I love you, Pop Pop." The secure future that 30 years at a good job brings to the table and the opportunity to enjoy a retired future with those you love.

Yes, with all of this, we'll bitch.

We'll find something wrong with this jacket or how the waiter served our burger. We won't like how someone looked at us, and hold it against him or her when maybe they were just having a bad day. Maybe they don't have it as good as we do. And I've been guilty of it. Wanting more. You make more so, you want more. Contentment doesn't seem to exist.

I've been in mansions and extravagant homes where despair, hatred and contempt reigned. And I've also been in small, old mobile home trailers where a husband, wife and three kids live a life together in happiness. A life supported by meager jobs that Mom and Dad work hard at. The appliances are old, but work. The kitchen linoleum floor is worn and cracked, but clean. The kitchen is tidy. The clothes are hand me downs, but laundered and folded. There are no fancy iPhones or the newest tablet. School books are on the clean kitchen table and a report card shows average grades. Paid bills lie on the same table waiting to be mailed. The family photos show cheerfully smiling people. They are content with what they have and happy to have each other. Do they have problems? Sure they do, just like everybody else. But they live their daily lives satisfied with the hand that life has dealt them.

In time, I learned to appreciate every single little thing I have; a warm blanket, oatmeal in the morning, a sunny day, a beer with friends, a good laugh, and the love of my family.

I stand there in the doorway of my kid's bedroom. Sometimes I give them a kiss. Sometimes I just smile. When I get into bed, I may give my wife a kiss or just lay my hand on her side thanking God that I have her. She'll mumble, "Don't even think about it." I'll chuckle and whisper back, "No, I know you've gotta get up early. And besides, this is just fine."

Chapter Ten
WTF?

A body was found in a quarry. Before we arrived, the term "dumped" got added to "body". He had been shot in the head and was lying face down in the middle of a big open area of the quarry. We arrived and started doing our thing. Unbeknownst to us, several investigators were tracking down all of the victim's drug and gang associates in an attempt to find a car that might have blood in it. It was believed that our victim was shot somewhere else and his bleeding body transported to this location and dumped. We didn't know where this theory came from, but we would do our job the way we always do it.

A couple of us had started with notes and basic photographs when our partner Tom showed up. He wasn't there thirty seconds when he asked, "What caliber is the casing?"

"What casing?" we asked.

Tom pointed to the ground near the body, "That casing right there."

We looked, and there was a 9mm spent bullet casing on the ground about four feet from the body.

"Oh! That casing. Didn't see it."

Now two lessons were learned at this crime scene. An extra set of eyes is always helpful. How many times have you searched furiously for something only to have someone else come along and say, "It's right there." It's a phenomenon that happens quite often because we individually process information very differently. No two people will look at the same photograph or drawing or crime scene the same way. It's just like that brain teaser exercise that instructs you to count the number of "F"s in the following paragraph.

FINISHED FILES ARE THE RE-

SULT OF YEARS OF SCIENTIFIC

STUDY COMBINED WITH

EXPERIENCE OF YOUTH.

A number of you will see 2, 3 or 4 "F"s, but there are actually 6.

How many times have you proofread the same material three times and still read right past the same typos? We try to have two people search the same area and, often, we'll look again. And then there's always the possibility that our minds weren't looking for a spent casing because we were told it was a dump job. That brings us to Lesson # 2.

The phrase "dumped body" was used by one of the first cops showing up at the scene and it took off from there. You now had lots of manpower wasting their time looking for blood in cars when in fact our processing of the scene showed that the victim had been brought to the quarry quite alive. He either laid face down on the ground, or was held down and then shot in the back of the head. The spent bullet casing at the scene and the bullet, that had exited the front of his head and lay in his pool of blood, proved it. A lot of legwork was wasted because someone mislabeled what they saw.

Being higher in the chain of command certainly doesn't exempt someone from doing something stupid. We responded to a stabbing murder inside a house where it looked like a teenaged foster child had stabbed or slashed his foster father to death. The knife was still sticking out of the guy. The body was in an upstairs bedroom that had two doors. It appeared that the foster son had fled out one of the doors, and had left a bloodied box cutter razor on the floor next to the other door. When we got there, it was obvious that someone had opened the other door thus sliding the box cutter along the floor leaving a thin blood trail. Did someone come in here after the murder? Did the foster son return? And why did he? It was a little baffling.

We continued to work the scene, and during one of our breaks we chatted with the uniform trooper who was securing the scene for us. He was a new guy and was keeping the crime scene attendance log up to date. The trooper heard us talking about the box cutter and then he said there was something we should know. He told us that there was an officer who had been inside the house before we got there. We told him that we had already talked to all of the responding cops, and they told us they used the first door and not the one that would've moved the bloody box cutter. He went on to say that this rather rotund higher ranking officer went in and told the young trooper not to put his name on the attendance log.

"Oh he did, did he?" We knew exactly who it was. Now the moved box cutter made sense.

Scott, who was our supervisor at the time, was livid and would straighten this out. Early the next morning, Scott approached this officer and let him know just how improperly he acted; firstly, by telling the trooper to keep his name off the crime log, and secondly, to go into the crime scene, move things and not tell us. To his credit, he fell upon the sword, apologized and further admitted that he touched the knife that was sticking out of the guy to see if it "was in there real good."

When Scott came back into our office and told us, we couldn't believe it. Yes, we've dealt with gawking cops and bosses who just have to have a look. And okay he inadvertently moved something, but what on earth would make you think you should touch, or give a little tug on the murder weapon that is sticking out of the victim? Even we in the crime scene unit don't do it. We bag him up and get him to a pathologist so that he or she can do their thing.

I've had bosses over the years that want to "see it". Hey, you're the boss. If you're the one going to be overseeing the entire investigation, I get it. Then there are bosses who just want to see the gore. You know, like your rubberneckers in traffic. This used to happen a lot more, but since the O.J. Simpson trial of the 1990's where proper evidence collection and scene security came into the courtroom spotlight, most bosses want to stay out of the crime scene. They don't want their names on that crime scene attendance log. One tactic we would use was to tell bosses that they had to put on one of our funky Tyvek suits before coming in. This will work on your vain, hotshot types who don't want to feel silly or take the chance that a photo of them dressed like this may wind up in the newspaper. One boss in full uniform knocked on the door and asked for a tour. I told him at the doorway that we had some faint footwear impressions and possible footwear debris just inside the door that we hadn't photographed or processed yet. Coming through there might contaminate it. I concluded that it might be a while before we got to it. He stared at me blankly, said okay and left, closing the door. I stifled a laugh as the other guys inside complimented me.

"Good one. Can't use that one on him again."

Hey, whatever it takes. We can't be stopping what we're doing to give tours to higher ups and district attorneys. Let us do our friggin jobs. We'll give you the photos later.

A lot of crime scene guys adhere to the strict "No one is allowed inside the crime scene" rule. But there are a couple of people I will allow in for the nickel tour. One is the DA, or ADA, who will have to prosecute this case and attempt to recreate this scene to a jury a year or two later. The other is the cop who is going to be in a room for hours with the potential perpetrator and that's up to him. Some interviewers would like to see the scene, others prefer not to. It depends on their style. Outside of these people, the rest can look at pictures.

Most people don't think like cops, so if you give them a tour you must remind them to either keep their hands in their pockets or wear the Tyvek suit and gloves. Don't lean on anything, watch every step you take, don't wander from wherever we are walking you. But I get it. It's not their thing. Not everyone does this for a living.

A murder victim was dying as he called 911 for help. He came home from work, walked into his home and was shot by someone who was inside his house. He collapsed and remembered the assailant stepping over him and leaving. He could reach a phone and called. The 911 dispatcher kept him on the line for about ten minutes while EMS and cops raced there. Later we listened to the 911 tape of this man's last agonizing ten minutes of life. The dispatcher did everything he could to keep him talking and alert, but cops listened more and more anxiously waiting for that big question to be asked, "Who shot you?" But he never asked. You could tell that this poor man was dying. He told the dispatcher that he could see the guy, and yet was never asked if he knew who it was that shot him. Finally, at the very end of the call, the dying victim mentions the perpetrator's name. People gave the dispatcher a hard time about it. But as I've said before, a lot of people don't think the way cops do. He has a different job than we do and that involves saving lives. He did that job as valiantly as he could.

It isn't difficult to find yourself sitting in a potentially dangerous situation if you don't follow the rules. However there do come those times when our back room guys want to sit a possible bad guy down in a room and go at him. Sometimes you want to make the interview appear informational as opposed to being an interrogation. You may not want the guy to think he's a suspect... yet.

A quiet man liked walking into the woods behind his house where he would find his nice secluded spot and have a peaceful smoke. When he didn't return for dinner, his wife went looking for him and found him shot to death and rolled down an embankment nearby. Soon the mentally unstable neighbor came into our sights. His property adjoined the victim's. Our guys wanted to ask this individual to come down to the station to "help them out" with this awful tragedy. In an attempt not to "hink up" an already paranoid personality, certain procedures were skipped. It worked out in that the suspect went along gladly with the whole, "Yeah, I'll help you guys." He drove to the station and sat down in a quiet room. After a while, the interview started to turn. It took some time. The guys would walk out of the interview room and let him think about things. Then they'd return with another round of questions. Eventually he confessed. He admitted to killing his neighbor because he believed that he posed some imaginary threat to him. Our guys got a written statement from the guy, stood him up and did the standard pat down of his body to start the arrest process. The pat down uncovered the loaded murder weapon revolver tucked into the waistband of his pants. Every cop there had an "Oh shit!" look on their face realizing just how easy it would've been for this unstable murderer to wreck havoc on everyone. I remember stopping back at the station after we were done at the scene and the guy being pointed out to me through a two-way mirror. He was wearing a big baggy sweatshirt that covered his waist.

Not patting him down for a weapon was definitely a mistake, but I understand why they didn't. Once again, you can't assume anything or try to use logic and think, "What potential suspect would bring the loaded murder weapon into a police station?" Luckily, this would-be scary situation turned out all right.

Procedures might have to be altered to get a job done, and other times there may not be any set procedures to follow to accomplish the task. A murdered girl's body was dumped in the freezing woods. A layer of snow covered her. It was imperative that we get her to the morgue and an autopsy started as soon as possible to determine the cause of death, type of weapon, and look for any kind of clues whatsoever in this whodunit crime. But she was frozen solid. You can't work on the body until it thaws and that would take time. More time than we wanted to spend. Most autopsies don't have to be done immediately so letting the body thaw inside a walk-in refrigerator usually does the trick. But we needed it done sooner, so the decision was made to leave the body on a gurney and out of the refrigerator in the room temperature autopsy room (Sort of like leaving that frozen roast beef out on the kitchen counter). It was determined that this procedure would hasten the thawing process some, but probably not by morning. So one guy came up with a solution. He rigged portable high intensity lights around the body inside the autopsy room. A cop would stand all night outside the locked morgue door.

One of our guys got there the next morning before the pathologist and met the cop. He wasn't a happy camper. The smell coming through the door was horrendous. Once inside, the good old smell of decomp was overwhelming. The originally well preserved frozen body was now already into decomposition. It also had a bit of a sunburn. A few more hours and it would've literally started to cook. The autopsy could be performed, but it was a bit of a mess.

When we try to hurry things up that shouldn't be hurried, we usually make mistakes. I can tend to be a bit impatient. It's always a part of our crime scene ritual to wrap things up with a final survey of the entire scene. Then we go over everything that we've collected and make sure we leave nothing behind.

There was a shooting on a residential street. The bad guy popped off several rounds at another guy and fled. The victim was taken to the hospital and although he was hit several times, it looked like he was going to make it. Paul and I were called to this outside scene where spent bullet casings littered the street and sidewalk. I was in charge of collecting the evidence. We figured out where the shooting occurred, photoed the scene, wrote our notes, started a crime scene sketch, and began collecting the evidence. Most of it would consist of the expended shells. We had also located a few lead projectiles that appeared to have missed their intended target and had hit a house, a garbage can, and a tree. Once all of the obvious evidence had been collected, we walked a grid search. Grabbing whatever cops were available, they walked shoulder to shoulder looking for more shells or any other evidence. The cops wore latex gloves that we gave them and, once the search was done, we collected the gloves and added them to our bag of garbage. It's common practice to have your own bag of garbage with all of your bloody gloves, evidence container wrappers, Tyvek suits, etc., and then take it away with you to dispose of properly. We felt good that we had completed a thorough job and I began wrapping evidence up. It's a good idea to package a number of small bags, like the casings and bullets, into larger bags to keep them together and more easily accounted.

We now started loading up the back of my van with our equipment and evidence. Just then a garbage truck was going by picking up the garbage from in front of each residence. We had already searched all of the garbage cans, so the timing was perfect. I figured this was convenient so I tossed our garbage bag into the back of the garbage truck. (There wasn't anything with blood on it so it was okay.) We left the scene and went back to the office to start processing the evidence. Once everything was brought inside our lab, I went right to the evidence, opened the bag.... and saw garbage. I looked at Paul, "Oh shit!"

His inquiring eyes soon widened as I explained my obvious screw up. Paul remembered the name of the garbage company and called them. I double checked my van. He came out and told me that their temporary transfer station wasn't far away and it should've been dumped already and would be waiting to be scooped up for compacting. We hopped into the van and took off. We were pointed to a pile of garbage that had been deposited from that neighborhood. It was dumped in a kind of open shed where it would soon be scooped up by huge front end loaders. The guys at the transfer station were great and let us look through everything. Of course, we might not have said that we were looking for mistakenly discarded evidence, but we did say that we were looking for evidence from a shooting in this neighborhood. Staring at the mound of trash, Paul and I had that "finding a needle in a haystack" despair. But the workers could actually narrow down an area of the mound when we told them what street we were on. They left us alone and went off to another pile. They were right on the money. Within fifteen minutes, we found my brown evidence bag, slightly compacted, but with all of the evidence intact inside it. Whew! We thanked the guys profusely and headed back counting our lucky stars.

I had learned my lesson. Don't be in such a hurry. Double and even triple check accountable items. It's a meticulous job we have. Treat it as such.

We all make mistakes. But the problem is when we refuse to learn from them. We all know a family member or somebody at work who just "doesn't get it". And you can try to explain it to them. They will nod and agree with you, and then they will go ahead and do it again. Thank God this is only a minority of people. Most people do "get it". If you help them out, they appreciate it. If you tell them, "Hey, don't do this again or you'll be in big trouble" they don't do it. When someone helps a cop out with something he's working on, the cop will usually have no problem going to bat for that person at a later time if they need it….. within reason.

Now I ask you. If you had an 88 mile per hour speeding ticket reduced to a minor equipment violation so that you received no points on your license and no raise in your insurance, would you learn your lesson? Would you realize that the cop used his word to a prosecutor he might not even know to help you out? He may talk to a fellow cop who isn't crazy about reducing anything, and had to listen to a ration of shit to get him to go along with a reduction for you. Would you take this break and be thankful? Or would you go out and feel free to do it again? I hope most of you would do the right thing.

I knew a gal who worked for a county agency that worked hand in hand with us on many cases. She got a speeding ticket and called me. She had definitely helped us out before, so I reached out for the cop who wrote the ticket. I did wonder why the cop didn't give her a warning because I'm sure he would've known her. A sergeant I knew picked up the phone and told me that the cop was off. When I mentioned why I was calling, his immediate response was, "Her? She called you? Did she tell you why she got a ticket?"

This didn't sound good, "Yeah, she did. She was speeding. Doing 81. Why?"

"Because she was doing a hundred and six!"

"What?!"

"Oh yeah. 106 in her hot rod Mustang, blowing people off the road. When she got pulled over, passing motorists were giving the thumbs up sign as they drove by. She got her break. He wrote her for 81."

"Okay. Forget it. I did not know that. Thanks for the heads up."

I called her up and politely read her the riot act and told her there was nothing I could do to help her out. She subsequently went to court and got the 81 reduced. Believe it or not, she called me again about two weeks later asking me if cops were upset with her. I asked why she thought that, and she answered that she got pulled over again in her Mustang and was given a ticket for doing 92. Incredulously I asked if she was doing 92. She admitted that she was, but she was late for an appointment. This ticket came from a cop at a different station who didn't know about the first ticket. Of course, she finally got around to the real reason for the call and I told her there was nothing I could do for her. It ain't easy trying to remain even remotely polite when dealing with people like this. It didn't matter how I explained it, she just didn't get it.

I was working the highway years ago in an unmarked car and got up behind a car in the left lane. I just wanted to get where I was going. I had no intention of pulling this car over. I just wanted to get by. There was no one else on the highway in the middle of the day. I tried flashing my headlights. Nothing. Okay. I had to get going. I passed on the right, glanced over and the gal looked right at me and flipped me off. I hit the brakes, let her go, got behind her and pulled her over. As I walked up to her open driver's window, I could hear her bawling.

"I'm sorry. I'm so sorry. I didn't know it was you."

"So if it wasn't a cop, it's okay to stay in the left lane and give someone the finger?" I replied.

She understood that the finger was a bit rude, but when I asked why she wouldn't leave the left lane, she didn't answer. She had been driving for years. She knew it was the passing lane. She understood that people shouldn't have to pass on the right. Yes, she had seen how it works. People in the left lane usually moved over for her if she was coming. But she didn't think she had to. And of course, that classic line came out.

"Well if I'm doing the speed limit in the passing lane, why should anyone be going faster than me?"

People who ask this need to remember that it's our job to enforce the vehicle and traffic laws, not theirs. It's their duty to obey the traffic laws. And let's be smart about this. Do you want to be in someone's way who heard that their house is on fire or their kid got into an accident? I'm not condoning speeding for any of these reasons, but let's use our head a little bit here. And then there's the big one. What if it's a cop?

One last speeding story illustrates my point best. I pulled over a woman who was speeding. She wasn't going that fast, but she was speeding. A man sat in the front passenger seat. They were both middle aged folks. I asked for the woman's license and registration. I could tell from our quick discussion that they were husband and wife. I told her that I had stopped her for speeding and that I would be right back. In my car, I checked her driving record and it was clean. They seemed like decent people who were on the way home from a family function and had been on the road for a bit, so I decided to give the woman a ticket for not wearing her seatbelt (which she wasn't) instead of the speeding ticket. I walked back up to the driver's window and explained that I had stopped her for speeding, but decided I would give her a ticket for not wearing her seatbelt instead. I went on to say that the seatbelt ticket wouldn't put any points on her license and it wouldn't raise her insurance premiums, but the fine that she would have to pay would remind her to keep a closer eye on her speedometer.

As I started to hand her the ticket and her documents, she looked up at me and said, "Well, I don't know why you have to give me a ticket at-----"

Suddenly the husband's arm shot across his wife's chest with the very distinct exclamation, "Shut the fuck up!"

His hand then gently reached towards me accepting the ticket, her license and the registration. He then leaned over, looked up at me, smiled and said, "Thank you very much, Trooper. Have a good day."

The husband gets it.

Chapter Eleven

The Tough Ones

I attended my first autopsy as a uniform trooper. It was common practice to send new guys to witness an autopsy. Upon arriving at the morgue, I was told that it was being performed on an infant. The parents had found the baby unresponsive in his crib and rushed him to the hospital. He was pronounced dead. There were no signs of trauma, so the death was a bit of a mystery. It was so strange seeing this tiny human being on the big metal table. He looked like he was merely sleeping. All I could think about was my own infant daughter at home.

The awful discovery of this beautiful child's unresponsiveness had to be horrifying for the parents. I kept thinking about that as the pathologist cut open this little body. I still remembered the joy and love surrounding my daughter's birth. Like this baby, it was only months ago. To see it come to an end on this cold silver table was so unbelievably sad.

It was determined that there had been no foul play. The cause of death was written up as SIDS which is being diagnosed less and less nowadays. I knew that the autopsy itself didn't bother me, but the victim tugged quite a bit at my heart.

Kids.... Your roughest, seen it all, hard line cop will have a tough time when he comes across a child victim. Every day cops deal with society's problems and the people who cause them: thieves, violent personalities, jerks and abusers of all kinds. When an innocent child is found amongst this mess, it's instinctual to feel sorrow. To want to protect her. I've known many, many cops who've grown hard-boiled and who truly believe the often cited eloquent verse, "Everybody is an asshole!" But kids have never been included in that assessment.

It doesn't happen often that a crime scene guy gets to travel. Road trips are usually for back room investigators, who are following up leads on investigations or traveling to another state to put hands on a bad guy and bring him back. But every once in a while, they'll need a crime scene guy to do his thing at some far away jurisdiction.

Similar to the television show "Storage Wars", a man in the Midwest bought the contents of a storage container. It had been left abandoned for a number of years and the storage place was legally auctioning it off. You couldn't look through it. You bid on it, took your chance and brought the contents home. Upon bringing it home and going through it, he found lots of personal items, children's clothes, playpens, high chairs, and a couple of cardboard boxes that had a very distinct smell to them. One box had another box inside it, and that one had one more inside of it. The last box contained tiny mummified remains. In all, there were the remains of three mummified infants. He immediately called the local Sheriff's Department.

The name on the storage container was tracked to a woman living in Pennsylvania, but they found out that she had lived most of her life in New York State. Our guys were contacted and a road trip was set up. Two back room guys and two crime scene guys would go. The back room guys would interview everyone that needed to be interviewed, and we would go through all of the contents of the storage container.

We would also arrange for the infants' return to New York State.

The good folks of the Sheriff's Department and the Arizona State Police met us. It's interesting when cops from one jurisdiction meet up with cops from another jurisdiction; everyone tends to be a little on guard. Cops are cops and we will always be suspicious, competitive, and not want to take any shit. At the same time, you understand jurisdictional procedures and don't want to step on anybody's toes. You also know that every police department, whether it's in the next township over from you or across the country, does things a little differently than you do. Now add to all of that, us New Yooorkers showing up in our suits at a police station where the men wear jeans, boots, and cowboy hats. We might work in rural upstate New York, a hundred miles away from the Big Apple, but New York will always be perceived as New York to the rest of the union.

In our very first meeting, we were introduced to the Sheriff; an older, weathered, good ole boy who welcomed us with a joke about New York cops vs. cowboy cops. He gave a briefing to everyone and threw in another shot at New York cops. We laughed and smiled, but it certainly didn't let our guard down too much. It was a good thing that the four of us were pretty easygoing guys. We realized that we were in their house and on their turf, so there was no point in participating in a "Whose dick is bigger?" contest. We had a job to do and we needed these guys.

As soon as the old time Sheriff left (and that was the last we saw of him), we started dealing with the detectives and troopers who actually worked the case. This gang of cops was gold. They immediately made us feel at home, and the cop camaraderie soon followed.

During breaks in the work, or while waiting around to pick people up, we discussed the differences in our jobs. It was very interesting. A lot of these guys were full time Sheriff's Deputies who also ran large scale farms and cattle ranches. These guys were real cowboys. And I mean the real deal cowboys. Feeding the hundred cattle they own in the morning, coming to work, and then going home to clean the barn and attend to missing or sick livestock. I asked them about a road sign I had seen on the way over that illustrated the silhouette of a mountain lion with the words "Endangered Species". They explained that there were lots of mountain lions around and when I inquired further if they were an endangered species, one of the cop/ranchers replied, "They sure as hell are when I'm around them."

At their homes, these cops were tending to cows on 300 acres of land. They needed so much land because the patchy grass didn't grow in their dry climate like it did for us back east. While roaming around looking for patches of grass to eat, a big cat would sneak into the pasture and grab a cow or heifer. One Deputy told me, "Lost twelve heifers this year to them damn cats!" This was a different world. But the cops? The cops were cops. Just like us.

The four of us split up. Two back room guys went off to interview everyone involved, and we went off to a State Police garage where the pull-behind-a-car trailer was being secured. The State Troopers had the trailer because they had been called in to do the initial scene work for the Sheriff's Department. The troopers were fantastic and gave us free reign to use, or do, whatever we needed. The infants' remains had been removed to the County Medical Examiner's Office, but the cardboard boxes that contained them were with the trailer.

It was quite evident by the condition of the boxes that the remains had been stored in them for many, many years. There were two rather large boxes. Inside the first large old box was a medium sized beat up box. Inside that box was a bathrobe that wrapped up one infant. Also inside this medium sized box was another smaller box with a second baby wrapped in curtains.

The second large cardboard box had the same medium and then small boxes inside. The third infant's remains were wrapped in blankets inside the small box.

Once we had enough photographs and notes documenting the boxes, we packaged them up and started on the contents of the trailer. There was box upon box of personal and household items that included men, women and children's clothing, baby blankets, bed linens, sleeping bags, tools, glassware, dishware, pots and pans, books, Christmas ornaments, toys, VCR tapes, games, knick-knacks, photos and photo albums, shoes, newspapers, magazines, towels, and lots of paper work. In between boxes were a folded up playpen, a disassembled crib, a kid's mattress, a baby stroller, and a sewing machine.

We read through every piece of paper and secured anything noteworthy.

It was a long process, but one that had to be done slowly. Whatever we decided was even possibly pertinent would get boxed up and go back with us. The rest would stay and go back to the guy who bought it. We were making decisions based on very limited information at the time.

All we knew was that this 50 year old woman was now living with a man in Pennsylvania. She'd been with him for many years and had eight children. We had the remains of three infants in boxes that clearly belonged to her. The guys had checked her background and found out that when she was a teenager, she had been questioned by police in connection with the discovery of another fetus. A junkyard owner was going through the trunk of a car that was scheduled to be junked. In the trunk was an old suitcase. In the suitcase was the body of a newborn fetus. The suitcase was traced back to this woman's family and she subsequently admitted to putting the baby in the suitcase and into the old car. The prosecutor at the time decided against criminal charges because the girl claimed that she kept the pregnancy a secret, had the baby by herself and that it was stillborn. She got scared and didn't know what to do with the baby's body so she hid it. Now 30 years later, we find three more babies, but these had been wrapped up, kept and carried around for probably a decade or two.

We took baby blankets, linens, clothes and any paperwork associated with identifying the contents to this woman. And of course, we couldn't rule out the possibility that there were other victims so we grabbed any and all papers that were associated with children; births, immunization records, medical papers, school report cards, any benefits received, anything at all. After hours of searching every box or container, and reading every piece of paper, we boxed up everything we had and made arrangements to stop at the Medical Examiner's Office the next morning on the way to the airport.

An early rise the following day had us grabbing our boxes of evidence from the great folks who had taken us in. The Sheriff's Department and State Police had been a tremendous help and their initial work on the case turned out to be quite valuable to the prosecutor's case. We thanked them and headed out to the ME's Office.

The doctor was ready for us and escorted us into one of their examination rooms. There, laid out on one of the tables, were the remains of the three infants. Two of them looked like tiny mummies frozen in the fetal position. The third was just an array of tiny bones. The four of us veteran cops stood there staring at these three little lives who didn't live much past birth over twenty years earlier. After a few awkward moments, I said that I'd like to take some photographs before packaging them up. After photos, the doctor wrapped each infant up and put each one in its own very small white plastic body bag. I'd never seen small body bags like that before. I had brought a bag for them so that I could carry it on the plane and keep it with me, on my lap, throughout the flight. Once back in New York, we'd drive directly to the Forensic Investigations Center in Albany, New York where they were taken into custody awaiting an examination by Forensic Pathologist Dr. Michael Baden.

The woman admitted to giving birth to the babies, but never

admitted to killing them. It was determined that one was a boy, one was a girl and the third's gender couldn't be determined. The trial was an emotional one that the newspapers followed daily. She was found guilty of murdering all three infants and sentenced to 25 years to life.

A child brings so much joy into people's lives. There are so many potentially great parents who for one reason or another, will never know the joys of parenthood. Here were four newborn lives. Not one, but four, who came into this world and a decision was made to end their lives. They weren't put up for adoption, or handed off to a relative, or even anonymously left on the proverbial Church steps. Four infants that could've been handed over to four couples who would've made their lives complete. Four little lives that any number of would-be parents would've taken, treasured and loved.

The death of a child at the hands of an adult is one of life's abominations. As a parent, I can certainly attest to the insanity that children put you through. They make you lose your mind. I can absolutely see how some parents "snap" and do something stupid. We're human. We make mistakes. Child Protective Services anywhere in this country will tell you of countless incidents where good parents lost it for a moment and did something terrible. I'm certainly not saying it's okay. I'm just saying that I can see how it happens. I've been there.

But the repeated beating, slapping, grabbing with force, shoving, and injuring of a child in any way is not normal. When I say repeated I don't mean numerous times, I mean even a few times. To intentionally inflict serious pain on a child is criminal. And I've seen it done by biological parents, step parents, boyfriends, girlfriends, and babysitters. There are people out there who should not care for young children under any circumstances. Unfortunately, some of these people are parents.

I've been involved in cases where mothers, fathers, boyfriends and babysitters have shaken a baby until he stops crying. A father who bit his infant son's back and dropped him on the floor to get him to stop crying. A boyfriend who pummeled his girlfriend's two year old daughter and left her body outside the back door to make it look like she snuck out and fell. Even a father who sexually abused his ten month old daughter and left her in the woods behind a grocery store claiming that someone grabbed her when he wasn't looking. There have been lots of others. These are but a few.

Home is where a child is supposed to feel safe. Two cases involving the deaths of young boys; one was two years old and the other was three, happened at home. The two-year-old had been left at home with his infant brother in the care of the mother's new boyfriend. By midday, a relative of the mother came by to relieve the boyfriend. He told the relative that the boys were sleeping in their room and went on his way. About an hour later, the relative checked on the sleeping boys and found the two-year-old to be cold and unresponsive. He was rushed to the hospital, but was pronounced dead upon arrival. A preliminary examination at the hospital revealed several bruises. The local and State Police were called. Once some initial interviews were conducted, it was determined that the residence was a crime scene and the back room guys started the process of obtaining a search warrant.

A call from my boss got me heading up to the house. I called Vinny and got him going to the hospital to get some photographs of the child and some info from the initial examination. All we knew was that a child was dead. No specifics. When a search warrant is signed, it's always nice to have some kind of idea as to what you're looking for in the house.

So many of these cases depend on medical examinations, history, and autopsy findings. Forensic Pathologists, as opposed to regular hospital pathologists, perform all of our autopsies because usually a crime is involved. If it's a suspicious death that winds up being natural, they can make that determination also. The death of a child or infant is one of the most important duties of a forensic pathologist. There is so much that a regular pathologist can miss or wrongly label. The law enforcement community, and every district attorney's office, depend heavily on the work forensic pathologists do when investigating any death concerning kids.

The search warrant was signed by a judge. We took loads of photographs and looked around for anything obvious. In the meantime, we tried to schedule the autopsy for as soon as possible. In this case, the soonest was the next morning. At the scene, we documented as much as we could without disturbing too much because we didn't have as much info as we'd like to tear the place apart. When we feel like we've gone far enough, we'll ask that a uniform presence secure the residence until the autopsy is completed. Hopefully the autopsy will give us a little more information as to how this child died and what we're looking for. Interviews that are going on outside the scene will also be a tremendous help.

The next morning, Vinny and I attended the autopsy. The boy had some obvious bruising that needed explaining. Every kid has bruises. They're kids. They climb and fall. They bang into things. Their siblings scratch and bite them. But there were some serious contusions that were not normal, especially a large one on his lower abdomen. Once the little guy's chest cavity was opened, the large pooling of blood inside proved massive internal bleeding. The examination went on to reveal a large tear to his liver and pancreas. Other injuries included a broken rib and bruises to his head, arms, and back.

Once we had this info, I reached out to the Major Crimes Senior Investigator. A couple of his guys were planning to have a sit down with the boyfriend. The autopsy results had not been released yet, so I wanted to give these guys a little leverage when interviewing the potential perpetrator.

Steve, the Senior of the Major Crimes Unit, is one of those low key, methodical cops. He quietly takes in everything and then sets out to accomplish the task. No big fan fare around this guy. He has no interest whatsoever in receiving credit for a job well done. I have worked with Steve on numerous big cases and he never gets rattled. It could be bosses calling for answers, or reporters covering a high profile murder, Steve stays calm and lets the pressure slide right off him. He just does his job.

As the supervisor of the crime scene unit who are the guys on the "inside" of the crime scene, it is such an incredible asset to have a guy like Steve on the "outside" running leads, gathering information and reading every statement. In many jurisdictions, cops outside the crime scene think nothing of keeping the crime scene guys in the dark. They usually don't do it intentionally. They get so wrapped up that they just don't think about us. And that's a huge mistake. Steve is one of those guys who keeps everyone informed. He gets the pieces of the puzzle as they come to him bit by bit, and shares the info with everyone, so that eventually someone comes up with, "Hey this person told me about that piece of the puzzle", or we at the crime scene can say, "Hey we found that missing piece of the puzzle here at the house". We in the crime scene are often forgotten or left out of that line of communication. It's happened before that crime scene guys totally disregard a valuable piece of evidence because it doesn't look out of place at the scene, while outside the crime scene there is information that makes it very important to the investigation. That's poor information sharing. A supervisor who doesn't relay important info isn't doing his job.

Steve knows the value of sharing essential tidbits. He and I will be on the phone numerous times during the processing of a scene. And it's beneficial to both sides. We may need to know what a suspect said, but conversely, we will often be able to give an interrogator some helpful questions from inside the scene. "Hey, why are there holes in the sheetrock walls of other rooms? Do you have a little problem controlling your anger?"

Steve's squad of cops is a seasoned lot of veterans who get called in to support and lend assistance to our backroom guys in big cases. They will also go out and do the same for any local law enforcement agency that needs assistance handling a full blown homicide investigation. This comes in extremely handy for us because we are often called in to do the crime scene work for smaller municipalities who may do things a little differently than we're accustomed. Having Steve and his guys there keeps things running smoothly for us on the inside.

I got Steve on the phone and told him about the severe trauma to the kid's abdomen. The bruising didn't show any definite markings like a belt or other instrument. It was caused by blunt force like a fist or being thrown against something. I let him know that this wasn't a one time injury. The kid had other severe bruises.

As the pathologist finished up, I decided to leave Vinny there and head to the house to start on the scene processing. Unfortunately, the autopsy didn't give us a hell of a lot more to go on. We wouldn't be looking for a particular kind of weapon or blood evidence. None of the injuries produced any exterior bleeding. I went into the house to do an overall survey after having just left the autopsy. Now that I knew what the boy looked like, I recognized him in several smiling photographs around the house. In one he's hugging his baby brother. In another, his mother holds him tight as he giggles. It isn't unusual to catch yourself staring at photographs like these or wondering if the boy had been playing with that dump truck at your feet earlier that day. The little boy in these photographs was a vibrant, full of life, tree climbing boy that was very different from what I saw on that metal table. Our jobs can often times become just that.... a job. We forget the human element of what we do.

I remember a financial planner complaining to me about his crazy hours and long days on the road away from his family. He tired of clients who bitched to him about the stock market and other things that were out of his control. And then he told me about a card he received in the mail from an elderly couple. They were his customers. The card was from Italy where they were on vacation. In beautiful handwriting, they thanked him for all the work he had done in helping them achieve a dream. Comfortable retirement. And part of that dream was one day having enough money saved and put away to go to Italy. They were two people who worked very hard their whole life and this guy had invested their retirement money wisely. He told me that he keeps their card on his desk. It's an example of the human element of his work. The pay-off. Why he does what he does.

The photographs of this little boy reminded me of why I do what I do. I could certainly say that it's a job that pays my bills and provides great benefits for my family, but that would be so wrong.

My daydreaming was interrupted by Steve. I told him that there wasn't anything out of the ordinary that would suggest a struggle. He told me to look under the twin bed in the boy's room. He went on to say that the inside railing of that bed should be held up by soup cans. The boyfriend said that they landed on the bed and broke it. Of course, his version described it as only wrestling. I told him I'd get back to him. Vinny had joined me and we slowly took the bed apart and photographed every section of it. It was evident that the bed slats and railing were broken to the point where two pieces of plywood had to be patched together to give the mattress a base on which to be supported. It wasn't much to go on, but it was another link in the chain of circumstantial evidence.

Steve's guys went at the boyfriend and got him to admit that he had become impatient with the boy a couple of times and had been rough with him. Then he lost it when the boy bit his finger. That was when the serious assault occurred. From that point on, the case would be a combination of scene evidence, statements and the testimony of the pathologist. A jury subsequently found the boyfriend guilty of second degree murder.

There had been some debate as to whether the biological mother had suspicions of her boyfriend's treatment of her son. Loneliness and needing to be loved can make some people look past a person's transgressions; even making excuses for them or justifying their actions.

A three year old boy was rushed to the hospital because he had fallen down a flight of stairs inside his home. He was unresponsive when paramedics packed him up for transport. Once at the emergency room, State Police were immediately notified. This was no fall down a flight of stairs. The kid's body was covered in bruises. The hospital was across the river from our Troop so our crime scene counterparts in that Troop responded to the hospital and took photographs for us. The boy never regained consciousness and died at the hospital. His little body was taken to the hospital morgue. The film was brought to us for immediate development (Yes, film. This was the 90's.) The developed photographs were brought to the crime scene. They were awful. The boy had bruises to his face, neck, arms, back, belly, buttocks, and legs. The bruises were different colors indicating to us that this battering happened over a period of time.

The biological mother lived at home with her son and her boyfriend. The boyfriend had spent a considerable amount of time in jail for various offenses. Their story was that they heard the boy fall down the stairs, went to him and found him unconscious. They then called the ambulance. Just looking at this kid's body made the case for severe child abuse. We got a search warrant and started on the house. It was disgusting. Old garbage everywhere. Cat and dog feces on the floor. A cluttered mess throughout. It was horrendous to think that a child lived there. Once again, the interviews would be paramount. Talking to the mother and boyfriend separately would hopefully turn one against the other. Soon the back room guys called and asked us questions like, "Are there two full gallon size jugs of Clorox in the living room, and do you see any evidence of cigarette smoking in the house?" Clorox bottles and cigarettes wouldn't normally stand out as important to us. In this case, the mother was telling our guys that her boyfriend sometimes burned the boy with lit cigarettes and when he continued to misbehave he would make the boy stand holding two full Clorox bottles out to each side at arm's length. If the boy lowered the jugs, the boyfriend would burn him again or beat him with a belt or with whatever he had handy. Then a simple question like, "Is there any hard candy?" The answer was yes to all of the above. The candy had been the reason for the discipline. The boy had taken candy that he shouldn't have.

Without this conversation, we wouldn't have known to take these items as evidence. Maybe at autopsy we would've seen marks on his body that looked like burns or marks from a belt. This house would again be a scene we would hold onto until after the autopsy.

Tom and I attended the post mortem examination the next day. When we arrived, a sheet covered that little form on the big metal autopsy table. It's a sobering sight. Under the sheet was the remains of a very young life that had endured physical abuse since the day he was born. It was not something to look forward to.

This was one of those cases about which I was often asked, "Doesn't it bother you to see that?" or "How do you deal with looking at that?" or "Doesn't that stay with you?"

Of course, there is a moment or two that is a mixture of horror, sadness, and anger. A moment where a slow shake of the head happens instinctually. But then something happens. Something kicks in. That anger turns into a kind of determination. And that determination makes you realize inside yourself that you are one of the people who can be instrumental in making sure that this defenseless victim finds justice. You can help make it right. The head shaking subsides, your gaze lifts and all you can think is, "Let's get the bastard who did this." Now you will look at this little body as a crime scene. You will analyze and document every bruise, and bloodstain, and tear in his clothing. You put emotion aside. Emotion doesn't do your job. It may fuel you, but your training and experience steps up and takes center stage. Every bruise, belt impression, burn mark, finger slap, scrape, cut, or unknown substance is methodically examined and documented in an attempt to build a case against the savage who did this to an innocent little boy.

Dr. Barbara Wolf would become one of my two favorite forensic pathologists. She had been called in to perform this autopsy. I knew that she would be the one needed to get this job done. It would be a monster of a task to document every injury and come up with an estimate as to how old each injury was. She would also be the perfect professional to present her findings in court.

Tom began the photography. He would eventually finish with hundreds of photographs. I took notes. Dr. Wolf worked without assistance. These days, almost every pathologist has an assistant who does the cutting and menial tasks. I miss the days of working one on one with the pathologist. I learned so much from them. It would be hours before we were finished.

Dr. Wolf carefully examined each mark on this child's body. Each was photographed with and without a scale. If there was a substance stuck to the skin, it was secured as evidence. Then the injury was washed and photographed again. Unlike other autopsies, Dr. Wolf needed more than just a cause of death. She had to establish a history of abuse. Each bruise's color was noted. The coloring and healing process could help determine age. She could tell right away that there were healing bruises and cuts that were weeks and months old. At some point during the autopsy, an x-ray technician arrived with copies of the x-rays taken before autopsy. Older healing broken bones were discovered. This kid would get beaten, heal for a little while only to get beaten again.

Dr. Wolf's examination would reveal that this boy suffered pulled hair, bite marks, punches, burns, a fractured jaw and elbow, (a broken rib was an old injury), a collapsed lung, lacerated liver and a brain hemorrhage. As if that wasn't enough, she found evidence of sexual abuse as well.

The final stage of this autopsy was something that's not usually done at most others. It was essential to estimate how old the numerous bruises were. You can't always see a healed bruise. On the surface, it's healing and may look like a simple red mark. But under the skin, the bruise is still there, taking a little longer to heal. To investigate this further, the pathologist has to slice back the skin in these areas to reveal the older, healing injuries. This child's body was so covered in bruises and injuries that Dr. Wolf had to slice back large sections of skin and tissue from the boy's legs, arms, and back. We now photographed and documented every single mark we could find on this now "skinned" child. It was the first time that I had witnessed this procedure and hoped I wouldn't have to again. It wasn't the sight of it. It was the reason that it had to be done. It seemed like one more abomination this poor child had to endure.

The cause of death would be listed as multiple blunt force trauma injuries to the head and torso. But in fact, this poor three year old was dying mentally, emotionally and physically from repeated severe abuse.

Dr. Wolf's incredibly thorough examination and subsequent report, coupled with professional courtroom testimony, revealed a young life who knew nothing but abuse for as long as he was alive. The mother and boyfriend were convicted and sent to prison for a long time.

I have attended many, many autopsies. Witnessing the results of the physical tortures inflicted on this three year old boy clearly made this the worst one I have ever seen. I've been to the autopsies of people cut up into pieces, burned beyond recognition, extremely decomposed, and viciously attacked in any way you could imagine, but none of them could hold a candle to the sick tortures this kid endured.

I don't care what some civil rights advocates say. There are people in this world that should not have children. How do you enforce that? I don't know. But the idea that unfit parents should keep their kids just because they are the biological parents is absurd. I know the courts do their best, but this was a situation where the kid should have been taken away before this could happen. There were enough instances and hospital visits and injuries. It's one of those cases that fell through the cracks and ended tragically.

A twelve year old boy, with baseball glove in hand, took his usual shortcut route through a small patch of woods toward the baseball field. The coach thought it unusual that one of his most dependable players didn't show up for a game without telling him. An hour later, a group of friends took the same shortcut through the woods and saw a baseball cap about 25 feet into the woods, off of the path. They ventured closer for a look and got the shock of their young lives. They ran for help.

We arrived and were led to a taped off section of woods not far from the ball field. The well worn path was a direct route from the boys' residences within a community of homes to the field. It was a nice, rural town in a somewhat affluent county. The victim had used the path numerous times before, as did many of the local kids. Our preliminary walk through brought us to the twelve year old boy's body lying on his back, clad in his Little League uniform. His shirt had been pulled up revealing several stab wounds to his chest and neck. It appeared that his body had been dragged a short distance. His thin built frame reminded me of myself at his age. I came to find out that he had been a much better baseball player than I ever was at his age.

This was someone's boy. There was a Mom and Dad going through unspeakable torments right now. "Are you sure it's my son?" "I just saw him." "Where? What happened? Show me." "Why did this happen?" "Tell me." Answering these questions is a huge part of a back room guy's job that I do not envy; facing parents and loved ones during a horrific time like this, trying to get answers, trying to figure it out, and not being able to tell them everything just yet. Watching a grown man cry like a baby. Seeing a mother's heart break in two and knowing that the tear will be there for the rest of her life.

Kneeling in the woods next to this boy's body brings these realizations to light. He looks like any twelve year old boy enthusiastically on his way to play America's game with his friends and be cheered on by his community. And then something happens. What? Is he met? Is he followed? Does he recognize his assailant? Which way did this person come from? What kind of an altercation is this? An argument? Or is it predatory?

The job again replaces emotion. Crime scene work is based on the "Principle of Exchange" first articulated by a French man of medicine named Edmond Locard. He stated that when two objects come into contact with one another, particles of each are transferred and left on the other. Furthermore, when something or someone is introduced into an environment, particles of that something or someone are left in that environment, and particles of the environment are taken away with the something or someone. In school lectures, I would use the simple analogy of an apple being hurled at a tree. Pick up the apple and you will find bits of tree bark embedded in it. Now look at the tree and you will find traces of apple attached.

It was this basic theory that filled my head as I knelt there in the woods.

"He was here. He left something behind. There is something of this animal left here. We've gotta find it. It's here."

We traced a few drag marks back to the spot on the path where the initial confrontation occurred, but we didn't find much. A couple of spots where dirt was scuffed, but that could be anyone coming through here or even responding cops. It was a very well-worn path and the surrounding woods were covered in old leaves, moss, and poison ivy. Usable footprints would be non-existent.

As with all violent altercations involving knives or sharp implements, there is the hope of finding blood that isn't the victim's. The more stabs wounds, the better possibility that the attacker cut himself. We would scour this entire section of woods for any trace of the killer. The search would begin on foot, shoulder to shoulder and then a group of us following them on our hands and knees.

Meanwhile, our back room guys, local cops and major crimes guys were talking to every single person they could find in this town's quiet community. Word of the crime spread quickly and residents became frightened for their children's safety. However, it was important to talk to as many kids as possible. The tricky part about talking to kids is that their parents have to be present. Rarely will a parent allow their kid to talk to the cops alone. It happens, but not that often. The tricky part comes in when a kid may know something, but doesn't want to say it in front of his parents. Usually they want to tell us, but it probably involves something sensitive, or doing or being somewhere they shouldn't have been.

A different case was a good example of this. A young boy went missing. Cops, firemen and volunteers searched the woods and surrounding roads and houses. The father started to get angry because a couple of our guys would keep asking family members questions over and over again. It wasn't until we got the younger brother alone that he admitted to watching his brother ride his bike into an abandoned pool that was filled with dirty, murky water and leaves. It was an accident, but the younger brother was scared to say it in front of his father because he and his brother had been scolded numerous times for playing near that abandoned pool.

There were a lot of kids in this town and a lot of activity that day. The weather was beautiful. The local baseball team had a game. Similar to our "He left something here" mantra, interviewing investigators always believe that "Somebody knows something". They knocked on every door and if no one answered, they noted it and came back another time soon. The community panicked and the newspaper ran front page headlines and stories of the terror that gripped this rural little town.

Three days later, something strange happened. A couple of local reporters were walking through that section of woods as part of a follow-up to their story when they came across a young man standing on a bicycle that was leaning against a tree. He was in the process of tying a black wire around his neck. The other end of the wire had already been tied to a tree branch above him. The two reporters got the wire removed from his neck and got him down off the bike. In broken English, the young man told the reporters that he had been attacked by a man in a black mask. The reporters had a difficult time understanding the young man's broken English especially when his account didn't seem to explain why he was attempting to hang himself. They walked the diminutive young man out of the woods and called the police. With a Spanish speaking State Police investigator, it soon became clear that there was no masked attacker in the woods. As he continued to talk to us, disturbing and confusing statements started to point to him as a possible suspect. Other investigators ran out and began canvassing this young man's neighbors and people that may have known him.

A number of neighbors knew who he was, but didn't really know him. Several interviews painted the picture of a loner type young man who no one trusted. He had been taken in by a local family as a foster child from Central America and was enrolled in the local high school.

His actual age was unknown. He could have been 18 or 23. He had been involved in a few violent episodes within the school that labeled him as a little scary and unpredictable. Not having much of a grasp on the English language coupled with his aggressive behavior made him an outcast within this community.

Cops intentionally waited to speak to the foster parents. Neighbors told us that the foster parents were doing their best trying to provide a home for a kid who came from an abusive family background in Central America. In later interviews, the foster parents would admit that he had problems, but they would never believe he was capable of murder.

The young suspect went on to make some very damning admissions. It became quite clear that this recluse had some very deep emotional issues. A search warrant was obtained for his room in the foster parents' house. There we would find lots of circumstantial evidence that included cut outs of every newspaper article relating to the murder, the date of the murder highlighted on a calendar and several disturbing comments written in Spanish and broken English on pieces of paper in his room. But nothing put him at the scene of the crime.

The young man was arrested. We had a solid defendant, but the case wasn't the greatest. It didn't help when all of his statements would subsequently be declared as inadmissible by the presiding judge. Now all we had was lots of circumstantial evidence and several items of the victim's clothing at the laboratory awaiting DNA results. We were hoping that DNA would come through for us... and it did. An unknown male DNA profile was found on the victim's baseball pants. We immediately asked the judge for a court order to secure a DNA sample from the defendant. He agreed. The DNA sample was sent to the lab to be compared to the DNA profile found on the boy's pants. More waiting. These lab tests never happen quickly and by no fault of the personnel. You just can't rush science.

It was a match. This crucial piece of evidence put the defendant at the murder scene and, combined with tons of circumstantial evidence;,a jury found the defendant guilty and sentenced him to 25 years to life. If he is ever released, he must be immediately deported to Central America.

Yeah, the bad guy was caught, prosecuted and put away for good. But this beautiful twelve year old life is gone. Those parents will never, ever be the same. There is a part of them that is damaged and will never, ever be fixed. They say that time heals. The truth is that time helps soften the hurt, but it never really heals. Some people will come to accept it as a part of their lives. But accepting it doesn't make your life whole again. They become one of those jigsaw puzzles where that one piece is missing and will never be found. It will always be missing.

I've seen hardened fathers and mothers in their 70's who openly cried as we carried out their adult children who committed suicide. It doesn't matter how old they are. It was still their child. There is no tragedy in this world like a parent losing a child. It's not the normal course of life. It's not supposed to happen that way. We expect our grandparents to die first, then our parents and the circle of life is supposed to continue on like that. Next it will be us when we are grandparents or great grand parents. But when life and death don't follow the script like we expect it to, we have a hard time reconciling with it.

I have been present at crime scenes where the rules of crime scene security were thrown out the window because of a child's death. Both were suicides.

One was a young man who ran from police, shot at them and then barricaded himself inside a house until he finally took his own life. He was Afro-American and racial tensions began to mount. Allegations and shouts that the police had murdered the man started to set the street outside the house on fire with hatred. Law enforcement was doing everything outside the scene and inside the scene by the book..... until the parents showed up. The District Attorney pulled us aside and asked if there was some way that the parents could see their son before the body was taken out in a body bag and held in the morgue until the investigation released it. The DA wanted to let the parents see him in the room where he had committed suicide. There was no way we would allow that. That would raise all kinds of legal questions later. How could you let anyone into the actual scene where the body was? What if we took his body out later and found something behind his body? We'd wonder if that was there before or could the visitor have dropped it there while hugging or getting close to the body. It might be done accidentally or intentionally. No one can come into the crime scene until we are completely done with it.

But what we did do was to tell them that we'd allow them into another uninvolved room in the house where we would have his body waiting for them. They would have to wait until we were completely done with the scene. By this time, we knew that we had a suicide. We packed him up and moved him to a room near the front door. We covered the wound to the side of his head as best we could without disturbing it. Crime scene guys then escorted the parents in with the District Attorney and gently asked if they would refrain from touching him in any way.

It was heartbreaking to stand there and watch two parents kneel down next to the dead body of the boy they loved and raised. He had been in trouble several times, but he was still their boy. We let them have as much time as they needed. The father helped his sobbing wife up and thanked us profusely. We escorted them back out.

The other time was similar in that a man in his 30's shot himself to death. He had been depressed. I oversaw the scene and we were just about done when I was heading out to my car to grab something. A man in his 50's approached me. He had a Catholic priest with him and introduced himself as the deceased man's father. He asked if there was any way he could see his son. I advised him that the body would be getting transported to the morgue shortly. He begged me to see his son before taking him to the morgue. Looking into this father's eyes broke my heart. Again, we were done with the scene and we knew it was a clear-cut suicide. I told him to wait outside the tape for a few minutes. Upon going back inside, I asked the medical examiner if he could leave the body in the uninvolved living room for a few minutes before it was picked up to go. He agreed. I asked a uniform cop securing the perimeter to escort the father and priest in. They were let inside the front door where the man's body was laid in a body bag. We covered the huge chest wound as best we could. Being a Catholic myself, I knew that the priest's involvement could get a bit wordy, so I grabbed him quietly and made it clear to him that his prayer needed to be short and to the point. He fully understood. The father, however, could take his time. Both men stepped inside and wouldn't move unless we said it was ok. They were brought to the body and the father knelt down beside his son and cried. He crossed himself as the priest very briefly spoke. The father gently touched his son's face, stood up strong and told the priest, "Okay, we can go." I walked them to the front door. The father stopped, took my gloved hand in his and shook it. He looked me in the eyes and said, "Thank you so very much." I nodded and told him how sorry I was. He walked away with his head up, strong in stride, but he was a broken man.

These two instances happened over a career of 30 years. In no way am I saying that this should ever be done. The security of the crime scene is paramount. You can not let anyone who is not involved in law enforcement inside the crime scene. In both cases, we had been called to a suspicious death. After working it, we knew one hundred percent that it was a suicide. If these were anything other than suicide, accidental or natural, there would've been no way that anyone would have been let near the bodies. In a suspicious death investigation, the body is still considered a crime scene and must be secured and protected all the way to autopsy.

Rules were slightly relaxed in order to ease a parent's grief. We in the crime scene world know it. We've seen it. There is no loss like that of a child.

My brother passed away at 30 years of age from severe asthma. I saw what that did to my parents. They were never the same. A part of them died with my brother. That was over 25 years ago and yet I will still see my 84 year old mother cry when she sees a photograph of my brother Paddy. Maybe it's my parents' pain I see in the eyes of these lost mothers and fathers. I don't know. Good parents give and give and give to their children. And I don't mean gifts and money and material things. I mean they give of themselves. Even when that child grows up and moves away, they still want the best for them. They would die for them. Good parents would.

And those of us who know this about our parents, who know that we will never, ever thank them enough, who realize the sacrifices they made, will usually have a tough time when they leave us. We understand very well that this is the normal course of life that they should pass on before us, but it still bothers us. It's hard to accept even though we know it's the way it's supposed to be.

I watched my mother-in-law and father-in-law pass away; two loving people who raised seven kids and treated me like their own when I married into the family. It took the devastating disease of Alzheimer's 12 years to take her, a woman who spent her life sacrificing and caring for others, including the elderly. On the flip side, my father-in-law lost his battle with cancer a few weeks after being diagnosed. Right to the end, he'd tell the grandkids wonderful stories about leprechauns and mischief, and make them laugh with the silliest magic tricks.

It was difficult for many in their big family to accept their deaths. Having to say good-bye to such devoted people. But soon I realized something that made their lives all the more memorable. I realized that in watching parents die, we receive yet another, and probably the most selfless gift of all from them. When generous, caring people like our parents pass away, the people who have given us so much, they poignantly teach by example one more lesson. In dying, they teach us to appreciate every moment of the life they gave us. It is their final and most touching gift of all.

When we experience the death of a loved one, we are presented with the cold, hard fact that life can be fleeting. We realize that no matter how long or short, life is always precious. We use the word precious to describe an infant who breathes life's little breaths as they slumber on your chest, both of you seeming to share the same heartbeat. And sometimes the same word can describe our elderly as they bravely battle devastating diseases. But the stark reality should be that life is precious every day. I know that sometimes problems and obstacles will overshadow this basic fact. Even the sun gets blocked out by the clouds every now and again. But the trick is to enjoy and appreciate its warming rays when it does shine. The treasures of being alive present themselves countless times throughout our lifetime. It could be spending that extra hour with Grandma so that she can spoil you with her favorite pie. Or taking that extra few minutes during a busy day to pick up the phone and call Mom or Dad just to say "Hi". It could be as simple as brightening a bad day for someone with a kind word or action.

These moments happen all around us, all the time. The tragedy is that most of us don't recognize them and don't take that extra step to savor them when they do occur. However, we will sit up and take notice of those times when the thought of losing life slaps us upside the head. It's sad that it takes the grim reaper being right up in our grill before we finally realize that unbelievable opportunities have always been right there in front of us.

Chapter Twelve
On the Table

It takes a very special kind of person to cut up human beings for a living. People ask me how I do what I do, but I really don't see the blood and gore every day. Pathologists do. I've worked with a couple of these doctors who averaged two autopsies a day. That's over 700 a year! I know there are probably pathologists in urban areas that are doing the same or more, but our pathologists are doing it throughout several counties, and sometimes across state lines. Not only were they traveling all over to conduct the examinations, but they had to go back quite often for court preparation and testimony. Now add to that the meetings with prosecutors and cops, preparing meticulous reports, sending out for lab work, and finally guys like me calling them up with, "Hey Doc, can you squeeze this really suspicious looking one in soon... like yesterday?"

When you find fantastic professionals to work with, the cops, coroners, and prosecutors will tend to keep using them.

These are the forensic pathologists as opposed to your regular pathologist who may work in a hospital or medical center. The forensic pathologist will have an extensive education and experience in crime-related deaths. They will be much more familiar with manners of death such as natural, accidental, suicide or homicide. It will be their findings that tell us a car accident was actually a natural death when the driver had a massive heart attack that caused the car to veer off the road. Or that a hanging was an accidental sexual act instead of a suicide. Or that a staged suicide is actually a homicide. They can tell us what kind of weapon was used on the body, or that a brain aneurysm dropped this person in their tracks as they were getting dressed. The forensic pathologist is a specialty like none other.

Your hospital pathologist is a valuable asset to a medical investigation. He can answer family's questions and apprise them of future medical concerns for other relatives. There have been a couple of hospital pathologists who have been very helpful in accident cases and natural deaths. But when the cops are bringing in a body under any kind of suspicious circumstances, a forensic pathologist is preferred.

One very simple example of this distinction is the removal of clothing. A hospital pathologist will cut right through clothing. A forensic pathologist will take the clothing off of the body thus preserving any potential evidence like tears, stabs, bullet holes or debris left on the clothing. One hospital pathologist cut through the down jacket of a murder victim. We had feathers flying all over and sticking to everything.

There are other instances where the deceased's identity is unknown. Tattoos and scars become very important. Cutting through these identifiers before they have been properly photographed hinders the identification process. This happens when a doctor gets there a little early and decides to start without the police being present. I showed up 20 minutes early to an autopsy where the unknown body was already opened up. Several identifying tattoos had been sliced through and the body had already been washed down, thus sending any exterior trace evidence down the drain.

As a crime scene guy (and the same holds true for medical

examiner's assistants and investigators), you know what you're supposed to be looking for, but a good forensic pathologist will show you and point out things you didn't even think of. And then they'll tell you why it's important. This has given me quite an education over the years.

I remember the first time I ever held a human heart in my hand. I thought, "Wow. This little thing has kept this body alive for 72 years." The heart is a truly amazing organ. On one suspicious death, there was no obvious trauma to the body and the Doc had gotten to the part where the organs are removed, examined and weighed. As he cut through parts of the heart, you could hear a crunching sound.

"Aha," came the response.

"Aha?" I echoed.

"Take a look at this," beckoned the pathologist.

He brought me in closer and exposed the interior section of the heart where the main arteries run. He was cutting through one of them.

"This is supposed to be soft. My scalpel should slice right through it like butter, but see this?"

He sliced through a soft wall and then hit something hard and pushed firmly through it. Then he moved about an eighth of an inch away from that hard spot and it sliced right through. He held up the artery for me to see, "Almost clogged shut."

He showed me the soft artery that was open about the diameter of a bar sip straw and then the clogged up part of the artery. There was a tiny hole through the center of the blockage that was maybe the diameter of a very small sewing needle.

He went on, "Imagine blood trying to push through that pin hole.

That's your heart attack waiting to happen." When I asked about a fix, he explained the whole bypass technique. It was quite fascinating.

One body had black lungs.

"What the hell is that?" I asked.

"A smoker."

I took a good photograph of it and later printed it out to bring home to my, then smoker, wife. She didn't appreciate it too much, but I'm happy to say that she kicked the habit a few years later.

Seeing what cirrhosis does to the liver made me have a few less beers on the weekend. Well, that weekend anyway.

And then there's the brain. Sawing open a person's skull and sending fine bone dust into the air usually propels the autopsy attendees back a few steps. Inhaling the airborne bone dust from some dead person's skull tends to shy some people away. But here are those pathologists and assistants standing right over it. You'd figure that if anyone knows the possible effects of inhaling this stuff, it'd be them, and there they stand. I soon realized that it's more the thought of sucking it in that freaks people out. Then the skull cap is popped off to expose the brain. Here is where it all happens.

A lot of unexplained deaths will be clarified as soon as the skull cap comes off. Bleeding will be immediately noted when a brain aneurysm occurs. It usually doesn't give its victim much time. It can drop you right there, or give you a couple minutes to sit or lie down and then, that's it. When I asked the doctor how it happens, he likened it to a garden hose that you buy, bring home and one day springs that pin hole leak. It's a weakening defect in a section of the wall and then one day the pressure of its daily use will make it pop and spring that leak of blood. Sometimes you can catch it on diagnostic procedures and sometimes you can't.

The forensic pathologist then takes the brain out, examines it, and weighs it. The first time I saw this, I kinda expected to see some intricate wiring or a complex control panel that runs this amazing piece of machinery. But there it is out on a table and it's just a mass of very soft tissue. You expect it to be so much more. How does this hunk of spongy, almost jello-like material do the unbelievable job it does? Staring at it, I imagine its contents. Decades of education, a lifetime of memories, fears, attitudes, calculators, emotions, stored photographs, images, and dreams. All stored inside this Nerf football-sized, grayish-colored water balloon. Wow.

Now he'll cut through it, examining the sliced cross sections for defect or injury. There may be evidence of past damage that healed or abnormalities that can be further studied. It truly is a fascinating slab of equipment, but it's also very fragile. That's why it needs to be protected inside our thick skulls, (Some much thicker than others). We cut through this tough, hard protective helmet to get to the valuable cargo inside. Even a fracture to this rigid exterior will still protect its contents. But smacking the brain around inside this defensive helmet can do it some serious damage. Ask those football players who have that hard-shell skull to protect the brain and then wear a helmet on top of that. A solid enough shot to the head can still cause a concussion that will have them seeing stars and reciting the alphabet as if they're waiting for the school bus.

Death is also a result of traumatic shocks to the brain as proven by the countless shaken baby incidents. Distraught parents or a babysitter rush an unresponsive infant to the emergency room claiming that they found the baby unconscious. ER doctors won't find any external trauma to the baby's body, but at autopsy, this little person's brain will show the telltale signs of being shaken too hard. Once the brain is out, you'll usually find bruising on the front and back of it from being slapped back and forth against the front and back of the skull's hard interior.

Examining a body that has been through various stages of decomposition or is completely skeletonized is another challenge to many a forensic pathologist. Decomposition by its very nature starts to destroy valuable findings on the tissue and skin. Knowing the difference between what decomp does to the body naturally, and what coloring or differences in the skin might be infliction related is one of their many specialties. You may have nothing but bones, but the pathologist's examination is just as meticulous, if not more so, than on a freshly deceased victim. Without the surrounding tissue and blood to clue you into where a wound is, the doctor now has to carefully examine each bone for the presence of a knife's nick or the graze of a bullet as it passed through the body. In both scenarios, it's possible that a bullet or blade did kill the person, but not hit any bone at all which makes it all the tougher for the doctor. Strangulation will leave no signs at all on a skeleton unless bones were actually damaged. And even then, when the vertebrae start to separate, you mightn't notice it at all.

Seeing a bullet hole in a skull and finding a projectile still rattling around inside is a big win. You have a probable cause of death and hopefully enough for a ballistics exam. But often times the loss of tissue really restricts a pathologist's ability to come up with an accurate cause of death.

Bodies that have been in the water for any length of time offer their own unique problems. First is identification. I used to love asking a group of high school or even college kids what the first question we want answered was when we find a body. The responses would range from, "How did he die?", ""Who did this?", "Where's the weapon?", "Is there DNA on the body?". Watching all of the CSI type shows on television tend to get these young minds jumping way ahead of themselves. They don't start with Step One which is what all good investigating cops, doctors and prosecutors do. The answer is, "Who is this?" Without knowing the victim's identity, there's a lot that we're missing right off the bat. So when we pull someone out of the water and can see that the water's effect has completely disfigured this person's normal appearance, we have a little work to do. Is it the guy who jumped off a bridge a week ago? Is it a missing elderly man with Alzheimer's who walked away from his house nine days ago? Is it a wife who has been reported missing? Or is this someone not from this area at all who winds up dead on a river bank? A "Yes" to any of these sends the investigation into four different directions right from the get-go.

The slim campground gal from an earlier chapter bloated up to a tremendous size. This will happen to all bodies as gas builds up inside them. Clothing will get stretched and it makes it difficult to take them off. The bloating also affects the face and makes it quite unrecognizable. Add to that, all of the hair falling out and you have a body that looks nothing like what it did. At one autopsy I attended, a guy was pulled from the river. His body was severely bloated. We knew of a bridge jumper five days earlier. The doctor and I discussed the possibility of this being the guy after only five days in the water. Of course, we couldn't rule it out because we knew that anything was possible when it came to bodies found in the water.

The bridge jumper had a brother-in-law who worked for the FBI. He did the right thing and figured that he'd spare the family the heartache and decided that he'd identify the body. He met us at the morgue just as we were getting the victim out of the body bag. I felt sorry for the guy. No matter how long he stared at the face, and we let him look as long as he wanted, he just couldn't say for sure if it was his brother-in-law. (It was.) And this body was in the water for only five days.

The longer a body stays in the water, the worse it gets. The bloating will further distort the body and any tattoos or other identifying marks. I saw one tattoo that reminded me of a friend's story. He and his wife had advised their 20 something year old daughter against getting a tattoo on her stomach. The daughter had a slim and athletic build so the butterfly tattoo looked very pretty just above her navel. That is until she got married, got pregnant and then had a beautiful baby. The proud grandma couldn't help but hit her daughter with the "I told you so speech". "Yeah, once it looked like a butterfly. Now it looks like a sickly amoeba."

This bloating makes undressing a body quite a chore. I was doing my best trying to help out at one particular autopsy. I said I'd get the boots off a floater as the Doc worked on the clothing. The boots were on pretty tight. I had them unlaced as far as I could, but they wouldn't budge. The skin above the boots was slimy and my gloved hand was slipping. Finally, I got a good grip of his lower leg calf in my right hand and the heel of his boot in my left and pulled apart as hard as I could and "Pop". I got it. Or thought I did. I looked down and the boot was still on his foot, but the guy's whole calf muscle came off in my hand. I looked at the pathologist with a pathetic, "Sorry about that, Doc."

"No problem Bill. Just leave it on the table next to where it belongs," came the reply from Doctor Michael Sikirica.

Doc Sikirica is the other forensic pathologist that tops my list. Any case that had a problem or big question wound up on his table. He is one of those guys who fielded the "Doc, we're not sure what we've got" calls and made immediate arrangements to help out. We had a fantastic line of communication with him and his staff. Knowing that Doc Sikirica was doing the autopsy always made us feel better about the investigation.

Of course, there was a boss who sometimes felt the need to throw his weight around, and in the heat of an investigation would declare that he was going to get Doc Sikirica to do the autopsy right now. Meanwhile, the Doc would be running all over the state doing autopsies and testifying, and this supervisor would leave the Doc a message stating that he needed to speak to him ASAP. We knew the Doc's availability for us, but never wanted to abuse that privilege because he really was quite busy. So once I'd heard this boss's spouting, I'd run to a phone and get the Doc on the QT.

"Bill, I hear you've got a body down there."

"Yep, Doc, we do, but I can tell you right now that we don't need this one done right away. We know who the guy is and he's been shot in the head three times. No mystery here as to his identity or the cause of death."

"Your lieutenant made it sound urgent in his message."

"Yeah, he does that."

"Okay. Thanks. I've got two more autopsies to do today and one in the morning. Is tomorrow afternoon all right for you guys?"

"Absolutely, Doc. Do what ya gotta do. Take your time. And I'll tell the lieutenant that you're coming tomorrow."

"Thanks, Bill."

Now if the circumstances were different and we really did need him as soon as possible, he'd figure a way to get to us or meet us halfway with the body to get the questions answered. Somehow, he'd arrange his waiting line of bodies and get us in. He gets the job done. Why in the world would you needlessly beat up a guy like this? Some people just don't get it.

Doctor Sikirica is a medical professional whose experience and know-how are truly invaluable to every single investigation he has ever been a part of. I have learned so much from this man and have come to have the utmost respect for him. Becoming a supervisor has taken me away from attending a lot of autopsies. I get to one here and there. But I do miss working them with the Doc.

Besides the educational aspect of attending an autopsy, there are also plenty of those "Check this out" moments that make them interesting. Like opening up a floater and finding three dead fish inside the stomach. They had swum their way in there, ate their fill and couldn't get out. Or the 18 feet of tapeworm found inside a guy's stomach who had died accidentally. That creeped me out. It reminded me of one of those slithering type creatures in gross horror movies. And then you get the big tough biker guy wearing women's panties and painted toenails.

The important surprises are the ones that help us out with the investigation. It's usually beneficial to hold the crime scene until the autopsy is done. As I've said before, the autopsy results can give you a direction to go in at the crime scene.

An elderly woman had been found dead in the backyard of a group home with her head bashed in. A bloodstained, broken concrete block laid there next to her. Blood was everywhere. We took the concrete block as evidence, but didn't find out till the autopsy that she had also been stabbed by a thin bladed knife. Now we were looking for a knife. Blood can cover up an awful lot and you can't be cleaning it away or disturbing too much of it until the autopsy. While at the scene, you give the body a good preliminary look and take lots of notes and photographs. Messing with the body too much at a scene can lose valuable trace evidence that can be secured properly under the more controlled environment of an autopsy.

If you can see two or three clear stab wounds at the scene, you'll probably find more later. One guy was found slumped over on his sofa with four obvious gun shot wounds to his chest. It wasn't until later that we saw the one to the top of his head at his hairline. It didn't bleed so it had to have been the final shot after his heart had stopped beating. It also let us know that we had a perpetrator that wanted to make sure the victim was dead before he left.

A woman whose bloodied body lay on her living room floor had numerous stab wounds to her chest. The knife, which had come from the kitchen knife block, was still sticking out of her body. A broken vase was shattered all over the floor and there appeared to be a laceration to the side of her head. At autopsy, we could piece together a violent chain of events that started with getting hit in the side of the head with the vase that had been in the living room. Then she was choked to death as she lay on the living room floor. To make sure she was dead, the attacker took a knife from the kitchen and stabbed her numerous times. He stabbed so forcefully that the knife tip would momentarily embed in the hardwood floor underneath her body. He'd yank it out and do it again. A lot of rage there. The availability of the weapons (vase and knife) at the house demonstrated a crime that may not have been planned as a murder, but escalated to it.

Most people are unfamiliar with death and how a body dies. It does not always happen instantly. It may take a little time and the body may still move slightly or make noises during the process. A killer who uses a hammer to totally destroy someone's face and head may see the eyes still open and hear what sounds like shallow breathing and then plunge a screwdriver through her heart. The mess created by the head trauma could easily cover the stab wound to the chest.

Television has conditioned us to believe that when a person is shot, or strangled, or beaten to death they don't move at all. But the act of dying can take some time. Anyone who has hit a deer with their car or has shot an animal while hunting knows what I mean. I don't want people to think that there is more suffering or that loved ones didn't die quickly. They probably did. What I'm talking about are natural processes going on in the body that may give the impression that someone is still breathing or alive.

This has certainly happened before when information at the autopsy led us to realize that another weapon was used but the crime scene had already been released. Sometimes you can get back in there and sometimes you can't. It's frustrating to see important evidence in crime scene photographs that you didn't know was important at the time.

In a few instances, the revelation of new information requires us to take another look at the body. And now it's been buried. Trying to get the family to go along with an exhumation can add insult to an already seriously injured family. And of course, if the remains have been cremated, you're really out of luck.

One exhumation was conducted because the medical examiner's office had forgotten to take inked fingerprints of the female victim. Latent fingerprints had been recovered from her house where she had been murdered and we needed her prints to eliminate a number of the latent fingerprints we had recovered. Obtaining post mortem fingerprints is a pretty common practice at most autopsies.

The process of "dead printing", as we've come to call it, isn't always that easy. In death the fingers tend to curl up. We have to straighten them out a bit, roll some ink onto their surface and then use a metal "spoon" that holds the white piece of paper that will receive the inked print. The curved surface of the spoon alleviates the need of having to roll the finger like you do with a live person. You gently push the curved white card on the spoon onto the inked finger. It may take a few tries to get a decent transference of the finger's ridge detail. You may have some natural oils on the fingers or they could be a bit slimy. Sometimes you've got to dry the fingers as much as possible and then apply the ink.

Now imagine dead printing a floater. We all know what our fingers look like after sitting in the bath tub for too long. The wrinkling causes a real problem. In those cases, we'll inject fluid into the fingers just below the ridges in an attempt to fill them back up and take out some of those wrinkles. Some hands that have been in the water too long start to shed that outer layer of skin. The outer layer stays intact but separates from the layers of skin underneath. When this happens, we often cut this separated cap of skin just below the finger joint. We'll have some ink and a full blank fingerprint card ready. This cap of skin can be worn over our own finger (with latex gloves on), and we can roll it in ink and then onto the corresponding square on the card just like you were fingerprinting yourself. We'd then put each finger tip in its own container and properly label it. If some fingers aren't as separated as others, we'll use a combination of the two techniques.

The natural curling inward of the fingers will protect the fingerprint details. We've gotten pretty decent prints off of some pretty decomposed bodies because of this. The same holds true for burn victims.

These great teaching moments don't always come along when you have a new crime scene investigator to train, so very often we'll photograph every step of these various procedures in order to have a mini-training manual on this particular topic. It's come in quite handy. We had already done our share of dead printing decomposed bodies, but didn't have photos of the procedure involving a floater so we figured we'd shoot this particular one. It's not a good idea to use the camera that's being used to take the photos for the investigation, so we'll usually have someone else pull out their camera for it. My partner was using his, so I went and grabbed my personal camera that I had in my car. It was the days of 35mm film. I loaded the film and took the first photograph of the severely decomposed hand of a floater. Then one of the other guys suggested that he take the photos with his extra camera while I help with the process. I said okay. I put my personal camera away and we went on to compile a really nice set of photographs of the entire process.

Now fast forward two weeks later to an evening when I get home after a long day. The house had just been cleaned up after a weekend Holy Communion party with all kinds of friends and family. For some reason, my wife didn't seem too happy. "What'd I do now?" I wondered.

She started with, "Got the pictures back from the Holy Communion."

"Great. How'd they come out?" I asked.

"Ummm interesting" she said, "I stopped by Roseann's after picking them up so that I could show them to her."

(I'll bet you can see where this is going.)

"Yeah. So did they come out all right?" I asked again wondering if they developed at all.

My wife pulled out the stack of photos and tossed them on the counter in front of me. She pointed.

"What is that?!"

The photos spread out a bit on the counter and right on the top of the pile was the picture of that decomposed hand from the autopsy. Right next to it was a photo of my beautiful daughter in her Holy Communion dress.

"What the---?" was my first reaction and then I recognized it. I tried to cover. "Oh. Hey, you know what happened---"

"That is just gross. Did you do that on purpose?"

"No. No. What happened was---"

"Roseann nearly puked. That is disgusting. What is the matter with you? It's Katie's Communion!" and she stormed off.

This work is not for everyone. But when you find a professional like these pathologists who live this work, who delve into it day in and day out, you have struck gold. I have learned so much from being around these medical intellectuals. Their experiences are fascinating. While writing this book, I had the opportunity to see Doc Sikirica on an exhumation from the 1970's that we were investigating. I hadn't seen him in years, but it was like we hadn't missed a beat. He examined the bones and we stood there shooting the shit. He said his caseload isn't as heavy as it was back in those days, but he still keeps pretty damn busy.

"How many overall, Doc?" I inquired.

"Over 10,000," he answered.

10,000 autopsies! You can't teach many of the things he has seen and believe me, he has seen it all. Like any profession, some are better than others, but when you find one who is truly like no other, you latch onto them. Ask any question that pops into your head. You never have to be afraid to ask anything. "Hey Doc, can I see that? What does that feel like? What the hell is that?"

The good ones don't pretend to always know that answer. They will say, "I don't know," and then they'll get back to you with the answer. Many of these doctors are fascinated by the work we do. They want to know the circumstances leading up to the crime. They'll ask if there's been an arrest on that last autopsy. They want our input. I've bounced so many scenarios off of people like Doc Sikirica and I've always come away a little brighter.

Sadly, many people don't feel comfortable asking someone else, "Hey what do you think about this?" when it comes to personal concerns. We'll ask for advice on just about anything else in the world. But things we deal with personally will stay locked up. A lot of cops do that. Men will have the attitude, "I'll figure it out on my own." You know what I'm talking about. The "don't ask for directions" mentality. And it certainly has something to do with not wanting to look stupid combined with an inability to approach others with a problem.

I can't even begin to tell you how many times I've had some fix-it problem in my house that I've bounced off the guys at work. Over the years, this bouncing it off different people has yielded numerous responses like, "Yeah, that happened to me once. I fixed it this way and it worked great." And I'd have my question answered. As I got older, I realized that these younger guys were more in tune with the latest gadgets and new technology that would save me time and money. There'd be some new mechanical fix to my problem that I didn't even know existed and I still wouldn't know (or have fixed it) if I hadn't reached out.

The proverbial leaky pipe was one such example where soldering would've taken forever because of where the leak was. A guy at work introduced me to those new snap into place pipe fittings. No soldering. One, two, three, done.

So many of us have that "leaky pipe" problem, but we don't want to ask for advice. The truth is that everyone has had some kind of leaky pipe problem in their life. People all around us go through the same things we do and yet we don't want to ask for help in dealing with ours. If a guy watches another guy pull a 15 lb bass out of a lake, he won't hesitate to ask, "Hey, what'd you use for bait?" When we see the results, we're quick to ask how to get that result. But when we struggle and search for answers to some of life's tough questions, we don't like to reach out and ask others. We don't realize that the gal sitting in the very next cubicle went through the exact same thing we're struggling with right now. It may not have worked out for her, or maybe it did. We need to have that light bulb go off in our head and say, "Hey, I can't be the only one who's gone through this. Of course I'm not. Let me see how other people have handled this."

We really are all in the same boat, facing many of the same waves, weathering the same storms, and enjoying the same sunny days.

But instead we keep it to ourselves with all of other "personal" stuff.

And it's called "personal" stuff because we think it's only happening to us. If it's tough to ask for directions, can you imagine what it would be like to ask someone's advice about something intimate?

How many times have you spent hours looking for something only to have someone else come along and point it out to you in plain view? Much like examining a crime scene, a different set of eyes is also a different set of perspectives. The doom and gloom of some situations can send you deeper and deeper into the abyss when reaching out to someone may illuminate your world to the fact that "Hey, you're gonna be all right. Yes, this is bad, but you are gonna be all right. I'm all right and I went through the same thing." Having that person, a living, breathing, speaking human being, who knows what you're going through is a tremendous relief. Talking about it with this fellow traveler who "knows" can be like lifting the weight of the world off your shoulders. You're not alone anymore.

Every day there are people all around us at work, in Church, at the ball game or standing in line behind us at the bank beating themselves up. It could be about not raising their kids right or having doubts about their marriage. They may be worried sick about losing their job, or maybe they're dealing with the crushing grief of losing a loved one to death, or dealing with the suffering of a long agonizing disease. When we experience these feelings, there is something so humanly basic within us that wants us to reach out. It knows that we should, but we resist it.

My closest family, friends and the gang at work have heard it all from me. (They should be writing this book.) Countless comforting words have either solved a problem, given great advice, or just put me at ease. Many times they just listened. And that listening lightened my load. They have been my priest, my therapist, my friend. They have come to know me and can be brutally honest with me. They are the people I label as "the ones I could bury a body with". And they know who they are. It's wonderful to have friends, but it is a true treasure to have people you can go to day or night with anything at all. When things go bad, you want them by your side. When times are great, you want to share every smile with them.

I sincerely hope and pray that I can one day be a fraction of the friend they have been to me..... and yes, I would bury a body with them and take it to the grave with me.

Chapter Thirteen
Bits and Pieces

I t's one thing when you do it for a living, but to cut up another human being after murdering them.... Well, that takes determination. Of course, on television dismemberment seems to happen with relative ease. Ever cut a chicken leg off with a knife and miss that joint between the bones? You can feel that you missed it and you try again, but in the process you made a bit of a mess of it. No, it's not that easy.

Some villains have thought to make it easier and cleaner by freezing the whole body and then cutting it up with a sawzall or band saw. In one murder, the guy bought a big freezer for the body and rented a backhoe to dig a hole in the backyard for the parts. These were the two business transactions that eventually sunk him. I never did understand his reasoning. If you're gonna dig a big hole, why freeze the body, cut it into pieces and throw it all in together?

Dismembering a person is usually done for one of two reasons. (I'll exclude the sickos who just like to do it.) Ease in transporting the body, or to slow down identification of the victim by cutting off hands (fingerprints) and the head (dental and visual). This latter reason is seen less and less nowadays with DNA on the scene for the last few decades, but it still occurs. In my earlier days on the job, a headless, handless and ,sometimes, footless corpse would be found wrapped in a tarp or blanket or carpet and dumped along a roadside embankment or into a creek. And yes, it could take months or years to identify the remains.

But now we can acquire a DNA sample from the remains and compare it to a DNA profile obtained from the suspected victim's hairbrush, toothbrush, or other personal items in their home. Lab scientists can also compare the unknown DNA to DNA taken from relatives. These scenarios would be avenues to pursue if we had some ideas as to who the remains might be. If we have no idea, there are DNA databases out there into which the DNA profile can be submitted. These databases will usually have criminals in them, but they will also have police officers, people who have freely given their profile as an elimination sample, lots of missing people and a few others. Even with this fantastic technology, we'll still have a few unidentified bodies on the books. Years later you might come up with a possible name but the person may not be in any of the databases. His residence, with toothbrush, hairbrush, etc., may be long gone, so there's nothing to which the DNA can be compared.

These days, dismemberment is usually done to move the body with greater ease to a place, or places, of disposal. Removing the arms, legs and head is difficult enough, but some of these butchers try to cut the torso in half. And that never works. You'll see the attempts at doing it on the body, but it stops when it becomes too tough and quite a mess. One guy took his girlfriend's body out to the woods and cut her arms, legs and head off with a hacksaw. He then took them out of the woods and dumped them in different places. Months later, we found the legs on a lake shore. Another lakeside homeowner thought he saw what appeared to be an animal carcass in a plastic bag in the water. He pulled it in, looked at it briefly and took it to the dump. After we found the legs, he came forward when area residents started getting interviewed about keeping an eye out for remains. We tried tracing it to the trash transfer station and landfill, but this garbage went to a facility that burned its trash. So much for recovering the torso. But the legs were enough to obtain a DNA profile and match it to the girlfriend. The hacksaw was found and tied the boyfriend to the girlfriend's blood. Unfortunately, the remainder of her body was never recovered.

Our cute, furry creatures of the forest can throw a wrench into figuring out whether a body was dismembered or not. Decomposing bodies attract our little friends and they can do quite a number on it. You'll find limbs pulled in different directions and pieces chewed off and dragged down into an animal hole. In many of these cases, we don't find every bone. It's pretty easy to tell that a body has been ravaged by animals, but we have to be careful not to overlook the possibility that certain parts may have been missing before John Doe made it into the woods. The skull is big and we usually find it. Not finding it nearby is a red flag. You don't have big animals or a gang of smaller ones picking up the head and taking it away. It doesn't happen. (Of course, anything is possible, but not normally.) The lower jaw does separate and many times is gone. And with it half of what we need for dental comparisons. The hands are made of many small bones and may get scattered, but we usually find some of them.

If there are no signs of hands, or the head or the face of the skull is somehow destroyed, then it's possible that you have a partial dismemberment. You have now officially ruled out any chance that this person wandered into the woods and had the big one. At autopsy, a close inspection will be required to ascertain whether saw or cut marks are present on any of the remaining bones.

One time I remember being in the woods with Terry trying to pick up as many pieces as possible of a scattered body. It had been found only forty feet into the woods off a very secluded secondary road. There was still a bit of a gooey mess left with some of the clothing. Disturbing it and packaging it all up sent that familiar aroma into the air. We finished up and decided to meet at the local police department that was handling the case. I took off first as Terry was headed toward his van. I got to the police department, hit the bathroom, made myself a cup of coffee and shot the shit with the local cops. Then I wondered, "Where the hell is Terry?" Moments later, he finally appeared to a few quandaries as to his whereabouts. He told us that he just got dropped off by a passing motorist. After a few "What're ya talking abouts?" he goes on to tell us that when he got to his van door, he realized that the keys were in the ignition and he had locked himself out. After some roadside cursing, he heard something from the woods on the opposite side of the road. When he looked to see what it was, he instinctively started backing his way around to the other side of his van. A huge black bear meandered out of the woods and crossed the road toward him and that aroma. To add insult to injury, Terry, who always wears his gun, had left it in his locked van this time. The bear ambled his way toward the van as Terry continued to hug the vehicle, keeping it between him and the beast. The bear continuously smelled the air and twice, stopped, looked directly at Terry and then continued on his way. Finally, after Yogi made his way a distance into the woods past the van, Terry waved down a car that thankfully picked him up.

A 3,000 pound hunk of metal flying down a highway at 60 MPH or even 40 MPH will demolish a 200 pound living thing standing or walking in its path. Most of the time, the severely broken pedestrian will stay intact. Some actually survive, but will live with painful reminders of this traumatic attack for the rest of their lives. Many die at the scene or later at the hospital as a result of massive internal injuries. The force of these collisions will tear vital organs apart as well as sever appendages, sending them a great distance or littering the roadway with them. So many of these collisions happen because of reckless behavior.

A 25 year old summer camp counselor drove five camp kids to a day of swimming a few miles away. The kids' ages were 12, 14, 14, 16 and 16. No one knows why she had to drive over a 100 MPH along a road she didn't know. Probably trying to impress the kids. She flew around a curve. Her speed made it difficult to keep the car in her lane and she veered into the other lane. In the oncoming lane was a town highway dump truck that had no where to go. The poor truck driver did his absolute best to swerve away from the rapidly approaching car, but her speed gave him no reaction time at all. His truck hit the car head on and even with the car's high speed, it was stopped dead in its track, driven backwards across pavement, crushing it over a distance of a couple hundred feet.

It was an awful scene to behold, but especially awful for anyone who was a parent. It was a poster scene for what parents and schools lecture to newly licensed drivers. The truck driver was okay, but horrified and incredibly saddened. It wasn't his fault, but he wished there was something he could have done. The five kids and the camp counselor were all killed. The car had been crushed and twisted and dragged along the roadway. Deep metal scrapings, car parts, bath towels and shoes littered the road. A trail of blood that was grounded into the pavement led to a forearm and hand that lay in the middle of this path of destruction. The mangled bodies of six young lives were entwined amongst each other and wrapped around sections of the car's metal framing. There would be no criminal charges, no arrest, no prosecution and no day in court. The person responsible for this carnage was also dead. It was one of those senseless scenes where every few minutes a different cop or paramedic or fireman would stand staring, shaking their head in sad disbelief.

What remained of the twisted hunk of metal would have to be cut up and sections of it pulled apart by heavy duty fire department extrication equipment to free the kids' bodies. The stark reality was that every person inside that wrecked car was dead, but you wouldn't know it by the way these emergency men and women worked. The bodies were a mess, yet every person working that scene and attempting to get these young bodies out of that car, made sure not to bruise them any further with their tools or machinery. Such intense care was taken not to "hurt" them anymore. These tough "seen it all" emergency scene professionals did their damnest not to leave another mark or bruise on any of their young already brutalized bodies. Once freed from the wreckage, firemen carefully carried and gently laid this tender cargo into body bags. At a scene so horrific you will still find kindness, compassion and love. Unfortunately, this uphill curving section of roadway will not be remembered for that. Its roadside flowers and decorations will be a reminder of something so tragic for years to come.

Not far away from these flowers is a roadside cross that marks the spot where a pedestrian lost her life. She was walking along the road late at night. A passing motorist stated that all of a sudden she saw a person crossing the road in front of her. She went on to say that she believed the person was dressed in dark clothes. Before she knew it, she was past her. Moments later, the darkly dressed body would be in the roadside ditch after being struck by a different car. The driver was on his way to work and said he never saw her. He knew he hit something, pulled over and found her.

There was a decent size area of newly paved shoulder outside the driving lane, but was she walking on the shoulder or in the roadway like the first motorist claimed? Could the driver have inattentively drifted off onto the shoulder and struck the pedestrian? And then why is this woman walking in the complete dark on an unlit road with no flashlight wearing dark clothing?

The victim was deceased with iPhone earplugs still in her ears. The iPhone was a hundred feet away where she was initially struck. She was wearing black pants and a black zipper top. The only light color was her pale Caucasian face. The roadside evidence and the damage to the driver's vehicle made it pretty clear that the woman was still in the roadway. Either still crossing or walking at the edge of the driving lane. The vehicle damage was to the right front headlight and the windshield at the very edge of the front passenger side. If she had been on the shoulder, she would've been fine. This road's speed limit was 55 and there was no indication that the driver was speeding. A person's head hitting the windshield of a 50 MPH vehicle will certainly cause death. The driver was run through the battery of impaired driving tests and passed. He was awake and on his way to work for a late night/ early morning shift. Speaking to the woman's boyfriend revealed that the woman would often have trouble sleeping. She would grab her iPhone and walk along the road at all times of the night. He tried in vain to stop her from this practice, but she would get up while he slept and do it anyway. This was an unfortunate accident.

We photographed the scene. Her body was twisted from the collision and having been thrown a great distance. As we examined her a bit closer, we could see the windshield impact to her head and broken bones to her legs where the car's bumper hit them. Then we noticed that the left leg below the point of impact was missing. Striking this leg severed it and sent it flying along with the body. This section of the road was surrounded by dense woods and it was still pitch black out. But we had to find her leg. Some collisions will actually knock people right out of their shoes. Shoes have remained at the spot of some impacts and other times thrown hundreds of feet away. It would be one thing not to find one of her shoes, but part of her body is another thing. We grabbed a few guys and started a search beginning with the area around the body and then fanning out. Once we hit the tree line, we had to make sure we looked up. It's rather common to find items from a crash hung up in tree branches.

Thankfully we found what we were looking for about 120 feet from the point of impact and about 45 feet away from her body. The shoe wasn't on the foot but the sock was. We gently bagged the lower leg section and brought it back to the body. A funeral home had been called, and the body was transported to the morgue for a later autopsy.

I know I've said it before, but I'll say it again. Walk along the side of the road that faces oncoming traffic. Walk during daylight hours. If you find yourself walking at night, have a flashlight in your hand. If you have something light colored to wear, wear it. Turn a coat inside out if you can. When walking, swing your arms. The human eye detects movement much more quickly than a slight change in coloring. And when you see a car coming, move onto the shoulder or off the roadway as far as you can. Just because it looks like a car is moving away from you or is staying in his lane, does not mean he actually sees you. Do not rely on drivers being attentive. Drivers could be tired or drunk. They may be texting or applying make up. They may be daydreaming. Don't ever assume that they see you. Most times at night, they don't see you until they are upon you so be off the roadway.

Working some outdoor scenes can involve a lot of prep work in order to actually do the job we're paid to do. We received information from a guy who was facing serious drug charges in New York City. He was hoping to make a deal in exchange for a reduced sentence. The NYPD had locked him up and relayed the info to us. He fingered another man for two murders explaining that the guy killed a man and woman and burned their bodies inside one of those city apartment building furnaces. Once burned, the guy smashed up the bones, shoveled all of the ashes and pieces out, boxed it all up and gave it to our guy to dispose of upstate. Our guy picked a creek into which to dump the remains. The dumping had occurred two years earlier.

It wasn't a big creek, but after a winter's meltdown or a heavy rain, it could certainly run heavy and fast. The width was about 15 to 20 feet and could rise a good two feet during wet seasons. Luckily, we were attempting to search the creek in mid summer, so it wasn't too high, but it still wouldn't be easy wading through shin deep water looking for the tiniest of human remains. We decided that the only way to properly search the creek was to build a dam further upstream and dry out the section we were going to search as much as possible. The lowering of the rushing water would definitely make it easier to search the sides and walls of the stream where most stuff would deposit and lodge.

We got several guys from the local Department of Public Works to dress down, boot up, and start hauling rocks and logs to the narrowest part of the stream above our search location. Our informant had come to the scene and pointed out where he roughly believed he spilled the box contents into the water. A couple of us had already gotten into the stream and did locate a few pieces of bone. We would venture a little more up stream and find another. When we stopped finding anything at all, we decided to dam the creek about 30 feet above that spot. We would work our way down stream from there.

Even at the narrowest spot, damming up the creek sounded easier than it was. Water is still going to get through and soon it will rise over the top. The DPW guys brought some hoses and pumps, and pumped away the rising water. Thankfully we started this prep work early. A couple of our guys began photographing, note taking and sketching, but we hadn't really started the full bore searching yet and it was getting into the afternoon. Soon the dam was doing its job. The water was lowering. Into the creek we went. We systematically searched every part of the sides and walls. We'd do the creek floor when the water subsided as far as it was going to go. Almost immediately we started finding gummy bear sized chunks of bone. (Can ya tell that I'm a Grandpa?) We documented our finds, photographed, and kept moving. We grabbed anything at all that looked like bone and that included lots of small rocks that we'd let doctors sort out later.

Arrangements had been made to get some kind of forensic doctor to show up and let us know how we were doing. By midday a forensic odontologist showed up and started examining our find. He was pretty impressed with what we had already recovered, especially the teeth. That began hours of "How about this, Doc?"

"No, that's a rock."

"Then how about this?"

We worked that creek without stopping, knowing very well that we couldn't leave it dammed up and come back the next day. After scouring about 200 feet of the creek sides, we worked our way upstream doing our best to search the creek bed that had a couple of inches of water running over it. We felt good about the areas we had searched. Of course, there may have been pieces that traveled further downstream, maybe hundreds of feet or yards, but you have to pick an end at some point. And by now, the doctor could say with reasonable certainty that we had a pretty good collection of small bones. He could further say that the remains were from two different people.

We finished in just enough time to disassemble the overflowing dam and let the creek return to normal. It had been a very long day. All of our bits and pieces were taken to a morgue. The next morning, they were laid out and examined. The whole collection covered the surface area of a large metal hospital gurney. The odontologist, accompanied by a forensic pathologist, began the meticulous process of examination and documentation.

Although we had only the smallest pieces of bone, and a fair number of teeth, lab testing would eventually reveal that we had the remains of a man and a woman. Further testing would confirm that the remains were in fact the murdered man and woman from the city. These findings combined with our informant's testimony were the icing on the cake that the NYPD needed to start building a solid case against the killer.

Various methods of DNA testing can determine identity from the smallest of samples. The US Department of Defense has an agency that uses these scientific miracles to help the families of so many U.S.

servicemen and women. If they receive a report of found remains that could possibly be a U.S. service person, they are on their way. And this could be anywhere in the world. They will fly a team of specialists into that location, document their findings, recover as much as they can, and bring it all back to their office in Hawaii where they will work their magic. They have identified remains from several past wars and brought closure to so many families.

I attended a fantastic week long course given by one of their guys. We received a few days of classroom instruction on the location and recovery of human remains. Then at week's end, we'd be sent out into a field where a pig's body had been buried the year before. In teams, it was our job to use our classroom instruction to find the buried Porky. The field was split up into quadrants and teams went to work. The pig wasn't in our quadrant, but he was found by that quadrant's team. I have used this training several times during my career and it has always been a tremendous asset.

The work that this agency does is truly amazing. We were shown slides (this was the 90's) of the numerous locations around the world where bones were discovered and brought home. It might be only a handful of bones, but these bones would be matched to some Mom's missing in action boy. The news is sad, and yet happy, in that many parents, spouses and sometimes children can finally know that a loved one is home. They can have that peace of mind having that final question answered. The work they do is a Godsend.

The same holds true for federal and state agencies that respond to disasters. They set up temporary morgues and arrange comfortable places for families to meet. They often provide counselors and people who know how to deal with the worst of situations. A huge part of their crew will include scientific and medical professionals who will sort through the remains of people who have been pulled from the ocean after a plane crash or pried free from the wreckage of a terrorist attack. They will use the best technology available to identify victims and help families get through this awful situation.

When 911 hit New York City, it was thought that body recovery would be an immense undertaking. The New York State Police sent uniform troopers to help shut down lower Manhattan. A couple of us were sent to help with body recovery. The massive scene itself was being handled by the FDNY, NYPD and the FBI, with countless other agencies assisting.

As we drove down and the Big Apple came into view, it was unsettling to see that huge, ominous cloud billowing from that island. We made our way past numerous roadblocks, parked our van and walked in. Showing up at Ground Zero on the morning of September 12, 2001 is something I will never forget. Emergency vehicles from all over the country were there. Equipment from private businesses was coming in. Dust covered workers were being cared for by nurses and paramedics near the river's edge where the airborne dust wasn't as prevalent. Walking down streets on the way toward Ground Zero looked like scenes from one of those apocalyptic movies. Devastation everywhere. Buildings were totally covered in a layer of gray concrete dust. Window glass was completely blacked out. From inside, you couldn't see a bit of the sun outside. The sun itself had a hard time trying to shine through that ever present cloud. Inches of the thick gray dust adhered to every vertical surface like sign poles, parking meters and metal fire escapes. It was only on the side that faced the Twin Towers; the side from whence came the rolling blast of a concrete storm down each street as the Towers collapsed. Cars on the street were all one color. Gray. On one minivan's big rear window was the message written in dust: "God Help Us." As we got closer to Ground Zero, more and more windows were blown out. The concrete dust became thicker and thicker. Parked cars were piled one on top of another. An ambulance was flipped over. A fire truck had cars on top of it. The concrete dust that covered the pavement was now inches thick like snow, and its airborne counterpart continued to harass our breathing.

The sights while traveling these few blocks were mesmerizing, but would be nothing in comparison to the Twin Towers.

Nothing compared to it because nothing was what we saw. Nothing. It's funny. You've heard all the news reports. You've seen all the video footage. You know they collapsed, but when you actually stand there and see for yourself that they are gone, it makes you sick. You feel this awful hollowness inside you. Why? Why? Why? You keep asking with no answer in sight. When you snap out of this momentary nightmare, you see the wreckage. Mountainous piles of twisted steel and concrete. Pipes stuck out of the pile at weird angles. Small fires still burned in pockets of debris. Sections of huge steel beams jutted out toward the sky in grotesque designs. And amongst this mountain of catastrophic rubble were people. People everywhere. Firemen, cops, ambulance people, construction workers, volunteers. They looked like ants on a giant anthill. All of them braving incredibly dangerous conditions to help. To help find any possible survivors. The manpower was astounding. It was a bit of a free for all that next morning, but you could see management start to take control. Teams started shoring up. Safety was becoming a priority.

We were introduced to a representative from the New York City Office of the Chief Medical Examiner. She was very appreciative of our offer to help. She pointed to the hundreds of body bags waiting to be used. She told us that the ME's Office brought all available staff into work to handle the numerous bodies that came in the day before; people who fell from the buildings, emergency workers killed outside the buildings and people killed by debris in the streets. That kept them busy all day and into the night. They assumed that pulling bodies from the wreckage would be the next huge influx.... but it wasn't. A body here and there would be found and brought to them, but that was it. They knew that there were thousands of people inside the Towers at that time of the morning, but they weren't finding bodies. They were buried. The vast majority of them were buried inside this concrete grave. That's when I realized something. On our walk through all the streets leading up to the Towers, I hadn't seen one office desk or chair. Not a single file cabinet. No tables, coffee pots, computers, or anything that you'd find in over 200 floors of offices. It was all buried. It was all gone.

We told the gal from the ME's that we'd hang around for the day and check back with her the next morning to see if things had changed. She thanked us. We walked around to see if there was something we could do in the meantime. You feel like a useless idiot not jumping in and helping, but the truth was that we'd only get in the way of the guys who knew what they were doing. We also had to stay available. The ME had our contact info in case they needed us.

Security heightened even more with planes having gone down in Washington and Pennsylvania. We spent the night at a relative's in Staten Island. The next morning, security measures almost stopped us from crossing the Verrazano Bridge. We finally did. It was so eerie being the only vehicle crossing the great expanse of this normally busy bridge.

Checking in with the ME's office brought nothing new. We made sure they knew to call us if help was needed. We headed home.

It's interesting how people of different backgrounds, different cultures and different opinions will band together against a common enemy. Liberal and Conservative will work hand in hand to fight a serious threat against our nation. Feuding agencies will set their egos aside and work side by side to find and save lost or injured citizens. And closer to home, residents who have no use for their neighbor will join forces and leave their grudges behind in their battle to keep a landfill from coming to their town.

The good that comes out of such unlikely partnerships is the renewing of friendships and the mending of old hurts. Unfortunately, that isn't the norm. Most times, once the threat has passed the old resentments and bad feelings return. We seem to forget all about that common good we were all working toward. During that shared partnership against that common enemy, we listened to each other and respected each other's words and feelings. We put aside all the negative feelings to achieve that greater good; a common betterment for everyone.

Family will do this all the time. Something bad happens. A serious accident, a scary diagnosis, a death. Family will come together and do what they have to do to get over the hurdle of fighting this common enemy. They will work together. They'll cook, clean, watch the kids, buy anything and do whatever needs doing. Then once life gets somewhat back to normal, the old grudges sneak back in. They're like that cancer that goes into remission and soon wants back into your life. Instead of working a little harder at stifling the ill will and setting aside the egos, we let the bad stuff back into our lives.

"She's not doing enough. I knew she wouldn't."

It's probably easier to slide back into the way it was. It's harder to take a few more deep breaths to get past a family member's imperfections. But hell, let's face it. We all have them. So many feuds remain active because one person refused to take that initial step towards reconciliation. These grievances will stay around for years because both sides feel that the other should make the first move. And no one does. The sad irony in this thinking is that when one does finally take the initiative, the other usually follows suit and years of fighting can come to an end.

And I'll let you in on an even bigger irony. Most people involved in these kinds of disputes view the idea of apologizing as a weakness. They see it as an admission of guilt and as a flaw to their character, when in fact it is the absolute opposite. Being the first one to pardon or ask forgiveness is a true testament to a person's courage. It brightly illustrates their capacity to forgive and to love. It shows true compassion. The person who steps forward to say, "Please forgive me. I'm sorry I hurt you" or "I forgive you" is the person who makes the world a better place to live in. Some family members will fall into a loving embrace. Others will require a bit more work. That's why the kindness has to be coupled with great patience in order to ward off some continuing blows. There are people who don't know how to handle reconciliation or sympathetic words. They're more comfortable feuding. They may answer back with negativities and rattle off times that "You did this to me" and repeat old comments made during arguments. It's because they really don't know what to say. Some people have a very hard time "letting go" of things in the past. That's when your patience has to kick in. It's hard enough to take that first step towards reconciliation, but it's even tougher to stick with it when you have an unwilling participant on the other end. It's important to listen to what they're saying. If they come back with spews of hatred and name calling, then you might as well walk away. Maybe you'll try again after some time has passed. But if what they're saying sounds more like confusion or like they're making excuses not to agree with you, give them a chance. See where it goes. Don't argue with what they're saying. Don't rehash anything at all. A great answer is, "I can understand why you'd feel that way." You don't have to settle everything then and there. It's a first step and they should be made to realize that as well. Too many good hearted and well-meaning folks have gotten up the nerve to settle an old score only to give up after meeting some initial resistance. Let's face it. If you're that person that had the courage and fortitude to do the right thing, then hang in there. Don't let that humanity and kindheartedness go to waste. Give it a chance to work.

Remember that your approaching them with the idea of making-up will probably come out of left field to them. They most likely won't see it coming at all, so be prepared. Do your thing even if it meets resistance, and leave the meeting still meaning what you said. It takes some people time to calm down, time to process something like that. Let them have their alone time with this incredible concept that you just dropped on them. It may take a couple days, maybe weeks. Many of these people have a lot of baggage they have to unpack and toss before they can face you. And you know what? No matter what the outcome, you tried. And you'll feel better knowing you tried. If it didn't work out, make sure that you harbor no ill feelings. The only feeling you should have towards that person is sorrow.

And to those of you who don't reciprocate when a hand is offered in forgiveness or reconciliation, all I can say is that you have a long, hard road ahead of you. You mightn't see it, but you do. Bitterness, jealousy and hatred are awful feelings to let build up inside of you. They are cancers in every sense of the word. They turn loving, caring human beings into ugly creatures. Grudges and resentments grow inside you like a disease. Some people don't know how to stop it. You know, if it was a disease, you'd go to a doctor and tell him to get rid of it. Yet when we see ourselves becoming unpleasant people who are turning away from family and people we love, we're oblivious. We don't say to ourselves, "Hey, she's my sister. I should be laughing and talking to her like we used to." We don't see how holding onto jealousy is affecting us. We're not sleeping. We break into a rash. We're always snapping at people. Then we justify it with, "Must be the stress of my job or raising these kids." Blaming these ill feelings on the two things in your life that keep you grounded is an even bigger mistake. Getting past these feelings and letting go of the baggage that weighs you down is not easy. Like that tumor spreading through you, get a doctor. Get help. If you refuse to see a therapist, then for God's sake, talk to someone you trust. Unload on them. Tell them everything. Don't keep it all inside. Talking about it is the first step in letting it go.

Life is going to throw some really tough curveballs at you. These are the times that'll be difficult. The death of a loved one, break ups, disease, financial ruin. They will be devastating. When these times come, do yourself a favor. In between the tears and depression, take a really good look at that grudge you're holding against your sister or mother or best friend. Examine it now in the context of what's really going on in your life. In most cases, it'll be small potatoes. Realize that and let it go. Now pick up the phone and cry to your sister. Bring flowers to your Mom and say you're sorry. Invite your best friend over for a stiff drink (no, a few stiff drinks!), and talk to them about what's happening to you. They want to be there for you. Now let them, you stubborn ole mule!

Chapter Fourteen
Murder in the Catskills

As a young crime scene technician, I wanted to learn as much as I could. I always told Don and Terry to call me out anytime. One summer day they took me up on my offer.

Sullivan County is home to a large Hasidic community during the summer months. Hundreds of Hasidic Jews travel two hours from New York City to spend July and August in vacation bungalows. These are closed communities with strict religious beliefs and practices. On their Sabbath, which starts on Friday at sundown and lasts till Saturday at sundown, there is no work whatsoever. No handling of money, no labor tasks, not even the turning on of a light switch.

They bring their children from the confines of a city apartment, usually in Brooklyn, to the picturesque expanse of the country where raccoons ravage their garbage and deer stroll their yards. These communities cater to families of all sizes. Husband and wife may occupy one bungalow. Then a family of six has the next with the grandparents in the adjoining one. The numerous families that comprise one bungalow colony will be a closely-knit group who will join together in worship and daily activities.

On a Monday morning in July, the calm and quiet of one such bungalow colony was disrupted with the cries, "They're dead! They're dead!"

A small one bedroom residence became the scene of a double murder that occurred during the night. With other occupied bungalows only 15 and 20 feet away, someone had entered the cottage of an elderly Hasidic couple and brutally murdered both in their beds.

The horrendous crime immediately received massive media coverage. Two elderly grandparents asleep in their beds were viciously attacked. The Sullivan County Sheriff's Office received the initial call. They immediately called in the State Police to assist. The Sullivan County District Attorney joined the investigation on Day One. Our crime scene unit was tasked with the scene. Don called me in to help. I was a uniform trooper and Sullivan County was my patrol area so I knew this vacation spot and the surrounding areas. The secondary road outside the gates of the bungalow colony was jam packed with police cars, newspaper reporters, and TV cameras. This was big news.

The elderly victims were from Poland and had lived through the Holocaust years of Europe. They made their way to New York. As a break away from the urban, gritty, and sometimes violent life of the city, they decided to spend a summer in the quiet, rural and restful calm of the Catskills only to be slain in their beds.

The involved bungalow sat further to the back of the group of modest cottages. Woods surrounded its rear and sides. There were a few wooden steps that rose to a small front porch. Inside that porch door was a cramped kitchen and eating area. A bathroom was at the back of this kitchen area. So far, everything looked normal. To the right of the kitchen area was a doorway into the one bedroom. Two twin beds lined each wall with a bureau between them on the far wall. Patterns, smears, and drops of blood covered most of the floor between the beds. The walls were decorated with sprays and spatters of blood. Each bed had its own pool of blood that had soaked into the mattress.

The 76-year-old man was crumpled and kneeling on the floor with his upper body still on the bed. Massive injuries were visible to his head and neck. The 67 year old woman was lying on her back on her twin bed. Her feet were off the foot of the bed and touching the floor. Her head and face were also severely disfigured. Lying on the bed above her head was a blood stained, wooden handled hammer.

From inside the bungalow, you could look out the front window and see the other bungalows so close by. Children who weren't told what happened played and laughed. Parents stood nearby keeping a close eye on the kids and stole glances at us as we walked in and out of the crime scene.

It was tight quarters inside and not easy to work. It's essential to treat every surface, whether it be a wall or table top or window sill, as a potential source of valuable evidence. In the dimly lit interior it would be easy to step on a footprint or a misplaced blood drop and ruin it. So, examining and processing the floor surfaces became an immediate priority. Once a multitude of photographs were taken of every kind of impression on the floor, we secured anything found on the floor so it wouldn't get kicked or stepped on. When the time came that we felt pretty good about processing the area, we covered it with a few layers of brown paper to further protect it. There would be other chemical processes to perform on the floor in an attempt to bring out more unseen details in the blood, but that would have to be done once the whole scene was processed and the bodies were out.

We had to leave our equipment outside because of the limited space inside. By now, meticulous notes had been taken and overall photographs were completed. We headed into the bedroom. In any kind of attack, it's urgent to come up with the type of weapon used. The hammer was definitely one of the weapons. Wounds to the bodies suggested that both the hammering end as well as the nail pulling claw end were used. Soon we saw stab wounds present on the man, so now we had two weapons. Remember stabbing or cutting doesn't always mean a knife. Did this mean two attackers? Something to keep in mind. Pieces of a shattered vase would become evidence. At the time, it wasn't clear if the vase had been broken during the attack, or used as weapon on one of the victims, or maybe the possibility that a victim used it in self defense. It was too early to tell. It would be nice to know that we had a bleeding perpetrator, but we had no such proof at the time.

Blood on the floor had definitely been stepped on by the attacker. Both victims were barefoot, and there was a very clear sneaker print in the blood on the bedroom floor. We immediately ruled out the person who had found them and any emergency personnel. This had to be the killer's footprint. And according to Edmond Locard's Theory of Exchange, the killer would have traces of their blood on the treads of his sneaker. A hopeful thought for us. Later chemical treatment of the floor would hopefully develop more detail on this partial sneaker print.

But until then we had to get the bodies removed and start processing every surface inside this bungalow. The Coroner was called and more photographs were taken of the bodies as they were turned over and moved. It wasn't a certainty yet, but the positioning of the 67 year old woman's body suggested another unspeakable act. It became apparent that she had also been raped. In our crime scene world, that awful realization brings a ray of light to our investigation. Maybe we'll be able to secure his DNA from the autopsy.

But getting an autopsy done on anyone affiliated with a strict religious sect like this isn't always possible. Complications started right there at the scene. The Coroner notified the rabbi of the community and advised him that the bodies would be getting handled and transported to the morgue. The rabbi had to be present. And more importantly to us, any autopsy, if it was allowed, or examination would have to be done immediately. Strict religious beliefs demanded that the bodies be buried by sundown unless the death happened late in the day. That was a problem we'd have to figure out. As we worked, the District Attorney (who happened to be Jewish, although not Hasidic) conferred with the rabbi, and the Hasidic community, and came to a workable compromise. One of us would leave the scene and attend the post mortem examination. It would not be a complete autopsy, but a limited examination and documentation of every wound and injury. A well known rabbi who often worked as a liaison with the State Police would be present during the examination.

Once the arrangements had been made, the bodies could be removed from the scene. We suggested that all the kids and anyone who would have a problem seeing the body bags come out be brought inside their cottages. The rabbi and members of the community appreciated the consideration. We've seen it all too often. People breaking down as they watch a black body bag being loaded into a vehicle, knowing that the contents are someone they knew or loved. It's a most unnatural sight for anyone and something that isn't easy to get over. Why in the world would anyone want to have to answer some child's innocent question, "What's in the black bag, Mommy?"

The bodies made their way to the morgue where renowned forensic pathologist Dr. Michael Baden would perform the examinations. Dr. Baden had also been instrumental in getting proper assessments done. He promised no intrusive procedures and with the District Attorney had convinced the rabbi that not allowing some kind of examination would seriously hinder the investigation that was currently a true whodunit.

As the examinations began with one of our guys present, the remainder of us stayed at the bungalow. The walls had been painted and re-painted numerous times over the years. These walls and the old wooden doors weren't surfaces that were very conducive to developing latent fingerprints. We dusted every single surface area inside that bungalow and every outside surface leading inside. The dusting wasn't giving us much until Don and Terry developed a print on the front surface of one of the bureau drawers. The bureau was between the beds and a prime location for possibly being the attacker's print. Part of our scene recreation revealed that at least one of the bureau drawers had been open during the attack because spatters of blood were present on clothing inside the drawer. The drawer had to have been closed after the attack. Was a drawer left open by the victims? Did the attacker quietly go through the drawers when one of the victims woke up? And did he close it after everything was over or did it close during the violent altercation? In any case, a drawer was open during the attack and it was closed when we arrived. This faint, partial print showed some promise.

Since the print was faint, and the wood surface of the drawer wasn't the greatest, Don and Terry decided against trying to lift the print at the scene so we took the whole drawer. Trying to lift a print with tape from a rough surface like that could destroy it totally. A nice smooth surface like glass or clean metal will normally lift all of the detail nicely. Remember that you're trying to lift every bit of the minutest details of a fingerprint; every ridge and individual characteristic. So much of this detail can get lost in the valleys of wood grain, especially as wood ages. After photoing the hell out of the print, the boys carefully packaged up the drawer as evidence.

Outside the crime scene, cops from the Sheriff's Department and State Police canvassed every single person in the area. Hundreds of people were spoken to, but nothing solid. A name might come up. Our guys would look into it only to have it lead to a dead end. The post mortem examinations confirmed what we already knew. Both ends of a hammer and a knife. Our further suspicion was also verified. The woman had been raped. We dead printed the bodies to use as elimination prints.

As night fell, the scene was held secure by uniform troopers. The next day brought a team from our crime lab in Albany to process the floor with chemicals. Our original sneaker print was as good as the impression got. No other ones developed.

When the crime scene was finally released, we had a handful of latent fingerprints, a sneaker print in blood, one of the murder weapons and possibly some DNA from our female victim. There was lots of other evidence, like the shattered vase, that we collected to process for prints, but those were the big ones.

As our crime scene investigators worked on the evidence in our lab, the investigation outside was stalling. A Hasidic man came forward and confessed to the crime, but his story didn't add up. A history of mental illness took him off the short suspect list. We had printed up several life size photographs of the sneaker print and gave them to our Major Crimes guys. They tracked down the sneaker company. Nike was very helpful and sent us the exact sneaker model that bore the tread design from the scene. One lead that surfaced was a neighbor who said she heard a motorcycle start up in the very early morning hours of that night. She listened to it drive off. It sounded like it had been parked right outside the bungalow colony.

Soon a list of every registered motorcycle in the county materialized. It was quite a lengthy list. Investigators would go through it to narrow it down using obvious elimination methods. Another part of this course of action was to have uniform troopers stop every motorcycle they saw on the road. Every one of them. Upon stopping them, they'd get the registered owner's name, operator's name and address, and take note of the footwear the operator was wearing. If it was sneakers, what brand. By now, the investigation was a month old. There were many cops who felt this was a waste of time, a grasping at straws tactic to show the press that we were doing something.

Meanwhile, the hammer had gone through a battery of tests for prints and blood types other than the victims'. No luck. The same result occurred after processing the vase pieces. Even the DNA from the victim was only a partial profile, basically a blood typing. Not the 20 billion to one ratio you get today with DNA testing. The media and State Police brass were all over the investigation. The full court press was coming down hard from above. And then a miracle happened.

A Long Island kid who decided to become a trooper a few years earlier had graduated the State Police Academy and was sent to the State Police station in Liberty, New York. SP Liberty had been handling the double murder investigation with the Sheriff's Department. As a young trooper, Sean was full of energy and did his job well. He was always around the action. When he was told to start stopping motorcycles, he wasted no time. The end of every shift brought the information of numerous bikes he stopped. But one particular motorcycle stop just didn't sit right with him. The male driver drove a red Kawasaki and wore brand new looking Nike sneakers. He got as much info as possible and then complimented the guy on his sneakers. The driver said that he had just bought them within the last few weeks.

The motorcycle driver was a kitchen worker in one of the nearby big hotels. It wasn't far from the scene of the crime. A check of the guy's name showed that he had no criminal record so no fingerprints would be on file. Our guys would have to talk to him. They made it look like they were talking to all hotel workers as part of the investigation. He was still a long shot, but there was more to this guy. He admitted that he had traveled that road by the bungalows. One of our investigators asked if he would voluntarily give us a set of inked fingerprints. He said he would.

The fingerprint on the bureau drawer became the focus of the investigation. The dead prints of both victims had already been eliminated as the source. The inked fingerprint card of the motorcycle driver was brought into the crime scene unit office. Don and Terry closed the door. Terry sat down with it first. It took a little while. Then he stood up without saying a word and let Don look. Don took his time. Soon Don looked up. They both started nodding. The latent print on the bureau matched the motorcycle driver's left thumb.

I had just stopped by headquarters in Middletown to drop something off from Liberty and figured I'd see what was up with the guys and the case. Don and Terry had just told the bosses and let me in on the huge secret. It was the guy. He'd have to explain why his fingerprint was on a bureau drawer inside this bungalow. The wheels were put in motion to have another sit down with the suspect. The flurry of activity was intense. After weeks and weeks of dead ends, we had a guy who was inside the bungalow. A guy who drives a motorcycle and wears Nike sneakers. He had already been locked into making the statement that he had never been to that bungalow colony or inside any of the cottages.

He agreed to come in on his own and talk to our guys. While that was going on, a search warrant was obtained for his apartment and a team of guys descended upon it. But it didn't yield much. Jewelry was missing from the bungalow. There was no sign of any at his place. However, one interview with a female acquaintance turned up a bracelet that our guy had recently given to her. The elderly victim's family identified it as Grandma's.

Pieces were starting to come together, but a confession would answer a lot of questions. The cops in the room with the guy tried every angle, but the guy wouldn't budge. He never admitted any involvement. The interview turned shitty and the suspect said it was over. By now, we had enough to arrest him. The clothing or sneakers he wore that night were never recovered. However, the brand new sneakers were the same type. A knife that matched the wounds was also never found. His blood would be taken and compared to the blood type found on the murdered woman.

The DA was handed the case with a lab result indicating that the suspect could not be excluded as the donor with a 35-1 ratio that it could be someone else. Not that 20 billion to one we would've liked. He also had a bloody sneaker print that was the same model of Nike, but not the exact tread design. What the DA did have was no alibi for the suspect's whereabouts on the night and early morning of the crimes, he drove a motorcycle, a piece of jewelry from the murdered woman, and the most damning of all was still the latent fingerprint impression of his left thumb deposited on a bureau inside the bungalow and between the two bodies.

The suspect had pled not guilty to two charges of murder and one count of rape. The defense would hire a fingerprint examiner to conduct his own comparison. He couldn't dispute our findings. It was a tough case with a lot of circumstantial evidence. The newspapers would cover the trial as witness upon witness took the stand. The defendant made the mistake of insisting upon defending himself. The judge would only allow it if a court appointed lawyer sat at the defense table with him. The newspapers loved this. Many times, his nasty attitude toward the court and witnesses drew warnings from the judge. Finally, when cross examining one of the first responding police officers he made an incriminating remark that placed him right there at the doorway to the bungalow. A stunned jury stared in silence as the suspect realized his mistake. He sat down and asked that his lawyer continue for him.

Terry testified to the fingerprint match. All of the defense's attempts at discrediting his findings fell upon deaf ears. The jury found the defendant guilty of a slew of charges that included double murder and rape. Since he never admitted to the crime, it could only be speculated that he walked into the unlocked cottage to burglarize it. The occupants woke up and it went bad from there. The hammer was found to have been there in the bungalow. It was unknown if the knife was brought or also from the residence. The sexual attack appeared to be an after thought; an angry, vicious act committed by an angry, vicious thug who displayed that side of his personality many times during the trial.

Not once did the police agencies or district attorney's office ever give up their search for this violent predator. When the investigation hit numerous dead ends, they tried a different route. When no new leads developed, they went back over old ones. No idea was ever discarded. No suggestions were ever blown off. Even if cops thought that an idea was a long shot, they tried it regardless. This case was solved and an extremely violent criminal was put away for a very, very long time. Good, hard-working, never-stop-till-it's-done police work did that. Luck had nothing to do with it. Many times along the way, it seemed hopeless. Expectations were low. But you keep at it. You keep going.

Life is going to hit a dead end here and there. Life is going to pound you in the gut. Your first response has to be, "I'll get through this!" because you will. Take it from me. Believe it or not, we're pretty damn tough sons of bitches. If you were weak, well now you're going to get stronger.

After that pounding, you have to take however long you need to catch your breath, to heal. Then you must take whatever good you can siphon from that knockdown and learn from it. You must learn from it. Make sure that in some way, this bad experience makes you a better person. Yes, a better person. Walk away from it a little smarter, a little more aware and respectful of life's unpredictability. And don't ever forget that punch in the gut. Some experts will instruct you to forget it, put it behind you, get past it. Yes. Get past the bad feelings and depression and negative thoughts, but always remember the event that made you a better person; remember how you got past it. Don't forget any of that because a day will come when you can be there for someone else who gets the wind knocked out of them by life.

When people suffer, they want desperately to talk to and be

with others who have felt that same gut punch. Others that can offer support, advice or just be an understanding ear. Doing that for someone else does make the world a better place.

Chapter Fifteen
The Whodunit

The rural countryside of upstate New York offers the most spectacular of natural settings. Our State Parks show off magnificent waterfalls, picturesque mountains and sun setting lake views. The hiking and walking trails go on for miles and miles through God's creation where it's not uncommon to run into deer, bears and rattlesnakes to name only a few. One such park isn't that far at all from the concrete jungle of the Big Apple. You would think you were on another planet.

Three young men took a nature hike that made its way around a gorgeous secluded lake. They decided to stop at this one particularly pretty spot that overlooked the lake from a large rock ledge at the water's edge. The rock ledge was the perfect spot for a restful break as evidenced by a small extinguished campfire nearby. They stood at the expansive rock ledge's edge and gazed out over the calm water of this beautiful lake. The water's surface was about five feet below them. The sun shined brightly making visible the many fish in the water. There seemed to be quite a number of fish in the water. And then they saw something quite out of place. A mannequin was floating in the lake about ten feet away from where they stood. They joked about the oddity of a store mannequin making its way out here. Some practical joker went to a lot of trouble for this. One of the young men climbed down the rock ledge to get to the water's surface and had a closer look.

"Holy shit. It's not a mannequin."

He could see some kind of bleeding wound to the floating man's shoulder. Their more alerted senses now saw what looked like the butt of a rifle under the water near the body. It looked like the rifle's barrel was pointed down into the rocky bottom. The butt of the rifle was a short distance from the rock ledge, so one of the young men decided that he'd try to retrieve it. He grabbed a long stick from the woods, reached its curved end into the water and attempted to hook the rifle and pull it out. The stick caught on something. He pulled and "Boom!" The rifle discharged under water, but stayed in place.

Okay. Now it was time to call the cops. Luckily one of the three had some kind of cell phone service in this remote area and called the State Park Police.

While this was happening, I was at a meeting that was dealing with a missing person case at another state park. The State Park Detective had been sitting in on the meeting that was now ending when he got the call about a floater in one of their lakes. That was all he knew at the time. We beat him up a bit with, "Hey aren't your state parks supposed to be restful places of calming serenity and discovering your peaceful inner beauty? What's with the missing people and floaters? Can ya do a little something about that?"

We laughed and headed our separate ways. I let him know that we were around if it turned out to be more than a drowning victim who had too much to drink. Little did I know how suspicious it would be.

It was hours later before I got the call to head out there. The sun was starting its descent and impending darkness would soon become a major factor. Some of our State Police back room guys were on the scene. The reason for the hold up in calling was because at first it looked like an obvious suicide. But that idea turned to shit. The scene wasn't easy to get to in a timely fashion, so I called to the guys at the scene and asked them to conduct a thorough walk through of the entire area at the water's edge and note every little thing they saw. They were told to note its location, but leave it where it was. Having people search the scene for us would save valuable daylight. I further told them to get the Medical Examiner's Office on the way. I was told that they were already there and that they were a big reason for this turning to shit.

Vinny and I arrived at a rural roadside and parked our vehicles on the shoulder. We packed up as much as we could for what we were told would be an extremely slow ride through some rough terrain that would take about a half hour. Park Rangers greeted us. Being the old guy, I sat in the front seat of the jeep with the camera cradled in my lap. Poor Vinny got the wooden bench in the jeep's open bed with the equipment bag. The jeep roared and headed out along a path that could hardly be called a path. Even at a very slow speed, Vinny and I had to hold on for dear life as the jeep bounced and knocked us around. I kid you not when I say that there were a few times that I saw Vinny's feet come off the floor of the jeep's bed. I thought we lost him until my twisting and turning head would hear the repeating phrase, "Still here." Of course, a few times this wiseass had to add comments like, "That all you got?"

After a 30 minute ride that literally kicked our asses, we got dropped off and hiked another 20 minutes through the woods and along the edge of this huge lake. The sounds of nature and its calming effects were soon replaced with "It's about time." and "What took you so long?". Five cops and two ME investigators stood at this scenic location giving us the usual cop harassment that makes the day go by. We were then quickly brought up to speed on the current situation.

The body had been pulled out of the water and laid on a short shore like section of the rock ledge. The white male was fully clothed and had a large wound to his left chest and arm area. The cops told us that they weren't sure if this wound was the result of firearm damage or the pecking away of a large snapping turtle that was sitting on the body when they arrived. They said it was quite a sight. This prehistoric looking monster perched on the chest of this floating body occasionally taking a chomp out of his shoulder area and then defiantly looking up at everybody as if to say, "Go ahead and try to take this snack away from me." The park rangers used some kind of stick to shoo the beast away as ME investigators pulled the body out. But our annoyed dinosaur friend stayed drifting nearby.

We started doing our thing. All pertinent items were pointed out to us and we quickly photographed everything. It was pretty obvious that the body had not been in the water that long. It was in fairly good shape over all. He probably went into the water earlier that day or possibly the day before. A back pack was found hidden in the bushes, and it contained a few personal items and a small screwdriver. It also had an empty canvas zipper case that usually holds a camera's monopod. No monopod, just the empty case. The cops had already located his car in a parking lot that serviced the trail that led to this spot. Taking a quick look inside the cluttered vehicle, a cop saw a monopod on the front seat.

His identity was checked and a call was made to a family member who said that the unmarried man in his forties had left home two days earlier, but didn't say where he was going. The relative went on to say that the man had been unemployed for quite some time and had been very depressed. Without knowing the circumstances, she went on to ask, "Did you find him? Did he commit suicide?" When asked why she would ask that, the family member explained that he had always been a loner, but as of recently he had become even more reclusive and stayed in bed all day. He broke off all ties with people. The most surprising was a nephew with whom he was very close. The cops further established that the deceased man did own a couple of long guns. We wouldn't know yet if the one in the water was one of his, but up to this point, this was looking like a straight up suicide.

Dusk was on the way so we went to the body. The two ME investigators showed us the wound to the left upper chest and arm area. It was hard to tell what it was, but his shirt was torn up around the wound. A few cops at the scene were familiar with people who have committed suicide by shooting themselves in the chest. It doesn't happen often but when it does, it's usually women who shoot themselves somewhere other than their head or face. But it was certainly possible. Holding the barrel of any long gun up against any part of the body where the explosion would hit bone first could certainly create a torn-apart gaping contact wound. Then our dinner guest would have went straight to the blood and made an even bigger mess.

But it seemed like a weird angle for a self inflicted entrance wound and without the rifle yet, we didn't even know if he could reach the trigger holding the rifle like that. It was odd, but we had to look at all possibilities. Then the ME investigator turned the body over and showed us what had turned this apparent suicide upside down. There was a small hole in the back of his shirt and a corresponding small, black lined hole just left of his spine.

The words automatically came out of my mouth, "Oh shit. There's an entrance wound in his back."

The gal from the ME's Office who was kneeling alongside me looked right at me and said, "Thank you. That's what I've been trying to tell these guys."

I got up and addressed the cops with the words they didn't want to hear, "This is a problem."

Vinny and I got all kinds of, "Hey maybe that's the exit wound" and

"Maybe the chest wound was a small entrance until this turtle did his thing."

Without getting into arguments, I told them that an autopsy should be scheduled for as soon as possible. And if the forensic pathologist went along with their theory, then I would. But we knew what it was. This guy was definitely shot in the middle of his back. Was it from the rifle in the water? We now went about carefully getting the rifle from the water.

As we did and unbeknownst to us, cops were coming up with more and more information that all came to the same conclusion. This guy's life was spiraling downward. He was depressed and family members wouldn't be surprised at all to hear that he had taken his own life.

The rifle was gently pulled from the water. It was too murky to see if there was a spent bullet casing in the water. We could check for that later. The rifle wasn't that long, so it fueled the self-inflicted chest wound argument. There was an expended shell casing in the chamber. If the young men's story was true, this would be the casing for the bullet that they accidentally discharged. The rifle's unstable positioning would prevent it from recycling properly and it wouldn't eject that casing, so this made sense. The casing to the shot that entered our victim had to be somewhere else. All info on the gun was given to the back room guys so that they could perform all the checks on it.

Soon a small boat came to the scene so that the ME folks could take the body back to their morgue. The autopsy would be conducted early the next morning. We secured the rifle, the back pack, and every cigarette butt that was found in the area.

The sun had set and a dimming sky was upon us. We noted our exact location and headed out. It was our hope that the autopsy would shed some light on the series of events that led to this find. We trekked out and got another half hour of punishment in that jeep. It was dark by the time we got to our vehicles at the roadside.

Day Two

The SP case investigator pulled into the parking lot of the medical examiner's office as we did. Brendan is one of those astutely perceptive back room guys who can pick up on the slightest vibe. He has a great cop's head that keeps an open mind in any situation. His diligence would be instrumental in this case's resolution. As we walked in, he let us know that the rifle did belong to the victim. Further interviews continued to paint the picture of a very lonely man who had been exceedingly depressed.

"Billy, this guy committed suicide. I know it," Brendan stated firmly.

"It certainly sounds like it, big guy, but I gotta explain how he gets an entrance wound to the middle of his back," I countered.

The pathologist had already been apprised of the suspicious circumstances and was ready for us. Overall photographs were taken and the examination began. The wound to the upper left chest area and arm was first. It did have a couple of clear snapping turtle chomps to it, but there was definitely severe damage below the chomps. The shirt was ripped apart considerably, but there was no blackish, soot stained areas of the shirt or skin that would be consistent with a contact wound had this been the entrance of the shot.

When a gun goes off, all kinds of soot and gunpowder fly out of the barrel along with the bullet. A lot of this debris will usually sprinkle out into the air and deposit onto surfaces in front of the barrel including the target if it's within 3 or 4 feet. That debris is called gunshot residue. With handguns especially, a lot of that residue will blow backwards towards the shooter and deposit on his hand, arm, shirt and other clothing. Depending on how close the barrel is to the target, varying gunshot residue patterns will be left on the target surface around the bullet hole. When that surface is skin, it may look like a spray pattern of black specks and tiny burns caused by the hot particles of this debris.

Now if the barrel is held right up against the skin, two things may happen. I explained earlier how a barrel held up against a hard surface like your skull will cause a tearing, star shaped wound because of the initial explosion's contact with the resistant hard surface. It then blows back some of that explosion's force towards the shooter and tears apart the entrance wound. The black residue will be present on and under the skin where the barrel was placed. The second scenario would involve holding the barrel up against a part of the skin that is not directly over bone. If the target area's path is soft, the bullet will make a nice little hole. This little hole will be coated with a blackish ring of gunshot residue. It will also be present down inside the wound.

There was no evidence of gunshot residue on the front of his torn shirt or anywhere in the chest wound. The remainder of his clothing including footwear was noted. Then he was turned over. In the center of the shirt's back was a small circular hole with some black staining to it. Under the shirt and directly lined up with the shirt's hole was the corresponding circular bullet wound that also displayed the black ring to it. Black staining could be seen down inside the wound.

"There's your entrance," the doctor remarked, "He's definitely shot in the back."

Sighs escaped a few mouths. There were cops present hoping that it was the other way around. Vinny and I knew what it was, but we were still hoping that the remainder of the examination would give us a little more to go on. The autopsy continued as usual. The pathologist charted the bullet's path. It entered his back at 52 inches high from the bottom of his feet. It was just left of the spine; no bone behind it. It then tore through the chest cavity, but missed the heart. It destroyed the left lung and created massive bleeding. It then exited the left chest and upper arm area at 53 1/2 inches high. It would have left a huge gaping exit wound. When asked, she answered that the exit wound would've bled profusely. Most of the damage to the chest area was the exit wound, not the turtle. I leaned over to Vinny, "Did you see any blood out there?"

"No, I didn't," he answered and added, "And I talked to every cop there that searched the whole area and no one saw any blood whatsoever."

We noted that. The autopsy ended. The pathologist let us know that this was going to be ruled a homicide. She said that it would be a few days before she filed the official findings. We left there with our photos and measurements. Outside, Brendan insisted that the guy had killed himself. We told him to keep us informed about anything at all that he found out. Our job wasn't done yet so we promised the same. Vinny and I went to lunch to draw up a battle plan.

As crime scene investigators, you document your findings and at some point, you lay them all out and then try to re-create the series of events that led to the incident. This re-creation can not be speculation. It has to be a series of events that you can prove. In some cases, it becomes a theory because you may not have substantial proof. If that's the case, that's how you present it to the case investigator. It has to be presented as a list of findings so that the crime scene guy, or case investigator, or district attorney can then add what they find in an attempt to fill in the missing pieces of the puzzle. When someone along the line puts their own spin on it, the puzzle pieces start to get jumbled.

Vinny and I went to lunch to have a sit down and decide our next plan of action. It took no time at all for us to realize that we had to go back to the scene with what we knew. A call was made to the office and measurements of the rifle were given to us. We also decided that we would walk the path that this guy used to get to that spot on the lake. The Park Rangers showed us the parking lot where his vehicle had been parked and instructed us how to follow the correct path that would get us to that spot on the lake. There were several paths but each had markers. They also let us know that it was quite a hike, but we knew we had to walk the way this guy did. Maybe we'd get something out of it. We packed up as little as possible and headed out. It really was a beautiful day for a hike. The well worn path soon turned into a rocky, rough and sometimes confusing trail. Very often the trail crossed other trails and we'd have to double check that we were on the right one. It was a picturesque park with waterfalls, caves, huge rock formations, creeks, deer, butterflies and a huge rattlesnake. Oh yeah, that wasn't picturesque. Scared the shit outta me. I probably would've stepped right on it hadn't it been for a hiker coming the other way who warned us about the mammoth reptile on the path ahead.

After two and a half hours, we reached the site. It was good to be there with just the two of us. I remarked that it was quite a romantic spot. Vinny instructed me not to get any ideas. From our limited selection of supplies, we pulled out our camera and started shooting overall photos again. We noticed something right away. The large expanse of the rock ledge surface was very light colored, especially in the sunlight. With eight people searching this entire area and then standing and mulling around for hours as they waited for us, no one found any sign of blood or an expended rifle shell casing. The casing found in the chamber was from the young guy accidentally pulling the trigger in the water. We still hadn't found the expended casing of the shot that killed our guy. Of course, you have to keep in mind the possibility that he's shot with another gun, but we wouldn't go there yet since the autopsy did say that the entry wound size was consistent with the bullet size from the found rifle. More scene work had to be done now.

The autopsy told us that he would've had a huge bleeding wound in his left chest area after being shot. The lack of blood anywhere on the large rock surface indicated to us that he didn't fall onto the rock ledge or wasn't shot in the woods and dragged across the rock ledge and dumped in the lake. Maybe he was shot at the lake's edge and went directly into the lake.

It was a tranquil and yet striking view as you stood at the edge of this flat rock ledge and looked out over the calm stretch of this natural setting. Did the killer bring our guy to this ledge's edge, with the rifle pointed at his back, shoot him, sending his body into the lake and then throw the rifle into the water only a short distance away where you could clearly see it?... Maybe. Can't rule anything out.

Then we looked down to the water's surface that was four or five feet below us. In the bright sunlight, you could see through the still clear water. Directly below us was another flat rock ledge that was under water. It measured about four feet from shore outward and about eleven feet wide. A closer inspection showed that it was less than a foot below the water's surface. You could stand on it and be in shin deep water. Just to the left of where we stood was a graduating series of step-like rocks that led down to the water. We carefully stepped down to the water's edge to get a different view of everything. From this side view, we noticed a kind of rock "shelf" in the vertical surface of the above ground rock ledge. This rock shelf was about 43 inches above the under water rock ledge. The shelf itself was about ten inches wide.

Now we had some re-creating to do. We grabbed a few short metal poles that we brought and taped them together to make a replica of the rifle that was found in the water. Using some bright yellow tape, we marked the trigger's location on our replica.

Next, one of us would be getting down into the water. It would definitely be Vinny. Hey, seniority does have its benefits. Besides, Vinny was our deceased guy's exact height and Vinny's arm reach was actually an inch and a half shorter. One little problem we encountered before getting into the water was that our giant prehistoric friend was back. He floated around about 10 or 12 feet away watching everything we were doing. He seemed a bit annoyed. Probably because we had taken away his lunch the day before. I think he had eyes for Vinny once he saw him taking his boots and socks off. I didn't blame Vinny for not wanting to get in the water with that monster, especially after the Park Rangers told us that he's probably been around for more than a hundred years and that the force of this snapping turtle's bite could take your hand clean off. We threw a few rocks at him to no avail. That only seemed to piss him off more.

"How about I shoot him?"

I won't say which one of us asked that question, but we quickly realized that the loud echoing blast from a .45 caliber handgun wouldn't be a good thing. Finally, the use of some bigger rocks did the trick. He swam away, but we kept a constant eye open for his return. Getting rid of the dinosaur seemed to please the multitude of fish that watched from a distance. They could now inch a little closer. There had to be 40 or 50 fish twelve to fifteen feet away from us. Just watching us. Weird.

Before getting down into the water, a small piece of yellow tape was stuck to the back of Vinny's shirt just left of his spine and 52 inches from the ground. Then into the water he went. I held the camera, measuring tape, and replica rifle. He remarked that the under water ledge's surface wasn't slippery. I gave him the replica. With replica in hand, it would be impossible for one person to hold the rifle to the back of another and both stand on the under water ledge. There wasn't enough room. Remember we have to check every scenario, no matter how unlikely it might sound.

As Vinny stood in the water, another strange scenario started to form in our heads. What if there isn't another person with him in the water? The rock shelf was directly behind Vinny. The shelf was situated lower than the tape marked entrance wound on Vinny's back. Could the rifle sit on the shelf and be pointed at his back? A ten inch wide shelf would not hold the weight of the entire rifle, even though it was a short rifle. But if you placed the butt of the rifle on the shelf and then placed the barrel against your back, you could hold it in place with your weight pressed back against it. But could you reach the trigger from this awkward position? We tried it out.

Vinny could easily place the rifle and hold it there using his weight as he stared out at the beautiful lake. Viewing this set-up from the side did go along with the bullet's upward trajectory. I then went back on top of the rock ledge to get an aerial view of the next experiment. Vinny then tried reaching back toward the trigger with his left hand. He couldn't do it. No matter how he tried to twist or contort his left elbow, he could not touch the trigger area. It appeared that the barrel being set up against the left side of his spine made it impossible to reach back with his left hand. However, when he reached back with his right hand, two observations were noted. Not only could Vinny's shorter reach easily come into contact with the trigger, but the pivoting of his body illustrated the exact bullet trajectory that we saw at the autopsy; in the back just left of the spine and out the higher left chest and upper left arm area. I photographed this trajectory path from above asking Vinny not to move. As I pulled my eye away from the camera, I saw something else. The fish. The spatter of blood and tissue created by the exit wound would have showered the water and attracted these hungry little guys. As if throwing a bucket of chum into the lake. The rifle blast would've then sent the body into the lake. The rifle's recoil off of the rock shelf, or possibly our victim's finger still in the trigger guard would have sent the rifle into the water as well. This scenario explained why there was no blood or bullet casing found anywhere. It all went into the water.

We were beginning to feel that suicide was a very good possibility now, but we still had more to do. The next task was to take a closer look at the rifle. Once back at the office, Brendan reached out to us. He had been doing a little of his own homework on the rifle. He found out that the rifle easily disassembled into three pieces. Two of these pieces would fit inside the back pack. The barrel was too long and would definitely stick out. We looked at the back pack and its contents. The monopod zipper bag. That could be placed over the protruding gun barrel and nicely camouflage it. Also inside the back pack was the small screwdriver. That was used to re-assemble the rifle at the lake. This explained how a guy could walk two hours through the woods and past numerous other hikers with a rifle without raising suspicion.

Now we looked at the rifle and keyed in on the barrel's muzzle. It had a double ring design to it. We pulled out the autopsy photographs and held up the entrance wound photographs alongside the muzzle. The double ring design was obvious. We also noticed that the double ring impression on the skin was a lot more pronounced on the spine side of the wound. Vinny remembered that the spine side of the replica rifle pushed harder against his back when he pivoted to the right. The other side of the wound appeared to almost rise up off the skin a bit in the same pivoting movement.

The close up photo of the entrance wound afforded us one final detail. At the bottom of the entrance wound was a very unique looking mark. It looked like a tent top; sloping lines that flowed toward each other to a pointed top. This tent top pointed downward towards the victim's feet. Then we looked back at the muzzle and saw it. The rifle's sight. The sight was about an eighth of an inch in off of the barrel's muzzle. This impression of the rifle's sight imprinted on our victim's back revealed that the rifle was upside down when it was placed against him. Out at the lake, we had assumed that the rifle stock would've been laid on its side on the rock shelf. We could now see that propping it upside down made it all the easier to access the trigger. Clear as day on top of the wooden stock were scratches where the wood would've recoiled against the rock shelf when fired.

The next day had SP divers in the water to retrieve whatever they could. In a matter of minutes, the spent bullet casing was found. It lined up with where the ejection port of the rifle would have ejected it had it been fired while upside down.

All of our photographs, measurements, and reconstruction findings were brought to the medical examiner. Brendan brought along all the statements from relatives. As we sat down, she commented, "Don't tell me you're going to say that he shot himself in the back." We all smiled and asked that she just listen to everything we had to say. After a slow step by step show and tell presentation, she sat back, shook her head and said that she couldn't argue a single thing. It was a suicide.

As crime scene guys and gals you have to keep an open mind. You have to treat every death as a homicide until it's proven otherwise. Every human being deserves that from us. You can never believe the oft repeated phrase "No one would ever do that."

Tom Clancy said it best when he stated that the difference between fiction and reality is that fiction has to make sense.

I have seen people do things that defy any sort of logic. But they did it. After reading this chapter, people will ask the big "Why? Why did he commit suicide in this way?"

I don't know.

We can guess at motives. Maybe he wanted the police to think it was a murder. Why? Again, I don't know. We all have theories. Maybe he didn't want to see the end coming. Maybe he wanted that breathtaking view of the lake to be the last sight he ever saw. He had been to this place as a boy. Maybe a nice girl once spoke to this lonely guy at this very spot. Maybe he wanted his death shrouded in mystery. Maybe it would be a way to have others remember him and talk about him after he was gone. There are hundreds of other "maybes" to the very simple question "Why?"

Television likes to sew everything together in an hour. And I get it. It's entertainment. By show's end, you know exactly what happened and why it happened. You get to see the weapon, the perpetrator, and have the complex motive revealed to you. It all makes sense.

But true to our famous author's words, reality doesn't always make sense..... to us. It may make perfect sense to someone else.

"Always Be Humble and Kind" is the name of a Tim McGraw song. The beauty of its lyrics lies in its simplicity. When you're humble and kind, ego has no place to take hold. A true team spirit can not flourish when egos are present. They get in the way. Everyone involved in this case worked together to bring about a resolution. It was a sad resolution, but one that brought closure to a grieving family. Every professional involved in solving this mystery was willing to listen. They were willing to say, "I'm not sure what happened here. What do you think?" No one was afraid to admit, "I must be wrong. Let's look at it your way." That's when great feats can be accomplished. When no one in the room is looking to be the one to say, "I did it! I solved it!", that's when the team spirit takes hold and amazing things happen.

Being humble and kind takes practice. You know, as parents we wonder if our kids ever hear a single word we tell them. Take it from me. They do. Of course, not always, but you'd be surprised at what they do absorb.

In sixth grade, my son was playing youth basketball. He was a pretty good player. During one game, he had a break away. It was him and the basketball all alone on his way towards a sure lay up and two points. Standing under the basket was one of his team mates. This fellow sixth grader was handicapped and had a hard time keeping up with team members so he often hung back, not sure what to do. My son stopped under the basket handed the ball to the boy and said,

"Go ahead, John. Take the shot." My son then proceeded to hold off the oncoming opposing team as this handicapped young man tried to take the shot. The ball barely hit the rim and bounced into an opposing team member's hands and off they went. The boy was ecstatic. It lifted his spirits.

People in the audience paid wonderful compliments to my son and his coach said he had never seen anything like it at that grade level. As a parent, I couldn't be prouder.

It's funny. My son went on to play high school football. He was the varsity quarterback. Looking back, I really don't remember how many touchdowns he threw, but I do remember that in every newspaper interview he downplayed his performance and praised the efforts of his teammates (especially the offensive line who protected him like the crowned jewels!). I remember that as a high school junior he was awarded "Most Valuable Offensive Player" after a play-off game and then proceeded to find his senior receiver and gave it to him saying, "I wouldn't have gotten this without you". The team members who played with my son would do anything for him. They appreciated being recognized and treated with kindness.

I guess some of the lectures did sink in.

Chapter Sixteen

The Big Picture

M y young family was growing; a cute redheaded two year old daughter and my wife expecting our son in a couple of months. We had bought five acres of land and were putting in the concrete foundation for our new home. First, I had to figure out the measurements for the concrete footers that would support the concrete walls. The dimensions had to be just right for the modular house that was being delivered in a couple of weeks. As always, scheduling got a little tight. We had to get the footers done because the guys doing the concrete basement walls were coming the next day. We finally finished the footers, only to have one of the guys re-measure it all and inform me that the footers were wrongly placed. My calculations had been off. The basement walls wouldn't sit on the middle of the footers. They would run along the very inside edge of the footers. The concrete guys had a suggestion that would add more concrete to two sides of the existing footers. Then you could shift the walls a bit so that they'd sit on part of the old and new sections of footers. It would work. But I was pissed. This was going to delay the entire process. I had run my ass off getting everything to this point.

I got in my car to once again run somewhere for more supplies. I was so frustrated and annoyed as I drove, bitching and complaining out loud. It was early evening when I drove by our local Catholic cemetery. It was a road I used every day. But this particular evening, I glanced over at the cemetery during my ranting. There in the very first row was a big black granite headstone. And on this headstone was the engraved image of an absolutely beautiful young woman's face. Her blonde hair blowing to an imaginary wind. I had gone to school with this girl. In high school, she had that gorgeous Farah Fawcett blonde hairstyle and an ever smiling face. At first you would think she was unapproachable, but quickly you would find out that she was as down to earth as you were. This made her even more beautiful. After graduation, and into her twenties, cancer took hold. She would lose that dazzling yellow hair, but never that smile even through her battle. The world lost this wonderful human being at way too young an age. The sight of her face on that headstone made me angry. Angry at myself. "What is wrong with you?" was all I could keep asking. If I could've stepped outside of my body at that very moment, I would've slapped the shit outta myself.

Dealing with the everyday minutiae of life is a given. Of course we have to, but zeroing in on it and letting it turn you into a miserable person is a mistake. It solves nothing. When you know its place in the grand scheme of things, dealing with it becomes much easier. And to do that, you have to take those two big steps backwards and take in the whole scenario. Envision this annoying situation as mere seconds in a lifetime. Objectively analyze this current issue and ask if it really is such a big deal. Is it worth my getting upset or losing sleep or becoming a jerk? Then make a rational decision as to how to conduct yourself. You have now successfully looked at "The Big Picture".

When you go to a Broadway show and sit in the front row, you are experiencing a different perspective of that production than you would sitting twenty rows back. Up close you can see the make-up is a little thick and that there are wheels under that moving scenery platform. You'll naturally key in on production stuff that you can see from being so close and sometimes this is pretty cool. But whether you know it or not, you're losing out on the "Big Picture" effect that the show wants you to experience. From fifteen or twenty rows back, the make-up is unnoticeable. You watch characters in a story. The details you noticed from being so close are non-existent. You can take in and enjoy "The Big Picture" as it was meant to be presented.

"We've got another body."

It's a common phrase in our line of work. We hop into our vans, drive to the scene, get briefed and do our walk-through, and "Yep. There's the body." The body. It's not until later when you're kneeling down next to this body that you find family photographs and a kindergarten made trinket key chain in a pocket. You look up from your kneeling position and instead of concentrating on the blood spatter and bullet holes in the walls, you now see the framed photographs. Photos of smiling kids, a black and white of his father in the Marines, and a wedding photograph. Construction paper colored with crayons is held to the refrigerator by magnets. We have a job to do and yes, we got another body. But it's a good thing to know that this body, in the big picture, was a loving father and husband and son.

The "Big Picture" outlook isn't limited to life's problems. It should be used every day during life's daily interactions. I can speak for cops. In general, we are a suspicious lot. We always have our guard up. We come across as grouchy or standoffish or just plain mean. But if people knew the big picture behind the everyday experiences that cops have with the human race, they'd understand their demeanor. In the course of a normal day at work, most people cops deal with are people who are not exactly forthcoming. Some will downplay their actions. ("I only had two beers" or "I was only doing 62"). Some will exaggerate the details ("Then he threw me across the room" or "She rammed my car in the parking lot"). Many will downright lie ("I wasn't there" or "I didn't hit her. She's lying").

Cops constantly, and I mean constantly, have to make determinations as to how much truth, if any, a person is telling them. Now add to this that he often comes into contact with the absolute filth of society; predators, scammers, thieves, and murderers. When he stops any vehicle at all, he has no idea as he walks up to that driver's window who this person is or where they just came from. However, the driver and occupants of the vehicle know very well that a lawman who can put them away for a very long time is about to question them. Cops deal with people who deceive them, lie to them, and try to hurt them. Many deal with it every day. So, if a cop or trooper isn't all smiles and touchy-feely with you, don't take it personally. It has nothing to do with you. They are the sheepdogs protecting the sometimes ungrateful sheep from the clutches of the ever lurking wolf. Remember that in the big picture when something awful happens, this grouchy, standoffish prick is going to be standing in front of you, protecting you and your family from harm.

I gave you a cop's big picture. But what about that guy at the counter who isn't getting your car part quick enough or finding the right shoe size for you in the ladies department? Yes, he might simply be a boob. Lord knows there are plenty of people out there who just don't know what they're doing. But there are lots more people out there that we will come into contact with every day who are having a tough time. And I don't mean the "I was up late. I didn't get any sleep so I'm tired and don't want to be here" bullshit. I mean the counter guy whose wife just left him for someone else. I mean that person in line who may growl a little because she knows she's about to lose her job, or the poor soul who is so out of it because he spends every other moment outside work at a hospital bedside where his terminally ill child suffers.

We run into something or someone who slightly inconveniences us and we blurt to ourselves, "What's their problem?" Believe me, in most of those cases, you don't want to know their problem. We're pissed off because we woke up late and now the kid at Dunkin Donuts is working too slowly for us to get us out the door to our secure job when he can barely pay his bills after coming home from Iraq.

The Big Picture theme is to be decent to everyone you meet. That sounds pretty general so how about this? At least give people the benefit of the doubt. Give people a chance. I'm not saying you have to kiss anybody's ass. Be decent. Be a little more patient. Now if you do all of that and the person still gets shitty or doesn't do their job, then say what you have to say and move on. Some people do need a wake up call, especially if fellow human beings are trying to be civilized to them. That is seeing the Big Picture from both sides.

And this goes for children as well. As adults we tend to blow off the little ones. We're too busy. Kids have to listen to a barrage of "Don't do this!" and "No, you can't have that!" And parents don't have the time or energy to listen to every single dissertation or string of questions that their kids come up with. That's part of a parent's big picture. But when another adult stops and takes the time to listen to what a child is saying and answer her questions, it really is a big deal. When a cop in uniform does this with a kid, it is truly magical. To a kid, it's almost like talking to a super hero. And when the cop agrees with the kid, or says that he likes the kid's ideas, the child goes home feeling ten feet tall. I once had a fantastic debate with a three year old girl about whether it was better to be a summer fairy or a winter fairy. That conversation of back and forth question and answers lifted my spirits that day. Later she brought me daises from the lawn and said Thank You. I asked for what? She just said, "Because you're nice." The big, tough cop in me had a rough time holding it together for the next few moments and then she was off on her next adventure. By the way, I chose to be a fair weather summer fairy and she chose the winter one because she had prettier wings.

You know that person you run into in the street that makes you cringe because you're about to get stuck listening to a few long stories that will have no end? They're usually good people who just can't help but unload on you or anyone else they run into. You politely listen for a few minutes and then find some excuse to get you the hell out of there without hurting any feelings. You usually walk away from that verbal assault feeling like you have just lost 15 minutes of your life that you will never get back. However, the talks that you have with a child, no matter how silly they get, never, ever feel like lost time. There is no doubt that as a grandparent I notice this much more now. As a parent, you have a million things going on and you are with your kids day in and day out. Taking them for granted comes easy. We shouldn't. We need to make as much time for them as possible. And in truth, when we do, it's a win-win situation. When you take the time to listen to them, you make them feel special. You give them the confidence to speak their mind and give their opinion. And in return, the experience will make your day.

Ya gotta love the honesty of little kids. They have no filter and don't worry about political correctness. They say what they mean and it is so incredibly refreshing. Every Christmas time for more than 20 years, I'd help out a dear teacher friend of mine with her kindergarten school play. Because of her tireless and dedicated efforts, Carol's plays became a sort of local tradition. The community loved them. I would either help backstage with the mob of crazy kids or play an adult role on stage. Part of my pre-production duties was to bring a batch of boys into the boys rest room and get them into their costumes. This was usually quite a task. I'd have eight or ten kindergarteners with sneakers off, costumes on wrong and somebody locked in a stall. You can imagine. And one time in the midst of this chaos, I was down on one knee tying this little boy's shoes. He was standing beside me with my head bowed down towards his shoes. I felt a finger touch the crown of my head accompanied with the statement, "You're bald here and here." At which point his finger moved to my receding frontal hairline.

I couldn't help but laugh out loud and told him, "Hey, thanks for pointing that out to me."

Their honesty is so absolutely invigorating in a society that tends not to tell things like they are. Another time, I had brought my four year old granddaughter to Church. She would get a little restless, but overall she was pretty good. During the homily, I told her to be quiet and listen to what the priest was saying. She stood on the kneeler in front of me as the congregation sat listening to our Vietnamese pastor. I could see her staring at the priest and then her face grimaced a little as her head started to tilt sideways. Before I could say anything, she simply asked, "What language is he speaking?" Thank God it wasn't that loud, but it was loud enough to elicit a few chuckles from some nearby parishioners who knew all too well how tough it was to sometimes understand our priest.

We badly need to extend this concept to teenagers. We all know the plight of a teenager. "No one listens to me" and "What I say isn't important" and so on. I know that it's a difficult task for parents. They are too close to the problem. But that's when an uncle or aunt or grandparent or family friend can really be a huge help. I've had some marvelous talks with these kids. After the conversation, it's so nice to hear parents remark that their teen enjoyed the talk and really felt that their opinion meant something to an adult. It was important to them when I'd ask for their input on something. These talks don't always have to be the "How are you feeling?" or "How are you and your parents getting along?" talks. Asking them what they think about a particular topic or incident will often give you quite a surprise. The depth and thoughtfulness of their answers will sometimes leave you speechless. Nurture that kind of conversation. Let's face it. You're sitting down with someone who is part of the future. Your future and the future of your children and grandchildren.

A "Big Picture" explanation I always taught in Sunday school to my class of eighth graders went like this. Each one of your parents wants you to become the kind of person who speaks their mind, stands up for what's right, and who is proud of their own special uniqueness. However, as you grow up from little kids into young adults under the same roof, speaking your mind, taking a stand and being unique is going to cause a lot of head butting. It's a fine line that's difficult for parents to see. Of course, they don't want you to be someone who just blindly follows the crowd. They want you to be that strong person who asks the question "Why?" We just don't want you asking us that question when we tell you to do something or else we're going to lose our minds. That's the "Big Picture" that both sides need to see.

It's the same outlook that helps me answer the questions that so many people ask me.

"How do you stand being around so much death?" "How do you live life seeing all that misery, all of that human violence?"

The answer is that you can't. If that's all you see. Because it's only a part of your life. The other times of your life have to be recognizing and enjoying the multitude of fantastic experiences that surround you every single day. Then you can find a very healthy and natural balance.

"Come on," you'll say, "Healthy? Natural?" You might break my chops over that answer, but think about it. Yes, seeing the misery that befalls so many people could lead to a hardened attitude. Yes, routinely witnessing the grief of family members over the seemingly senseless and sometimes brutal loss of a loved one can be depressing. Yes, picking up pieces and physically handling the remnants of what used to be a living and breathing human being can be a somber task and one that would turn most people's stomachs. Yes. I agree with you..... if you let it.

We tend to be a species that dwells on "shit". We let wonderful moments become fleeting, but we'll re-hash and endlessly ponder bullshit. We let it then turn us into anxious, complaining nincompoops. Extraordinary opportunities will constantly present themselves to us and we'll walk right by them, ignoring them, taking them for granted, and squandering a chance at feeling enhanced and becoming a better person.

The very nature of life is also death. With it brings great sadness and that's life. We must accept that. But while we're alive, we need to be aware that there is so much that is good, and captivating, and funny as hell in life. The trick is to keep a vigilant eye out for those treasures. When you come across one, stop what you're doing. It could be a rainbow over the sky scrapers, or a ray of sun shining like a bolt of lightning through the clouds. Stop. Take a good look at it and say, "Wow, that's pretty cool." Then you can keep going on about your day's duties. That few seconds will lift your spirits. It will prioritize things in some small way. Doing this helps you balance the good and the bad. If life were a football game, it would always seem as though the bad is outscoring the good and that's just so wrong. The good is all around us. The good is such a better team. Don't keep giving the ball to the bad. Give it to the good and let the good score over and over again.

In my case, encountering and experiencing all of the death and destruction that I have over the years has made me appreciate every damn thing in my life. Everything! No, not just the house and the car and the good job. That's all nice, but it becomes part of the bullshit stuff we worry about. When I say everything I mean gazing in awe at my sleeping grandson; sharing a laugh with a friend over a beer; asking a stranger "How ya doin?"; watching waves hit the beach; driving through a wintery tunnel of trees; re-hashing old memories with a parent or grandparent; smiling at someone you pass and seeing a pleasant reaction; smelling the freshly cut grass as you cut it; making silly faces just to hear a child's laugh; complimenting someone who's standing in line with you; walking an elderly person to their car and starting up a conversation; lifting someone else's spirits; beholding the reaction to the question, "Do you want a lollipop?"; feeling a child's embrace; peeking at a child as they figure something out; hearing the words "I love you"; staring into the eyes of someone you love; and knowing that titles like Trooper, Sir, and Senior Investigator can't hold a candle to the titles I truly cherish: Friend, Son, Dad, Pop-Pop.

CPSIA information can be obtained
at www.ICGtesting.com
Printed in the USA
FSHW020802190521

9 781388 029593